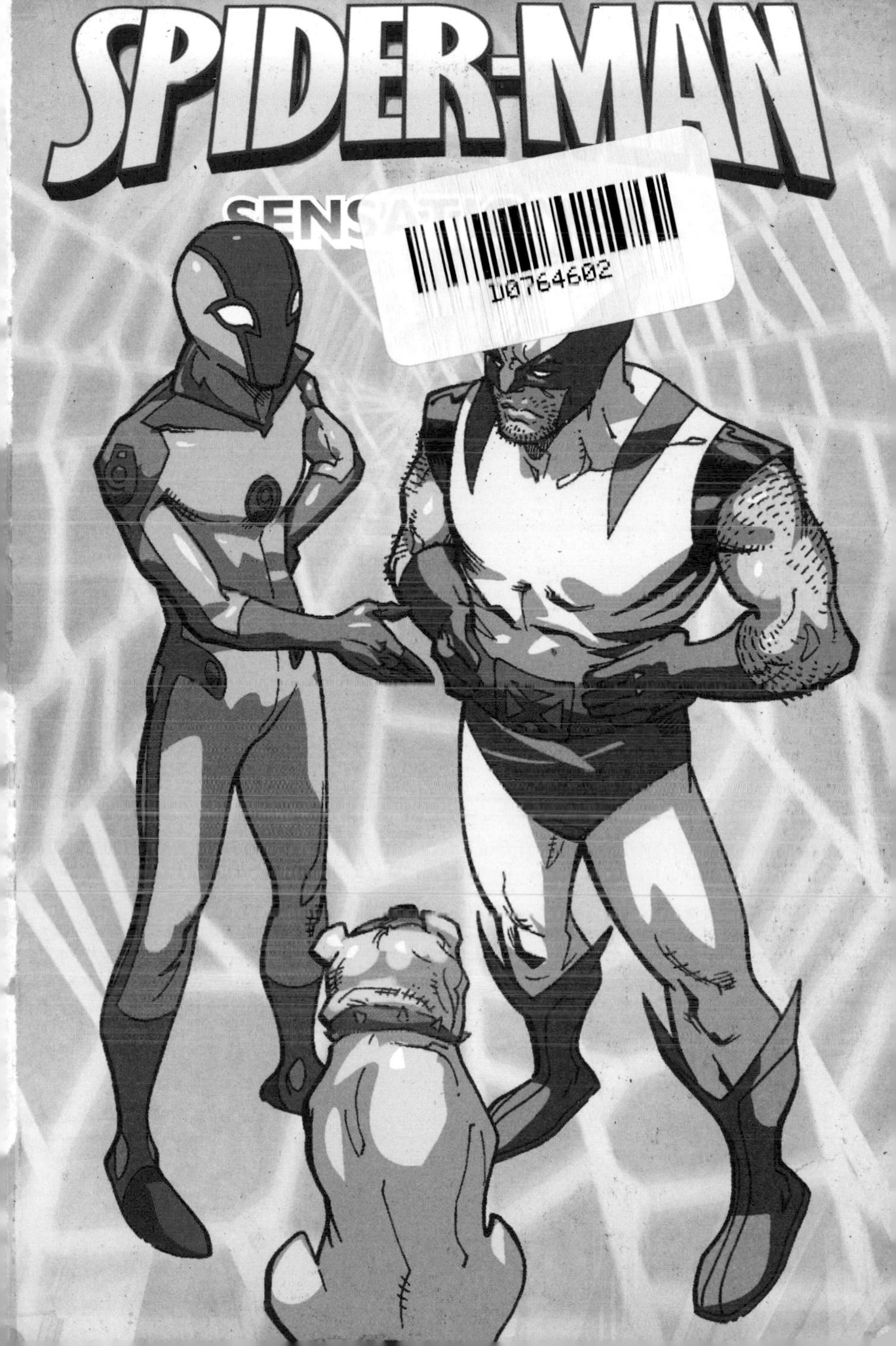
SPIDER-MAN
SENS

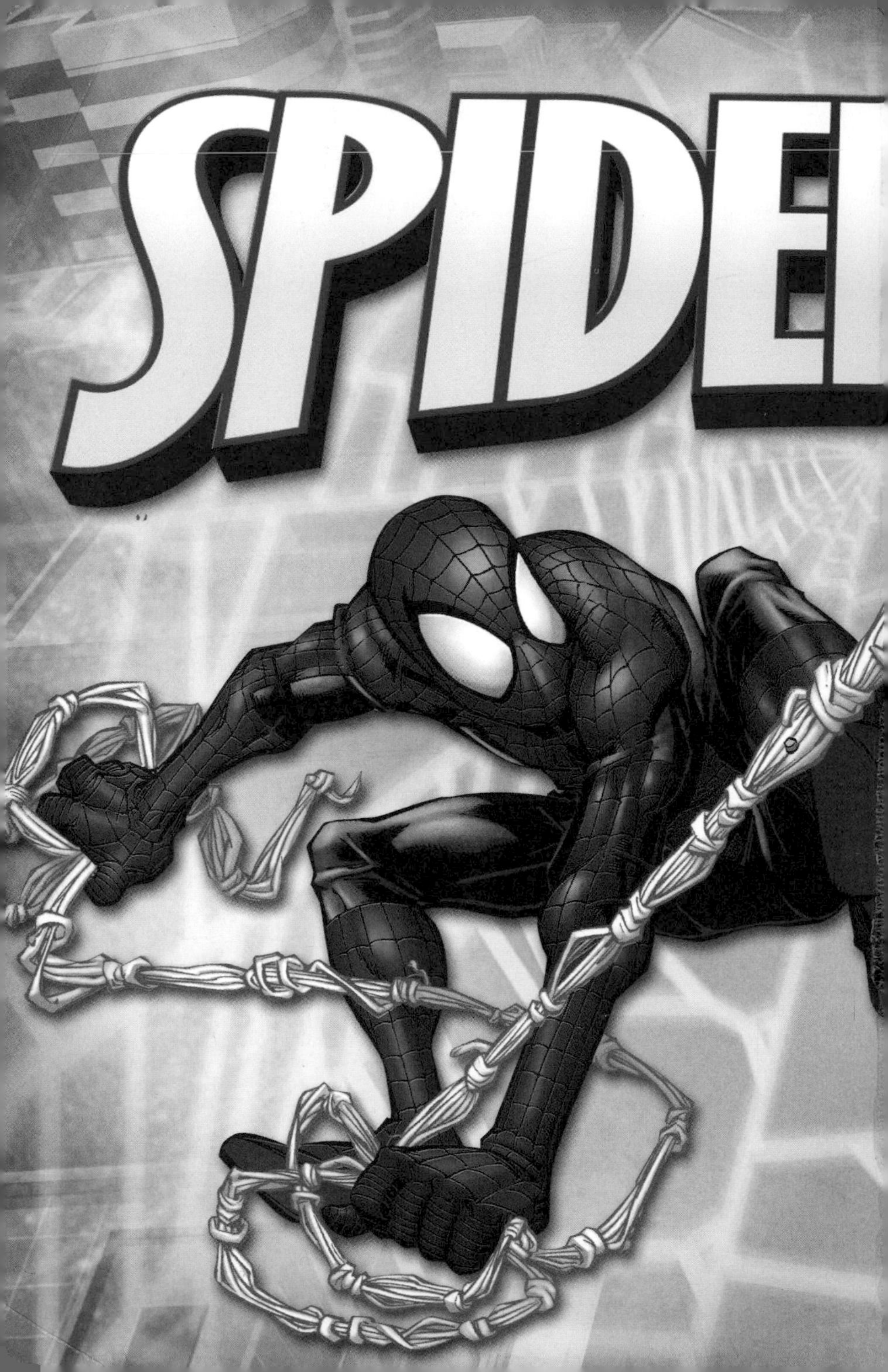
SPIDE

R-MAN

SENSATIONAL

Writer: **Paul Tobin**
Pencilers: **Matteo Lolli (Issues #9-10 & #12)**
with **Colleen Coover (Issue #10)**
& **Rob Di Salvo (Issue #11)**
Inker: **Terry Pallot**
Colors: **Sotocolor**
Letters: **Dave Sharpe**
Cover Artists: **Patrick Scherberger & Edgar Delgado**

Editors: **Jordan D. White, Michael Horwitz & Nathan Cosby**
Senior Editor: **Mark Paniccia**

Collection Editor: **Cory Levine**
Editorial Assistants: **James Emmett & Joe Hochstein**
Assistant Editors: **Matt Masdeu, Alex Starbuck & Nelson Ribeiro**
Editors, Special Projects: **Jennifer Grünwald & Mark D. Beazley**
Senior Editor, Special Projects: **Jeff Youngquist**
Senior Vice President of Sales: **David Gabriel**

Editor in Chief: **Axel Alonso**
Chief Creative Officer: **Joe Quesada**
Publisher: **Dan Buckley**
Executive Producer: **Alan Fine**

S

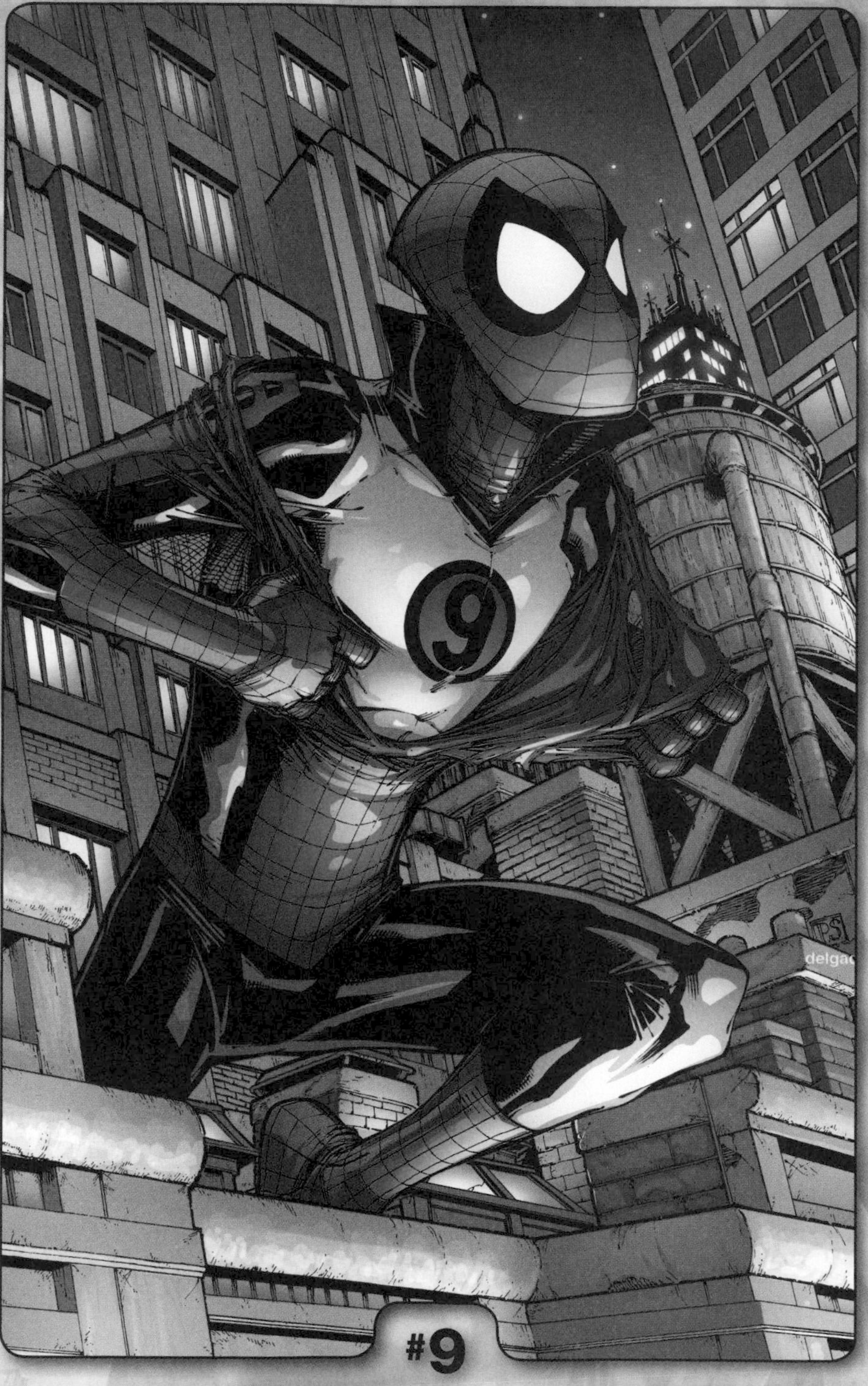
#9

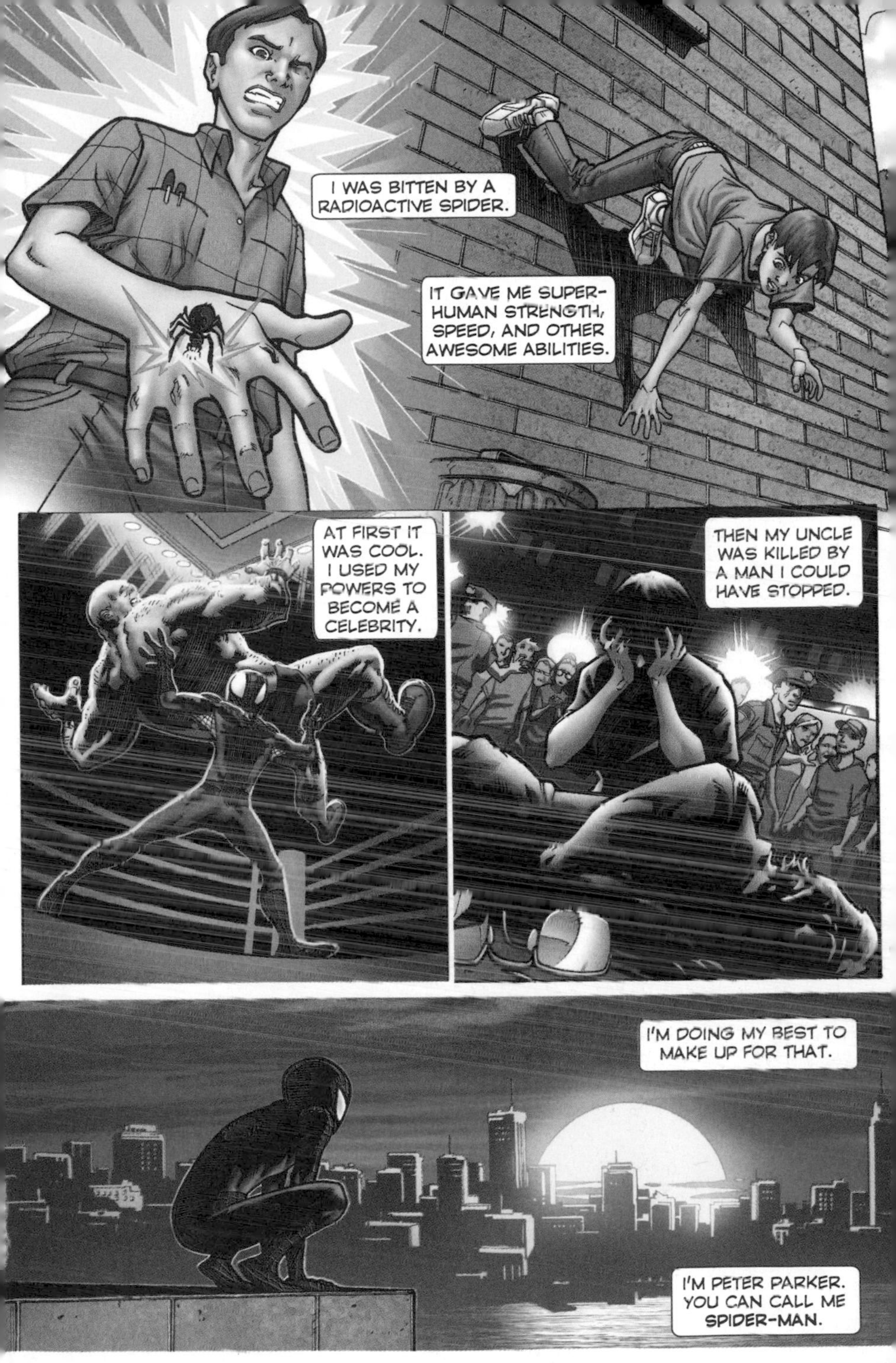
I WAS BITTEN BY A RADIOACTIVE SPIDER.
IT GAVE ME SUPER-HUMAN STRENGTH, SPEED, AND OTHER AWESOME ABILITIES.
AT FIRST IT WAS COOL. I USED MY POWERS TO BECOME A CELEBRITY.
THEN MY UNCLE WAS KILLED BY A MAN I COULD HAVE STOPPED.
I'M DOING MY BEST TO MAKE UP FOR THAT.
I'M PETER PARKER. YOU CAN CALL ME SPIDER-MAN.

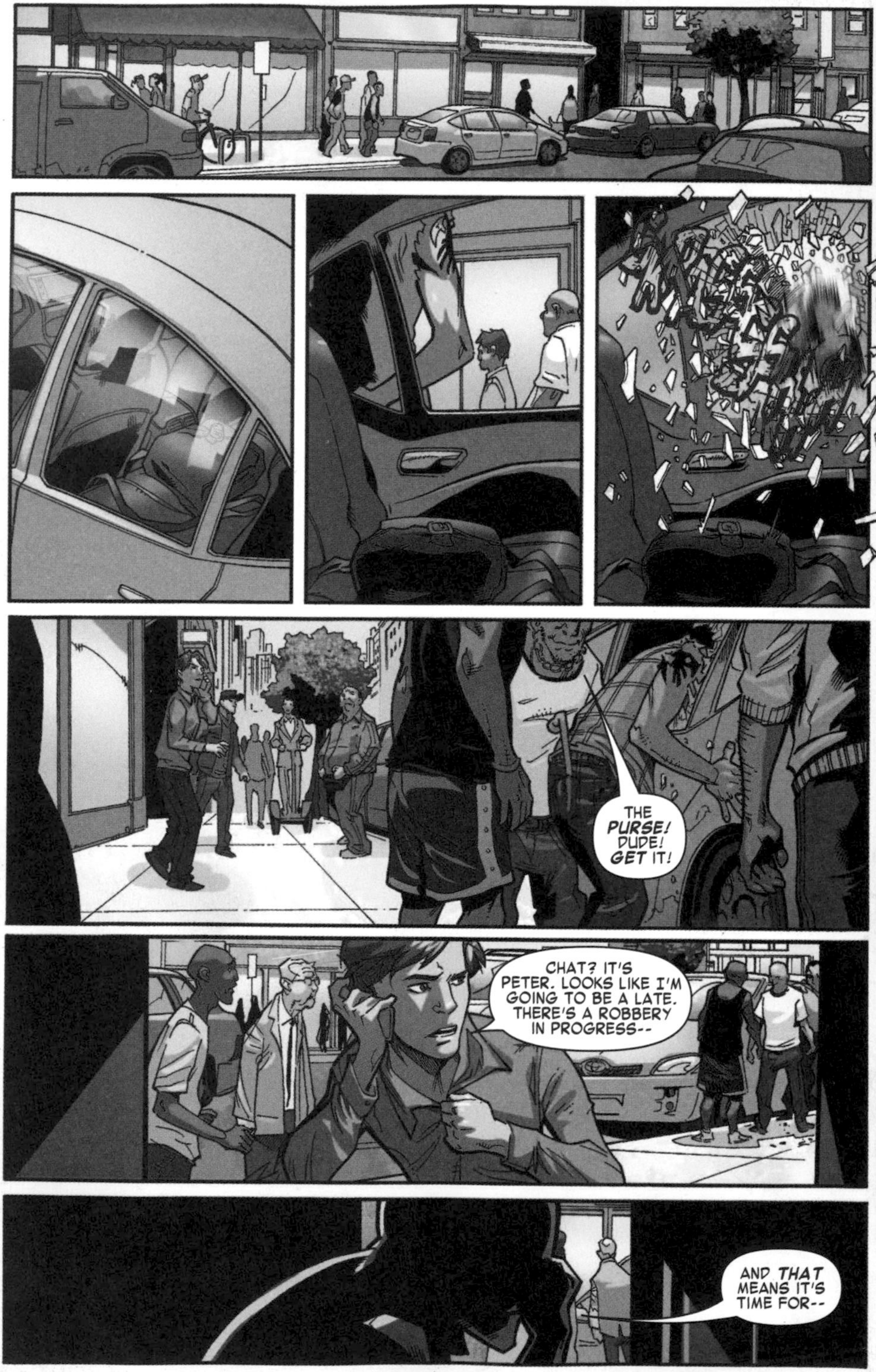
THE PURSE! DUDE! GET IT!
CHAT? IT'S PETER. LOOKS LIKE I'M GOING TO BE A LATE. THERE'S A ROBBERY IN PROGRESS--
AND THAT MEANS IT'S TIME FOR--

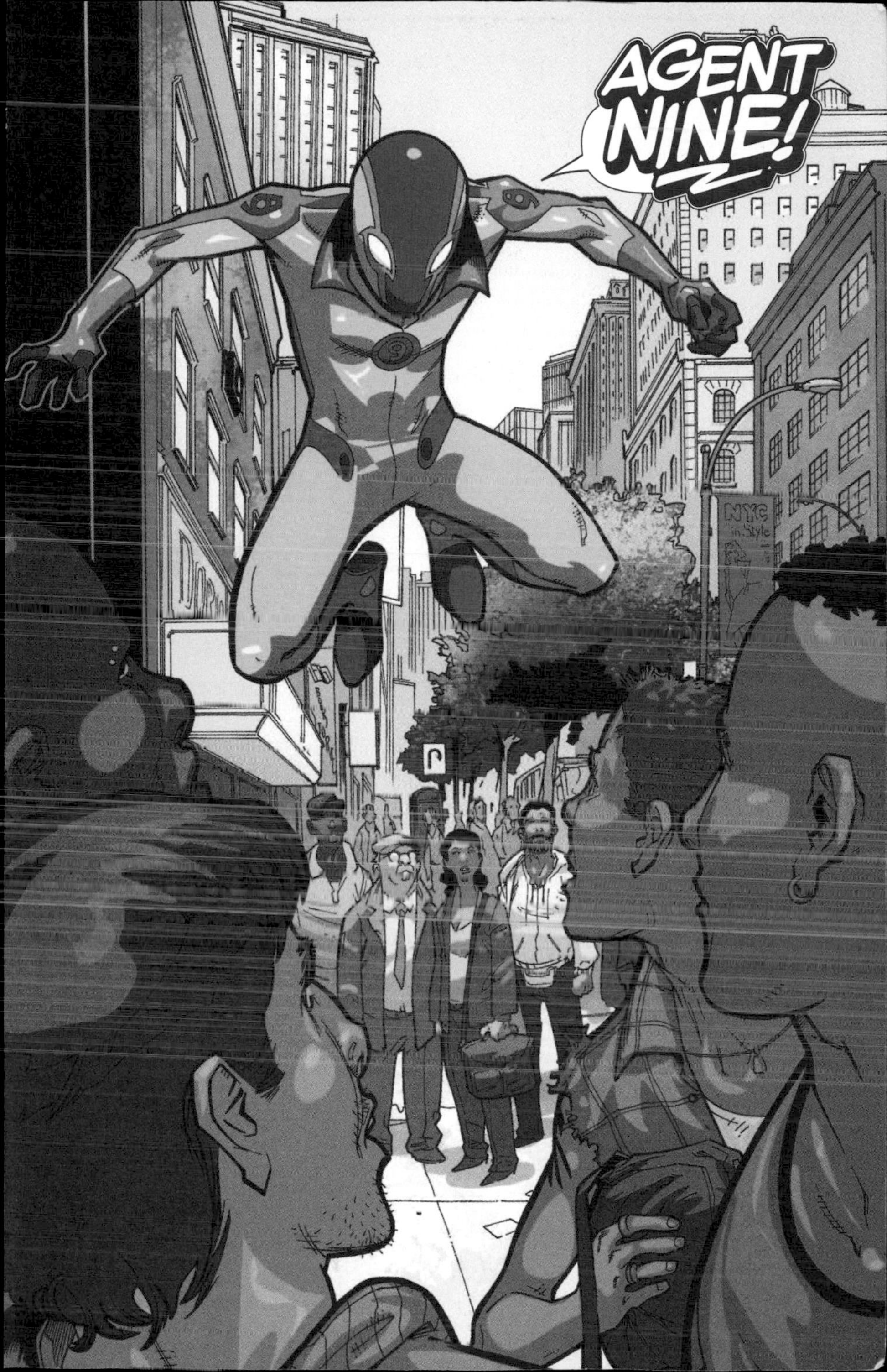
AGENT NINE!
NYC in Style

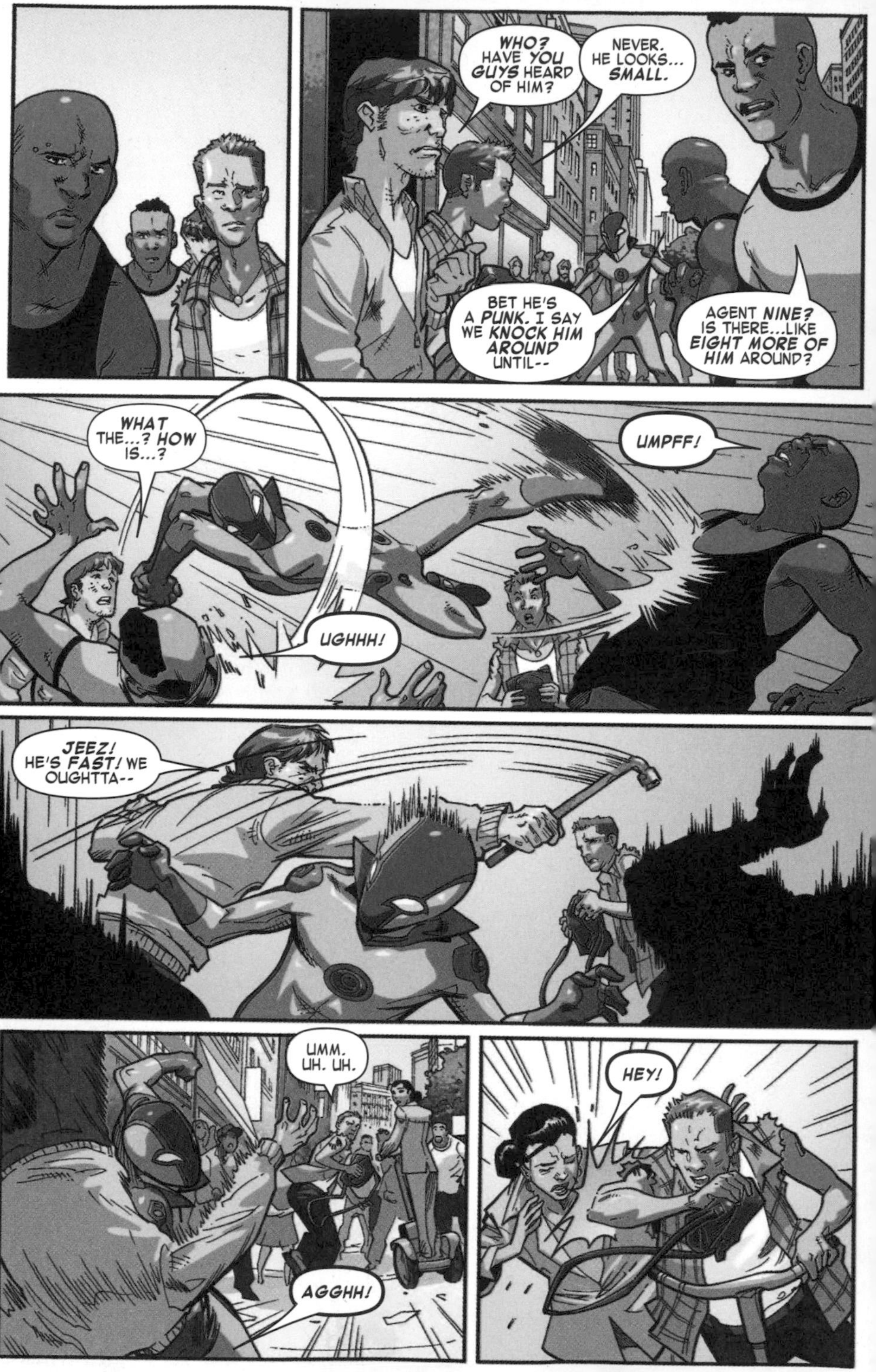
WHO? HAVE YOU GUYS HEARD OF HIM?
NEVER. HE LOOKS... SMALL.
BET HE'S A PUNK. I SAY WE KNOCK HIM AROUND UNTIL--
AGENT NINE? IS THERE...LIKE EIGHT MORE OF HIM AROUND?
WHAT THE...? HOW IS...?
UMPFF!
UGHHH!
JEEZ! HE'S FAST! WE OUGHTTA--
UMM. UH. UH.
AGGHH!
HEY!

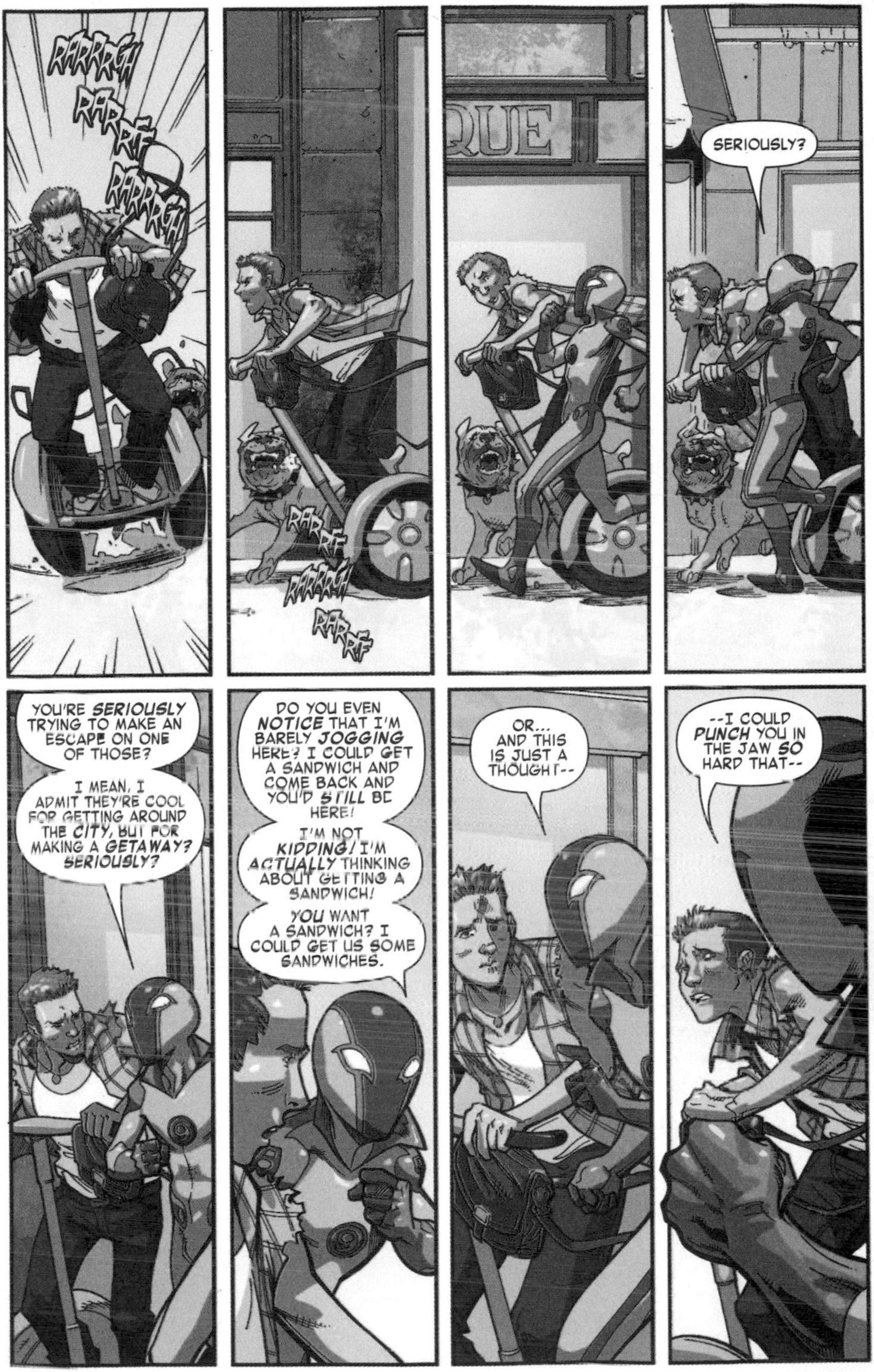
RARRRGH
RARRRF
RARRRGH
RARRF
RARRRGH
RARRF
SERIOUSLY?
YOU'RE SERIOUSLY TRYING TO MAKE AN ESCAPE ON ONE OF THOSE?
I MEAN, I ADMIT THEY'RE COOL FOR GETTING AROUND THE CITY, BUT FOR MAKING A GETAWAY? SERIOUSLY?
DO YOU EVEN NOTICE THAT I'M BARELY JOGGING HERE? I COULD GET A SANDWICH AND COME BACK AND YOU'D STILL BE HERE!
I'M NOT KIDDING! I'M ACTUALLY THINKING ABOUT GETTING A SANDWICH!
YOU WANT A SANDWICH? I COULD GET US SOME SANDWICHES.
OR... AND THIS IS JUST A THOUGHT--
--I COULD PUNCH YOU IN THE JAW SO HARD THAT--

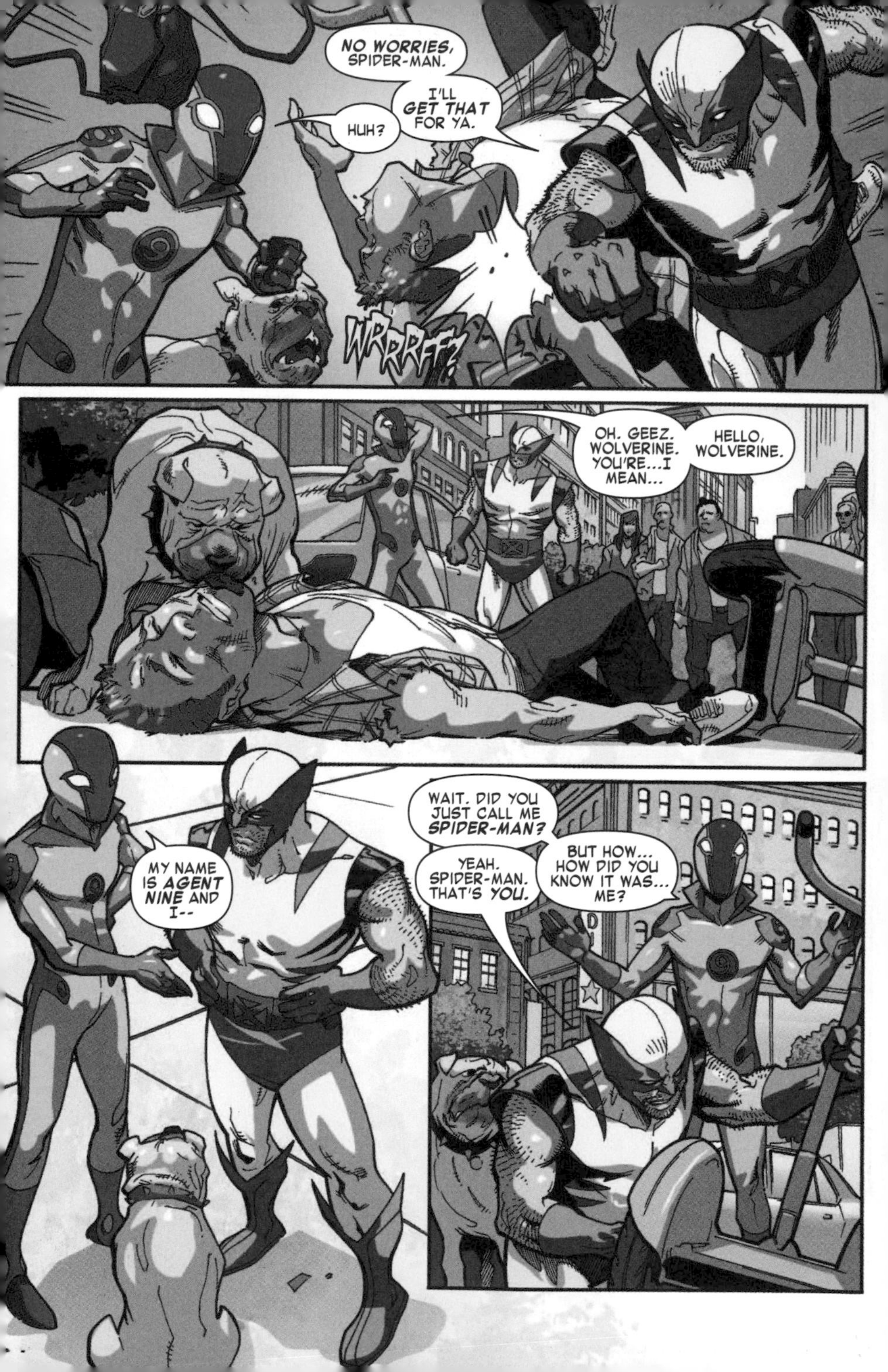
NO WORRIES, SPIDER-MAN.
I'LL GET THAT FOR YA.
HUH?
WRRRFF?
OH. GEEZ. WOLVERINE. YOU'RE...I MEAN...
HELLO, WOLVERINE.
MY NAME IS AGENT NINE AND I--
WAIT. DID YOU JUST CALL ME SPIDER-MAN?
YEAH. SPIDER-MAN. THAT'S YOU.
BUT HOW... HOW DID YOU KNOW IT WAS... ME?

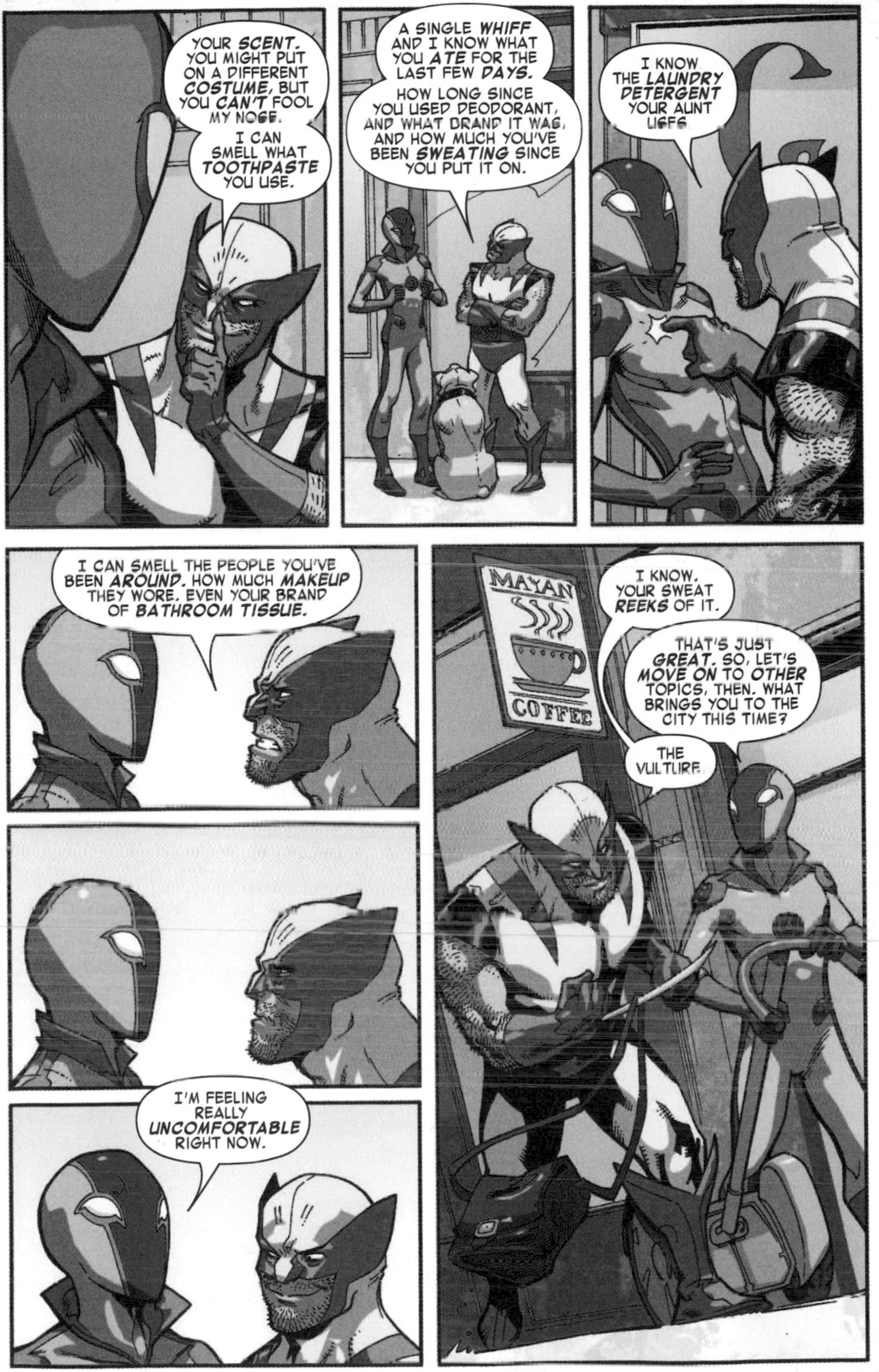
YOUR SCENT. YOU MIGHT PUT ON A DIFFERENT COSTUME, BUT YOU CAN'T FOOL MY NOSE.
I CAN SMELL WHAT TOOTHPASTE YOU USE.
A SINGLE WHIFF AND I KNOW WHAT YOU ATE FOR THE LAST FEW DAYS.
HOW LONG SINCE YOU USED DEODORANT, AND WHAT BRAND IT WAS, AND HOW MUCH YOU'VE BEEN SWEATING SINCE YOU PUT IT ON.
I KNOW THE LAUNDRY DETERGENT YOUR AUNT USES.
I CAN SMELL THE PEOPLE YOU'VE BEEN AROUND. HOW MUCH MAKEUP THEY WORE. EVEN YOUR BRAND OF BATHROOM TISSUE.
I'M FEELING REALLY UNCOMFORTABLE RIGHT NOW.
MAYAN
COFFEE
I KNOW. YOUR SWEAT REEKS OF IT.
THAT'S JUST GREAT. SO, LET'S MOVE ON TO OTHER TOPICS, THEN. WHAT BRINGS YOU TO THE CITY THIS TIME?
THE VULTURE.

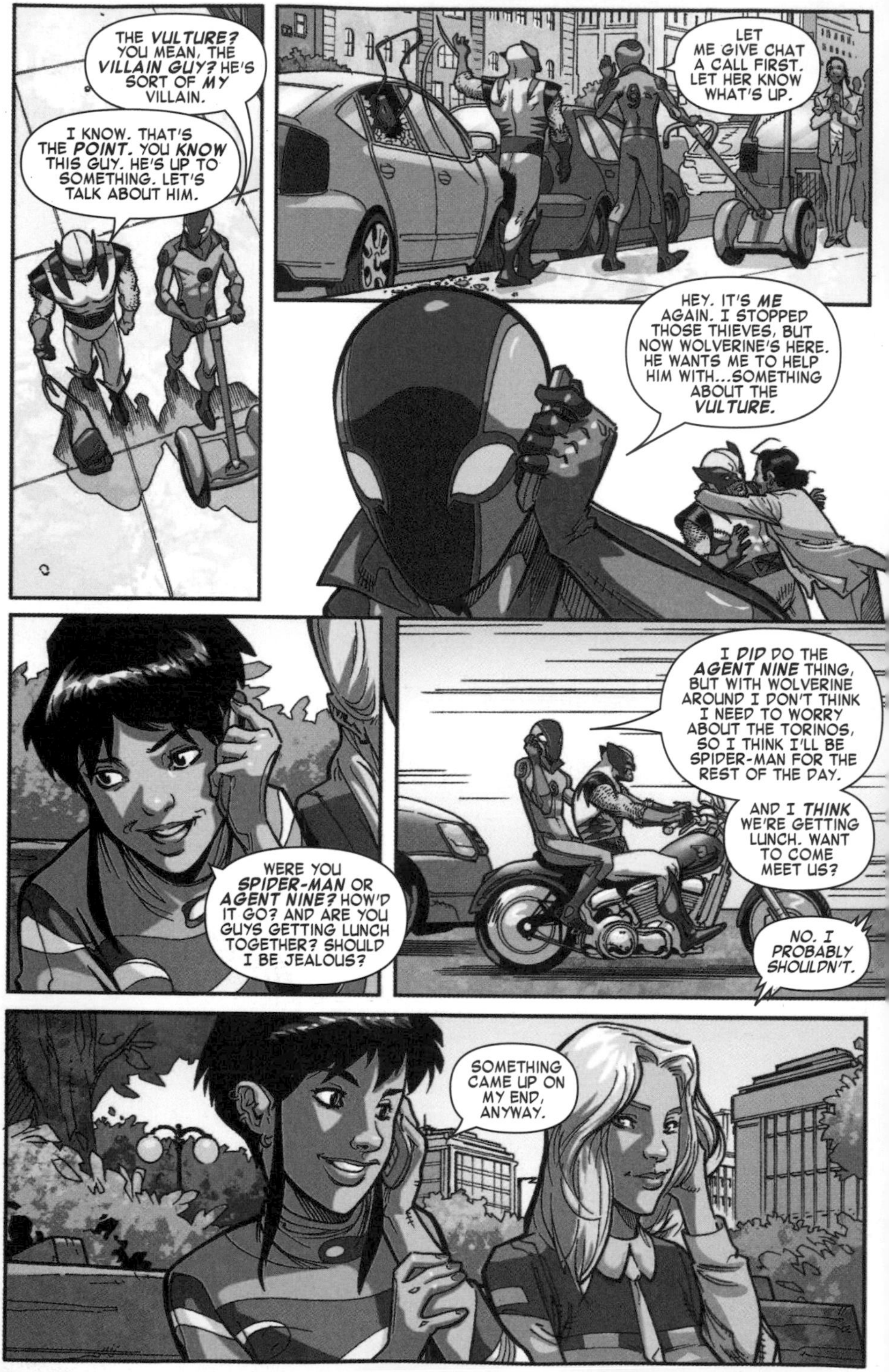
THE VULTURE? YOU MEAN, THE VILLAIN GUY? HE'S SORT OF MY VILLAIN.
I KNOW. THAT'S THE POINT. YOU KNOW THIS GUY. HE'S UP TO SOMETHING. LET'S TALK ABOUT HIM.
LET ME GIVE CHAT A CALL FIRST. LET HER KNOW WHAT'S UP.
HEY. IT'S ME AGAIN. I STOPPED THOSE THIEVES, BUT NOW WOLVERINE'S HERE. HE WANTS ME TO HELP HIM WITH...SOMETHING ABOUT THE VULTURE.
WERE YOU SPIDER-MAN OR AGENT NINE? HOW'D IT GO? AND ARE YOU GUYS GETTING LUNCH TOGETHER? SHOULD I BE JEALOUS?
I DID DO THE AGENT NINE THING, BUT WITH WOLVERINE AROUND I DON'T THINK I NEED TO WORRY ABOUT THE TORINOS, SO I THINK I'LL BE SPIDER-MAN FOR THE REST OF THE DAY.
AND I THINK WE'RE GETTING LUNCH. WANT TO COME MEET US?
NO. I PROBABLY SHOULDN'T.
SOMETHING CAME UP ON MY END, ANYWAY.

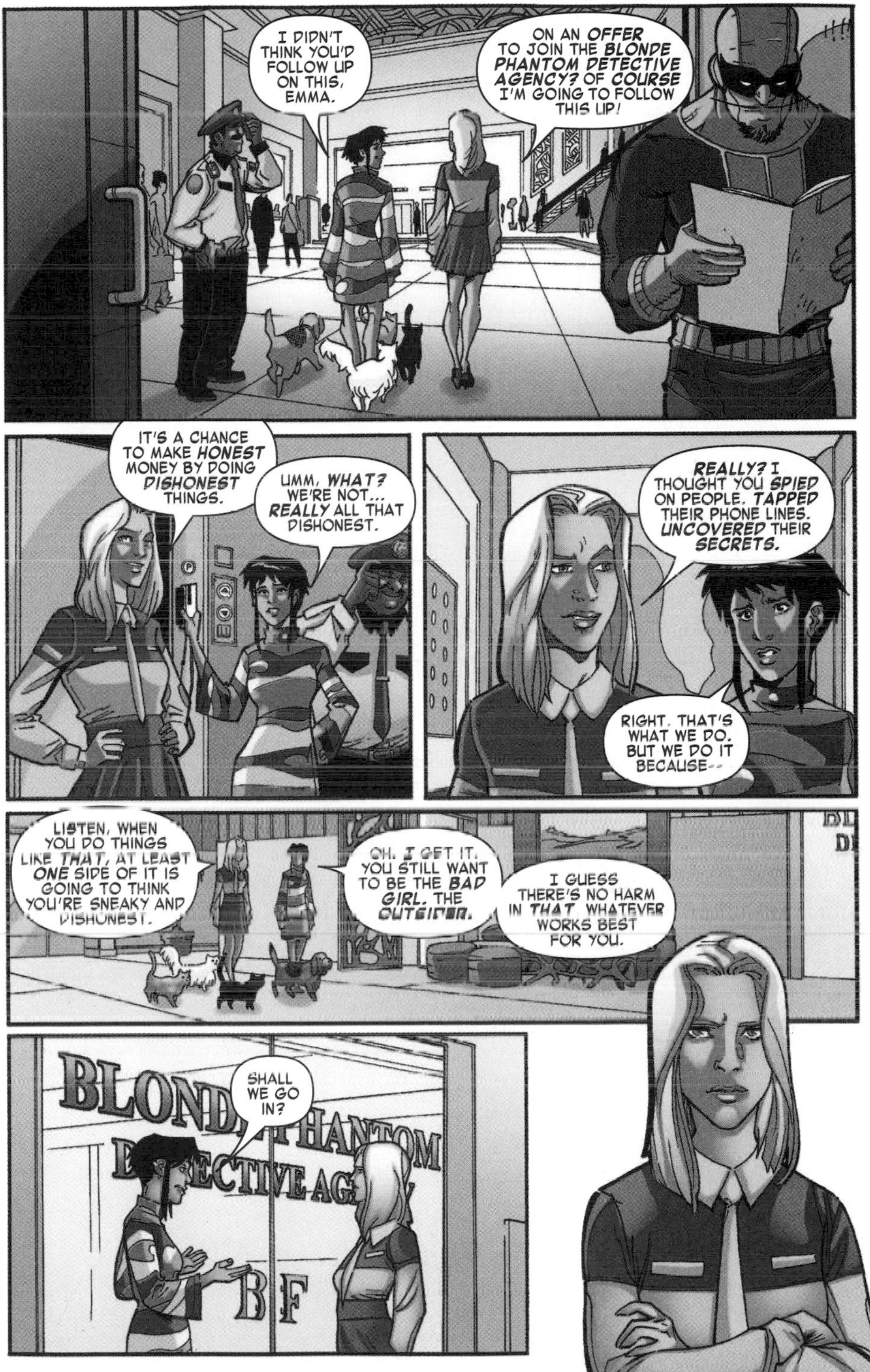
I DIDN'T THINK YOU'D FOLLOW UP ON THIS, EMMA.
ON AN OFFER TO JOIN THE BLONDE PHANTOM DETECTIVE AGENCY? OF COURSE I'M GOING TO FOLLOW THIS UP!
!!!
IT'S A CHANCE TO MAKE HONEST MONEY BY DOING DISHONEST THINGS.
UMM, WHAT? WE'RE NOT... REALLY ALL THAT DISHONEST.
REALLY? I THOUGHT YOU SPIED ON PEOPLE. TAPPED THEIR PHONE LINES. UNCOVERED THEIR SECRETS.
RIGHT. THAT'S WHAT WE DO. BUT WE DO IT BECAUSE--
LISTEN, WHEN YOU DO THINGS LIKE THAT, AT LEAST ONE SIDE OF IT IS GOING TO THINK YOU'RE SNEAKY AND DISHONEST.
OH. I GET IT. YOU STILL WANT TO BE THE BAD GIRL. THE OUTSIDER.
I GUESS THERE'S NO HARM IN THAT. WHATEVER WORKS BEST FOR YOU.
BLONDE PHANTOM DETECTIVE AGENCY
SHALL WE GO IN?
BF

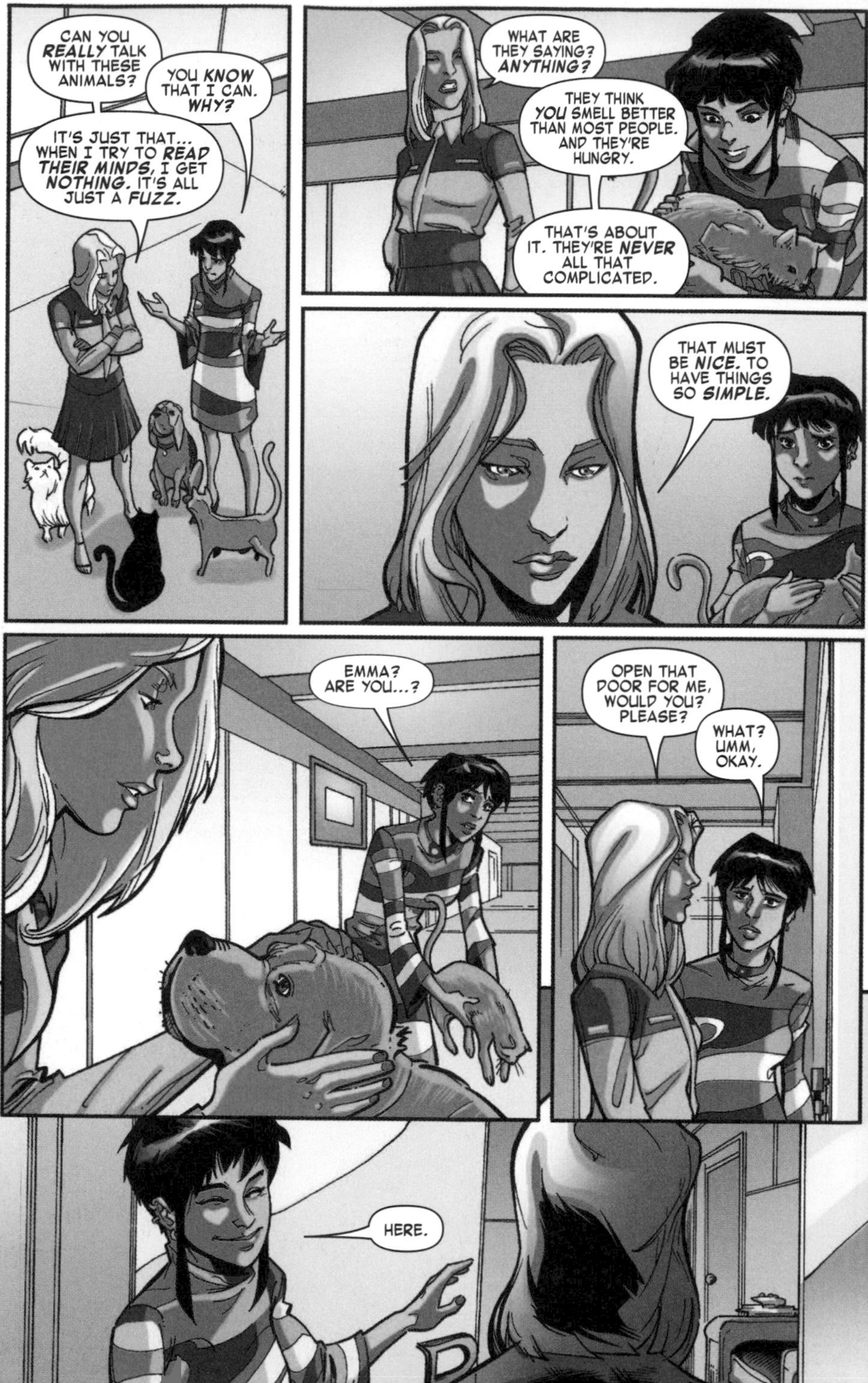
CAN YOU *REALLY* TALK WITH THESE ANIMALS?
YOU *KNOW* THAT I CAN. *WHY?*
IT'S JUST THAT... WHEN I TRY TO *READ THEIR MINDS,* I GET *NOTHING.* IT'S ALL JUST A *FUZZ.*
WHAT ARE THEY SAYING? *ANYTHING?*
THEY THINK *YOU* SMELL BETTER THAN MOST PEOPLE. AND THEY'RE HUNGRY.
THAT'S ABOUT IT. THEY'RE *NEVER* ALL THAT COMPLICATED.
THAT MUST BE *NICE.* TO HAVE THINGS SO *SIMPLE.*
EMMA? ARE YOU...?
OPEN THAT DOOR FOR ME, WOULD YOU? PLEASE?
WHAT? UMM, OKAY.
HERE.

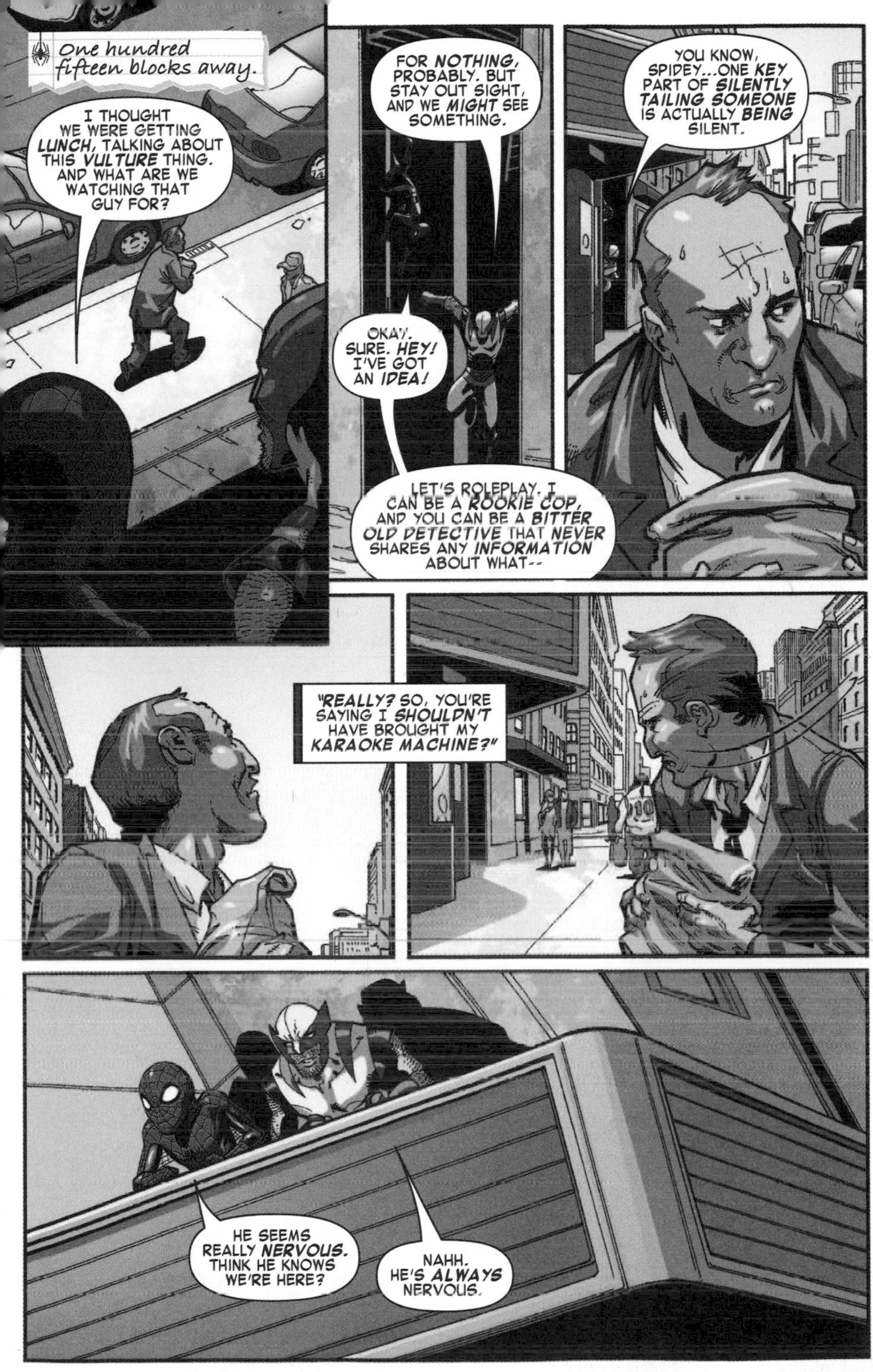

One hundred fifteen blocks away.
I THOUGHT WE WERE GETTING LUNCH, TALKING ABOUT THIS VULTURE THING. AND WHAT ARE WE WATCHING THAT GUY FOR?
FOR NOTHING, PROBABLY. BUT STAY OUT SIGHT, AND WE MIGHT SEE SOMETHING.
OKAY. SURE. HEY! I'VE GOT AN IDEA!
LET'S ROLEPLAY. I CAN BE A ROOKIE COP, AND YOU CAN BE A BITTER OLD DETECTIVE THAT NEVER SHARES ANY INFORMATION ABOUT WHAT--
YOU KNOW, SPIDEY...ONE KEY PART OF SILENTLY TAILING SOMEONE IS ACTUALLY BEING SILENT.
"REALLY? SO, YOU'RE SAYING I SHOULDN'T HAVE BROUGHT MY KARAOKE MACHINE?"
HE SEEMS REALLY NERVOUS. THINK HE KNOWS WE'RE HERE?
NAHH. HE'S ALWAYS NERVOUS.

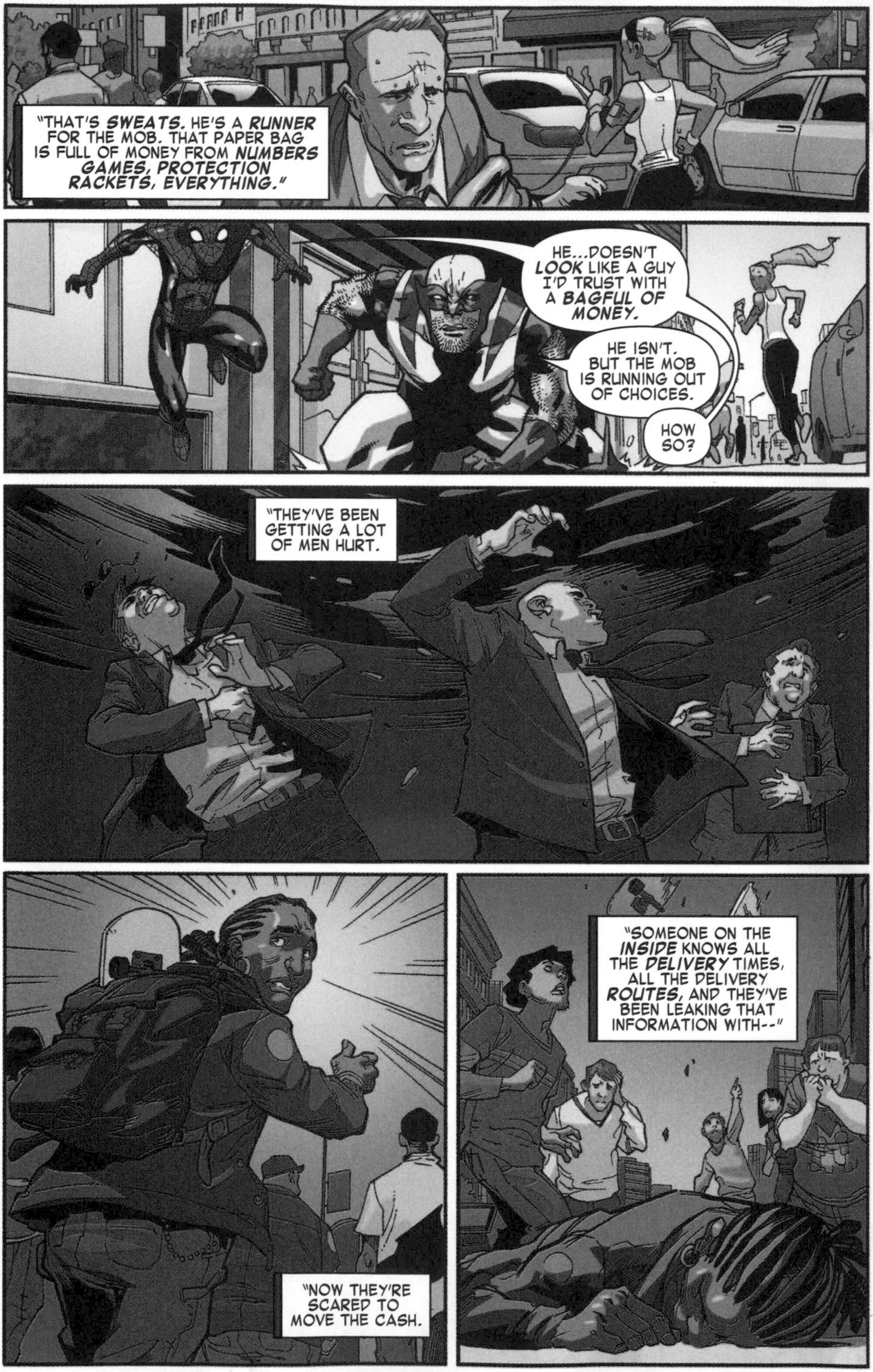
"THAT'S SWEATS. HE'S A RUNNER FOR THE MOB. THAT PAPER BAG IS FULL OF MONEY FROM NUMBERS GAMES, PROTECTION RACKETS, EVERYTHING."
HE...DOESN'T LOOK LIKE A GUY I'D TRUST WITH A BAGFUL OF MONEY.
HE ISN'T. BUT THE MOB IS RUNNING OUT OF CHOICES.
HOW SO?
"THEY'VE BEEN GETTING A LOT OF MEN HURT.
"NOW THEY'RE SCARED TO MOVE THE CASH.
"SOMEONE ON THE INSIDE KNOWS ALL THE DELIVERY TIMES, ALL THE DELIVERY ROUTES, AND THEY'VE BEEN LEAKING THAT INFORMATION WITH--"

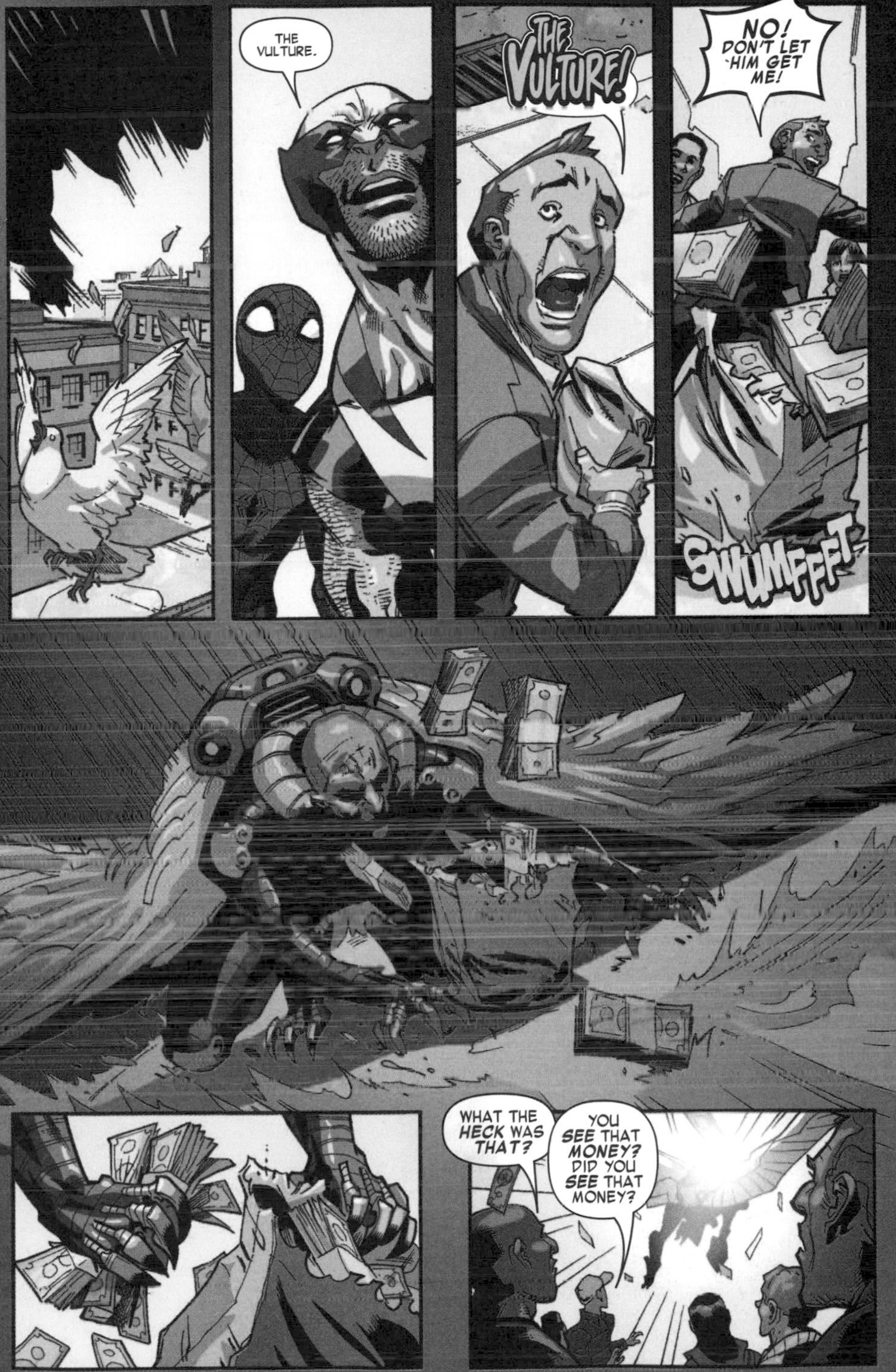
THE VULTURE.
THE VULTURE!
NO! DON'T LET HIM GET ME!
SWUMFFFT
WHAT THE HECK WAS THAT?
YOU SEE THAT MONEY? DID YOU SEE THAT MONEY?

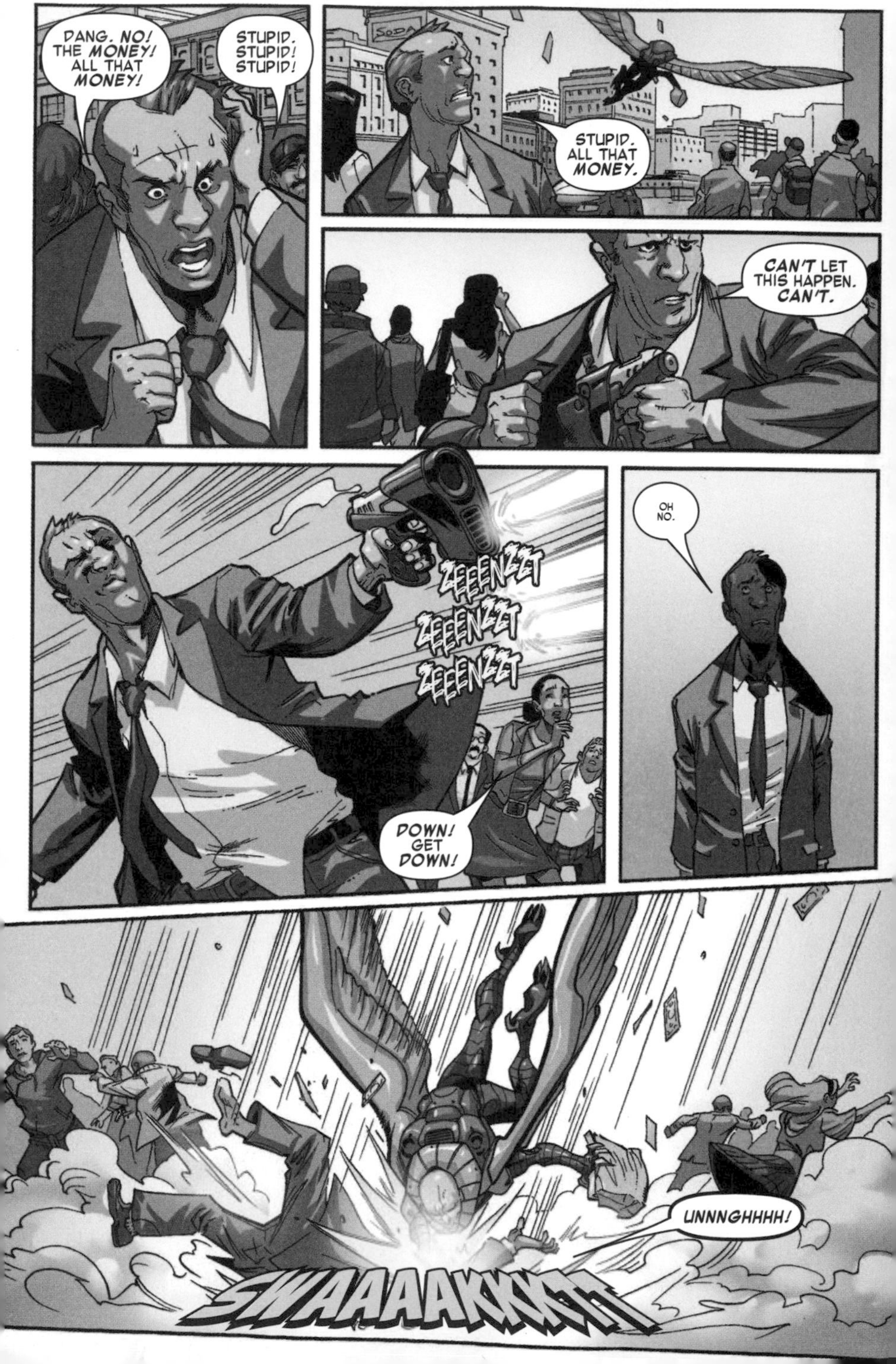
DANG. NO! THE MONEY! ALL THAT MONEY!
STUPID. STUPID! STUPID!
SODA
STUPID. ALL THAT MONEY.
CAN'T LET THIS HAPPEN. CAN'T.
ZEEENZZT
ZEEENZZT
ZEEENZZT
DOWN! GET DOWN!
OH NO.
UNNNGHHHH!
SWAAAAKKKT!

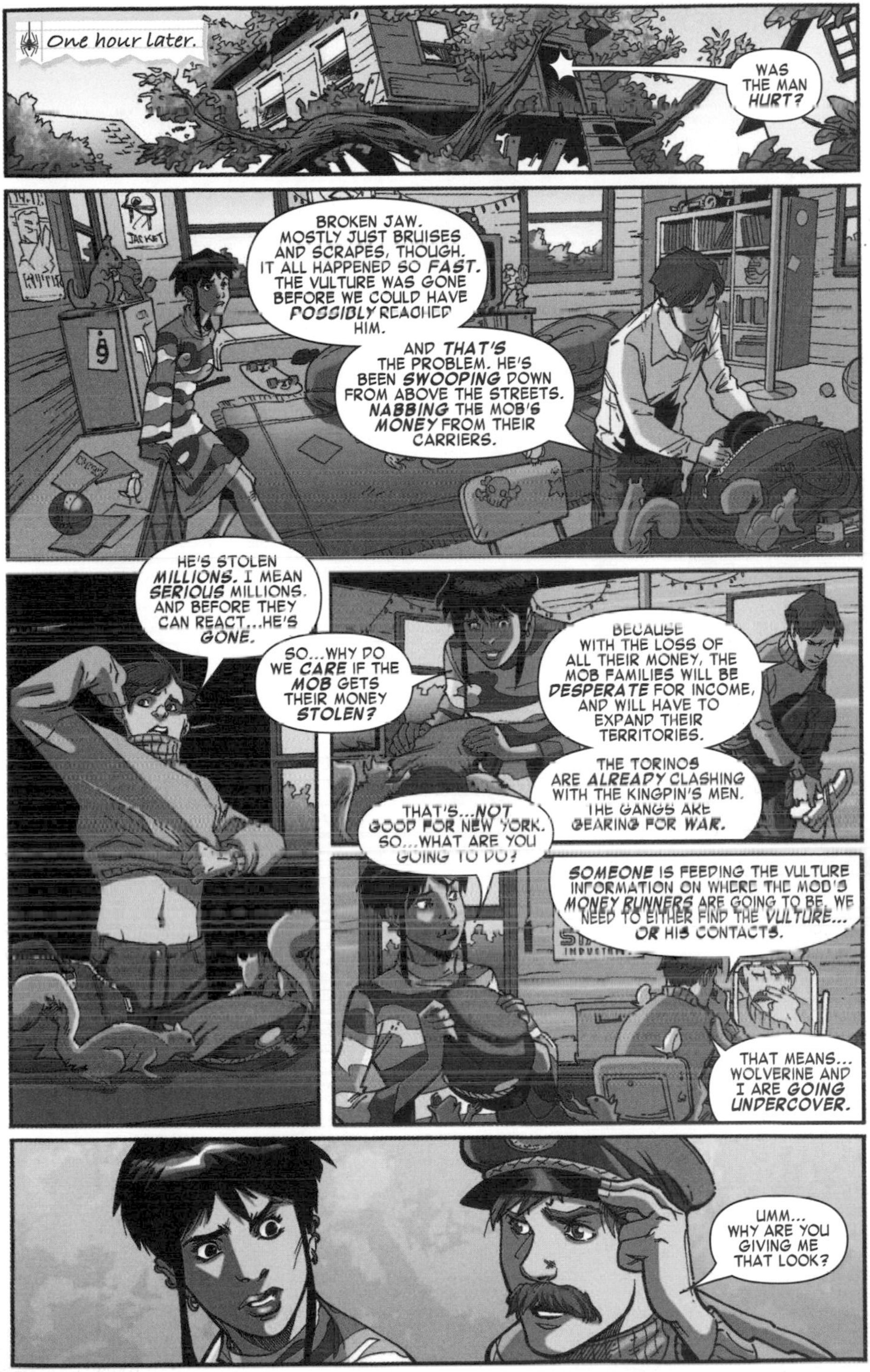
One hour later.
WAS THE MAN HURT?
BROKEN JAW. MOSTLY JUST BRUISES AND SCRAPES, THOUGH. IT ALL HAPPENED SO FAST. THE VULTURE WAS GONE BEFORE WE COULD HAVE POSSIBLY REACHED HIM.
AND THAT'S THE PROBLEM. HE'S BEEN SWOOPING DOWN FROM ABOVE THE STREETS. NABBING THE MOB'S MONEY FROM THEIR CARRIERS.
HE'S STOLEN MILLIONS. I MEAN SERIOUS MILLIONS. AND BEFORE THEY CAN REACT...HE'S GONE.
SO...WHY DO WE CARE IF THE MOB GETS THEIR MONEY STOLEN?
BECAUSE WITH THE LOSS OF ALL THEIR MONEY, THE MOB FAMILIES WILL BE DESPERATE FOR INCOME, AND WILL HAVE TO EXPAND THEIR TERRITORIES.
THE TORINOS ARE ALREADY CLASHING WITH THE KINGPIN'S MEN. THE GANGS ARE GEARING FOR WAR.
THAT'S...NOT GOOD FOR NEW YORK. SO...WHAT ARE YOU GOING TO DO?
SOMEONE IS FEEDING THE VULTURE INFORMATION ON WHERE THE MOB'S MONEY RUNNERS ARE GOING TO BE. WE NEED TO EITHER FIND THE VULTURE... OR HIS CONTACTS.
THAT MEANS... WOLVERINE AND I ARE GOING UNDERCOVER.
UMM... WHY ARE YOU GIVING ME THAT LOOK?

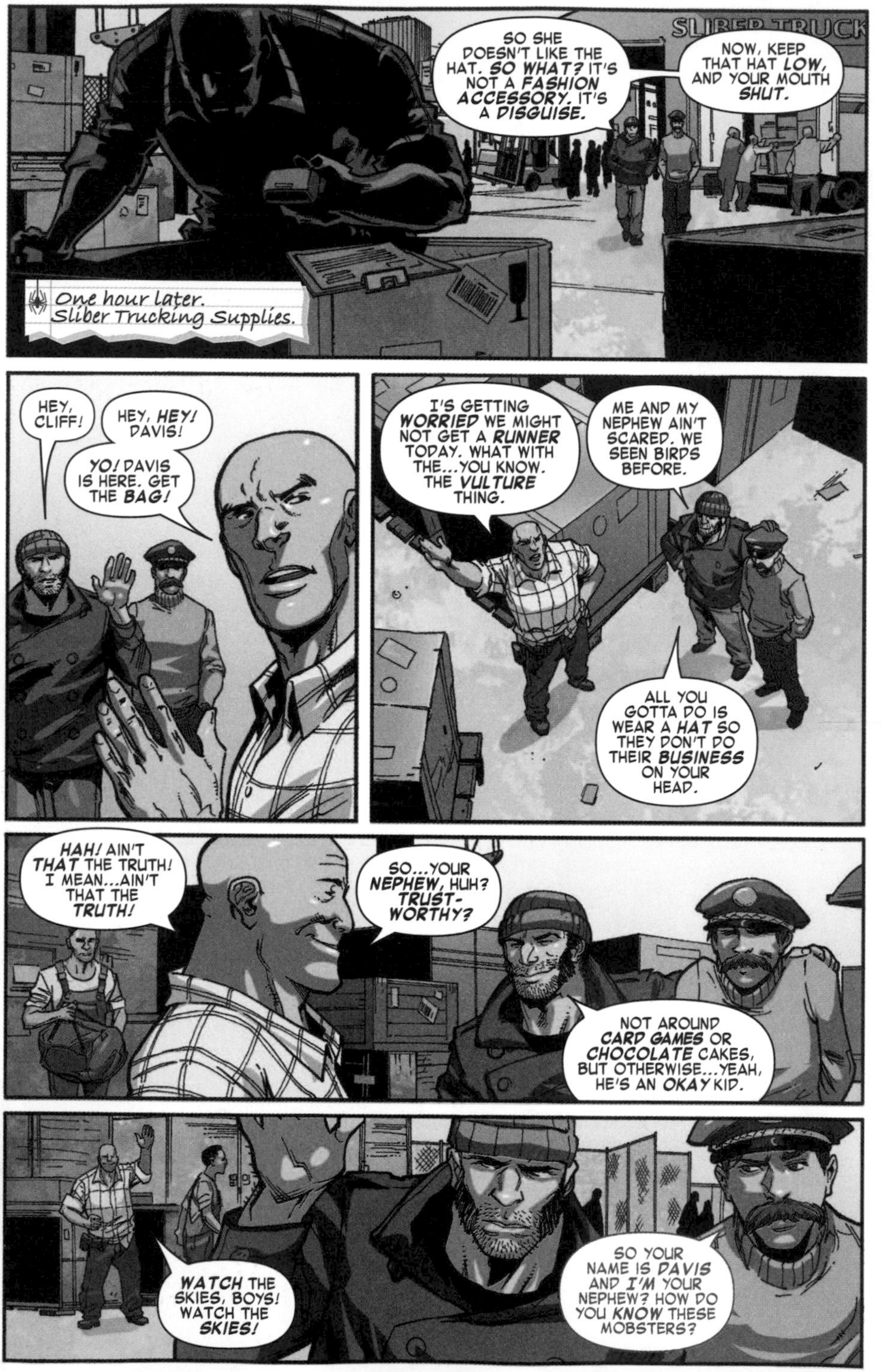
SLIBER TRUCK
SO SHE DOESN'T LIKE THE HAT. SO WHAT? IT'S NOT A FASHION ACCESSORY. IT'S A DISGUISE.
NOW, KEEP THAT HAT LOW, AND YOUR MOUTH SHUT.
One hour later. Sliber Trucking Supplies.
HEY, CLIFF!
HEY, HEY! DAVIS!
YO! DAVIS IS HERE. GET THE BAG!
I'S GETTING WORRIED WE MIGHT NOT GET A RUNNER TODAY. WHAT WITH THE...YOU KNOW. THE VULTURE THING.
ME AND MY NEPHEW AIN'T SCARED. WE SEEN BIRDS BEFORE.
ALL YOU GOTTA DO IS WEAR A HAT SO THEY DON'T DO THEIR BUSINESS ON YOUR HEAD.
HAH! AIN'T THAT THE TRUTH! I MEAN...AIN'T THAT THE TRUTH!
SO...YOUR NEPHEW, HUH? TRUST-WORTHY?
NOT AROUND CARD GAMES OR CHOCOLATE CAKES, BUT OTHERWISE...YEAH, HE'S AN OKAY KID.
WATCH THE SKIES, BOYS! WATCH THE SKIES!
SO YOUR NAME IS DAVIS AND I'M YOUR NEPHEW? HOW DO YOU KNOW THESE MOBSTERS?

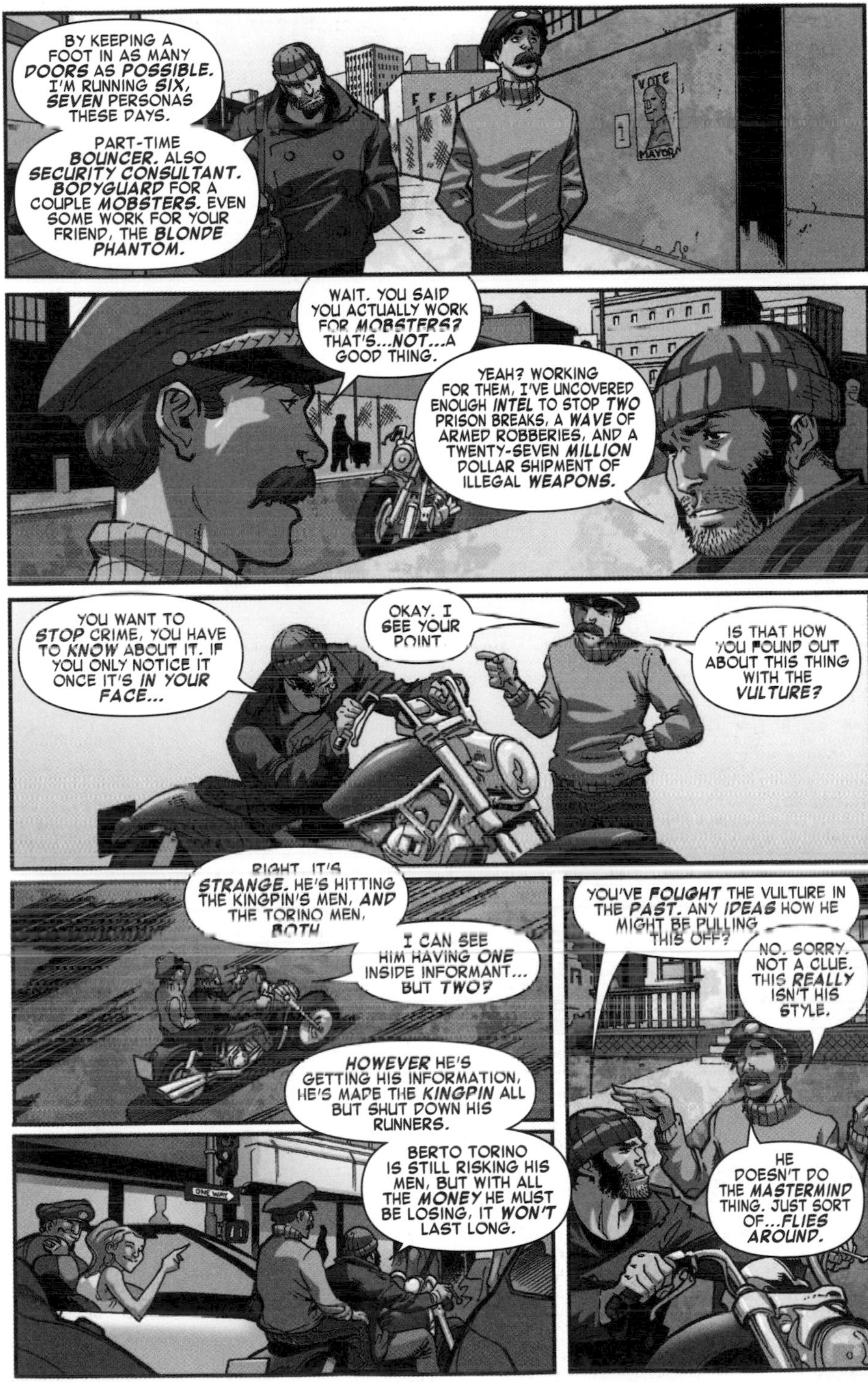

BY KEEPING A FOOT IN AS MANY DOORS AS POSSIBLE. I'M RUNNING SIX, SEVEN PERSONAS THESE DAYS.
PART-TIME BOUNCER. ALSO SECURITY CONSULTANT. BODYGUARD FOR A COUPLE MOBSTERS. EVEN SOME WORK FOR YOUR FRIEND, THE BLONDE PHANTOM.
VOTE
MAYOR
WAIT. YOU SAID YOU ACTUALLY WORK FOR MOBSTERS? THAT'S...NOT...A GOOD THING.
YEAH? WORKING FOR THEM, I'VE UNCOVERED ENOUGH INTEL TO STOP TWO PRISON BREAKS, A WAVE OF ARMED ROBBERIES, AND A TWENTY-SEVEN MILLION DOLLAR SHIPMENT OF ILLEGAL WEAPONS.
YOU WANT TO STOP CRIME, YOU HAVE TO KNOW ABOUT IT. IF YOU ONLY NOTICE IT ONCE IT'S IN YOUR FACE...
OKAY. I SEE YOUR POINT.
IS THAT HOW YOU FOUND OUT ABOUT THIS THING WITH THE VULTURE?
RIGHT. IT'S STRANGE. HE'S HITTING THE KINGPIN'S MEN, AND THE TORINO MEN, BOTH.
I CAN SEE HIM HAVING ONE INSIDE INFORMANT... BUT TWO?
HOWEVER HE'S GETTING HIS INFORMATION, HE'S MADE THE KINGPIN ALL BUT SHUT DOWN HIS RUNNERS.
BERTO TORINO IS STILL RISKING HIS MEN, BUT WITH ALL THE MONEY HE MUST BE LOSING, IT WON'T LAST LONG.
ONE WAY
YOU'VE FOUGHT THE VULTURE IN THE PAST. ANY IDEAS HOW HE MIGHT BE PULLING THIS OFF?
NO. SORRY. NOT A CLUE. THIS REALLY ISN'T HIS STYLE.
HE DOESN'T DO THE MASTERMIND THING. JUST SORT OF...FLIES AROUND.

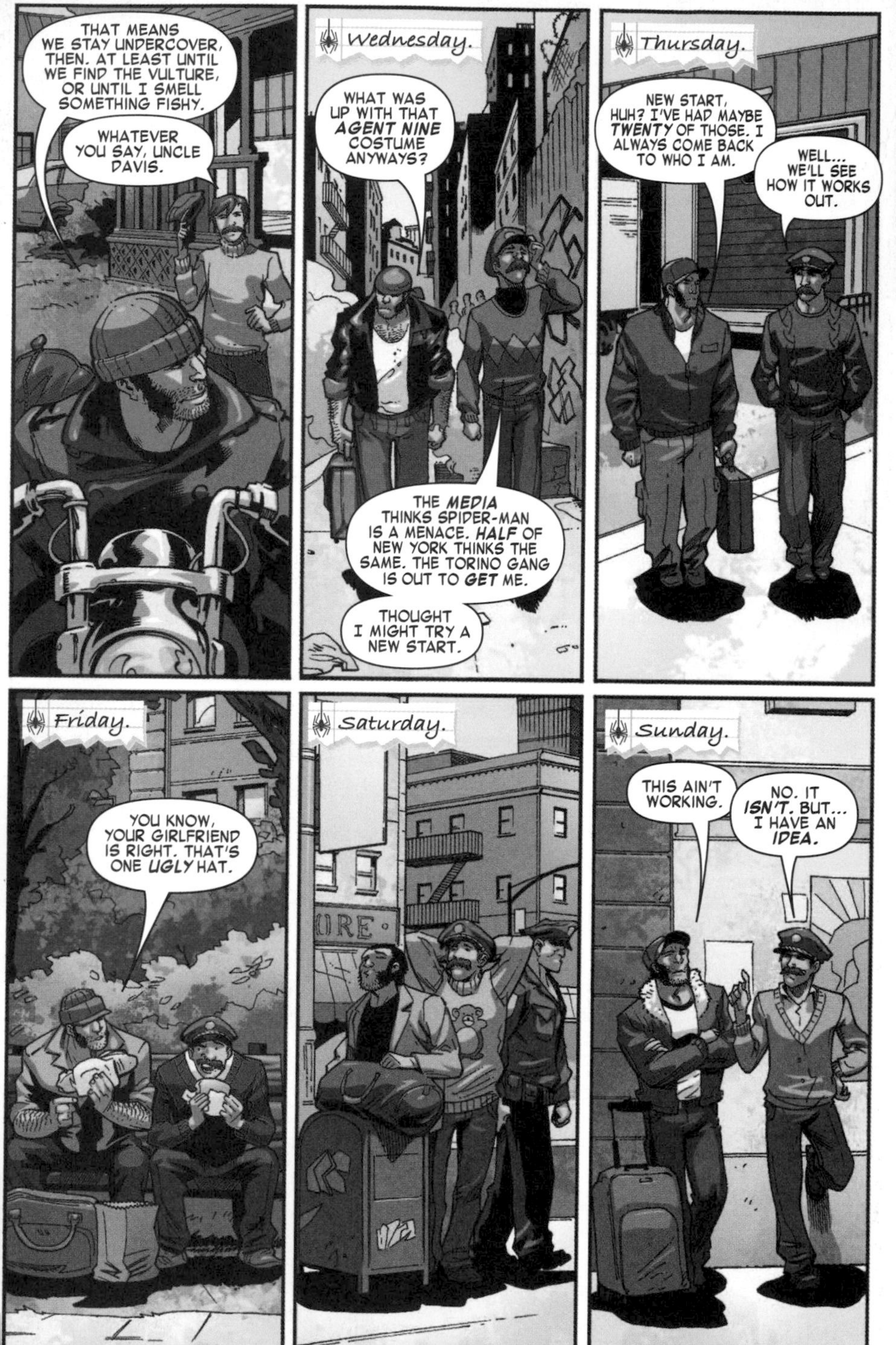
THAT MEANS WE STAY UNDERCOVER, THEN. AT LEAST UNTIL WE FIND THE VULTURE, OR UNTIL I SMELL SOMETHING FISHY.
WHATEVER YOU SAY, UNCLE DAVIS.
Wednesday.
WHAT WAS UP WITH THAT AGENT NINE COSTUME ANYWAYS?
THE MEDIA THINKS SPIDER-MAN IS A MENACE. HALF OF NEW YORK THINKS THE SAME. THE TORINO GANG IS OUT TO GET ME.
THOUGHT I MIGHT TRY A NEW START.
Thursday.
NEW START, HUH? I'VE HAD MAYBE TWENTY OF THOSE. I ALWAYS COME BACK TO WHO I AM.
WELL... WE'LL SEE HOW IT WORKS OUT.
Friday.
YOU KNOW, YOUR GIRLFRIEND IS RIGHT. THAT'S ONE UGLY HAT.
Saturday.
Sunday.
THIS AIN'T WORKING.
NO. IT ISN'T. BUT... I HAVE AN IDEA.

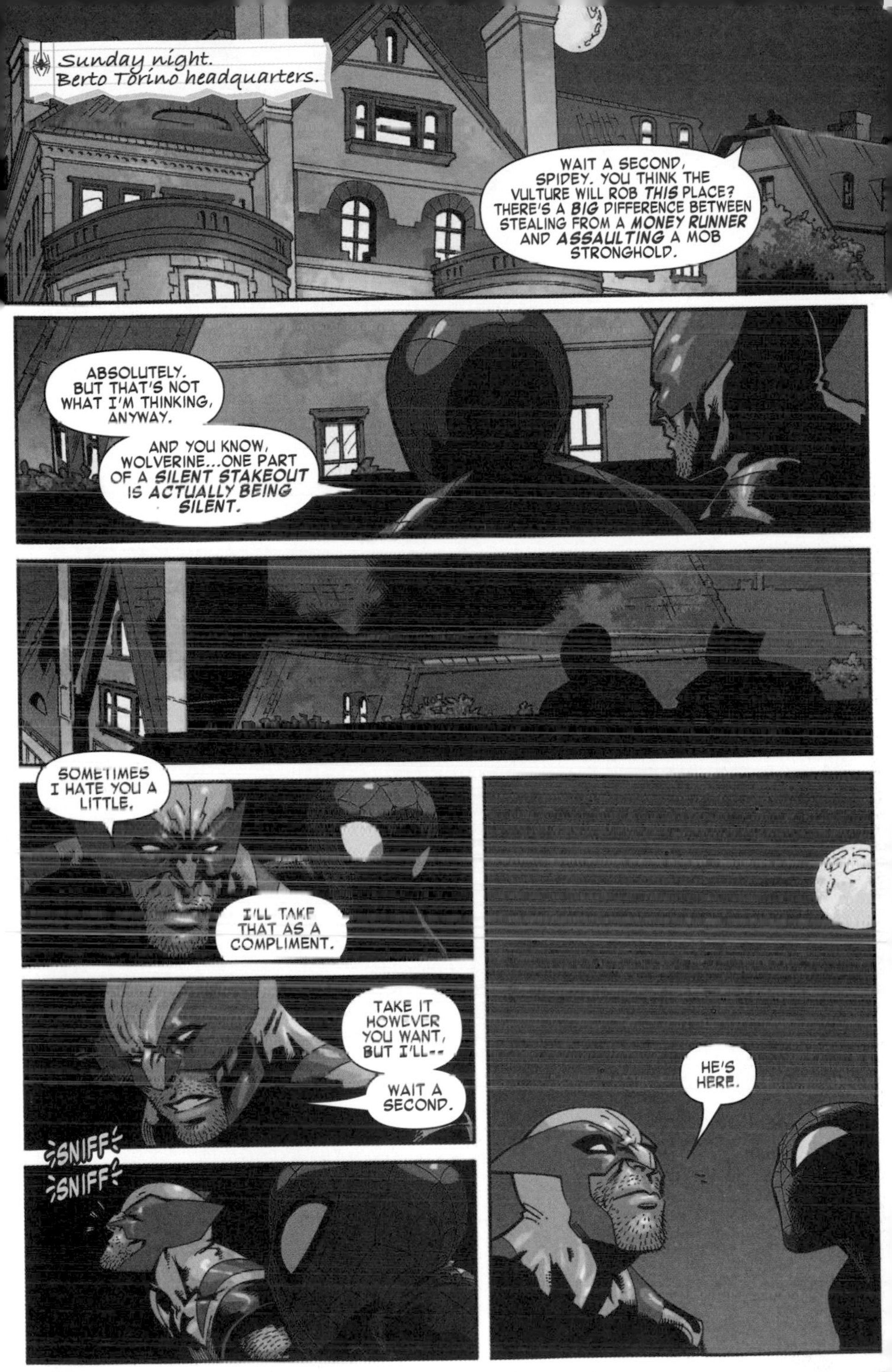
Sunday night.
Berto Torino headquarters.
WAIT A SECOND, SPIDEY. YOU THINK THE VULTURE WILL ROB THIS PLACE? THERE'S A BIG DIFFERENCE BETWEEN STEALING FROM A MONEY RUNNER AND ASSAULTING A MOB STRONGHOLD.
ABSOLUTELY. BUT THAT'S NOT WHAT I'M THINKING, ANYWAY.
AND YOU KNOW, WOLVERINE...ONE PART OF A SILENT STAKEOUT IS ACTUALLY BEING SILENT.
SOMETIMES I HATE YOU A LITTLE.
I'LL TAKE THAT AS A COMPLIMENT.
TAKE IT HOWEVER YOU WANT, BUT I'LL--
WAIT A SECOND.
SNIFF
SNIFF
HE'S HERE.

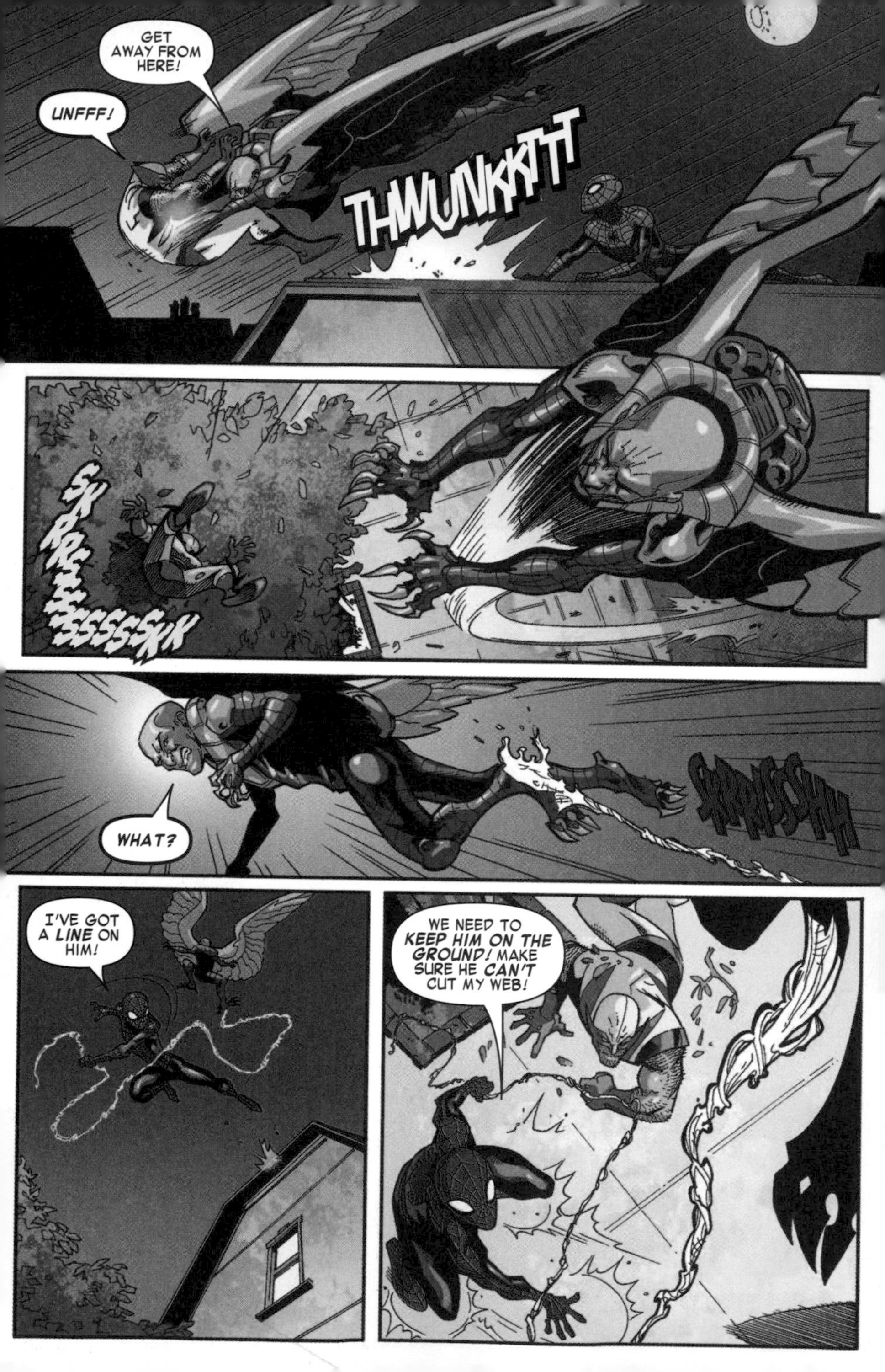

GET AWAY FROM HERE!
UNFFF!
THWUNKKTTT
SKRRSSSHHSSSSSKK
WHAT?
SKRRSSHH
I'VE GOT A LINE ON HIM!
WE NEED TO KEEP HIM ON THE GROUND! MAKE SURE HE CAN'T CUT MY WEB!

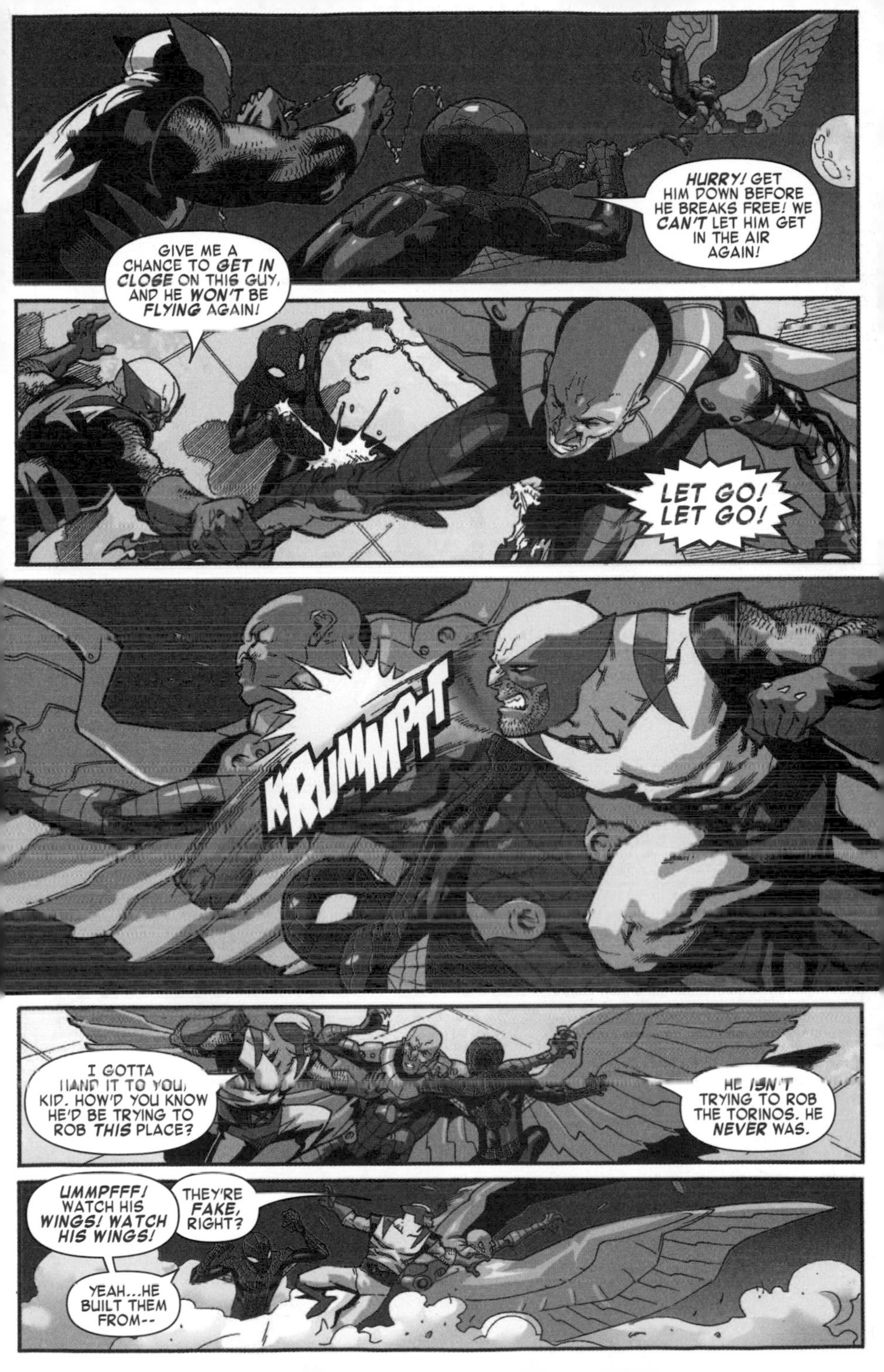

HURRY! GET HIM DOWN BEFORE HE BREAKS FREE! WE CAN'T LET HIM GET IN THE AIR AGAIN!
GIVE ME A CHANCE TO GET IN CLOSE ON THIS GUY, AND HE WON'T BE FLYING AGAIN!
LET GO! LET GO!
KRUMMPTT
I GOTTA HAND IT TO YOU, KID. HOW'D YOU KNOW HE'D BE TRYING TO ROB THIS PLACE?
HE ISN'T TRYING TO ROB THE TORINOS. HE NEVER WAS.
UMMPFFF! WATCH HIS WINGS! WATCH HIS WINGS!
THEY'RE FAKE, RIGHT?
YEAH...HE BUILT THEM FROM--

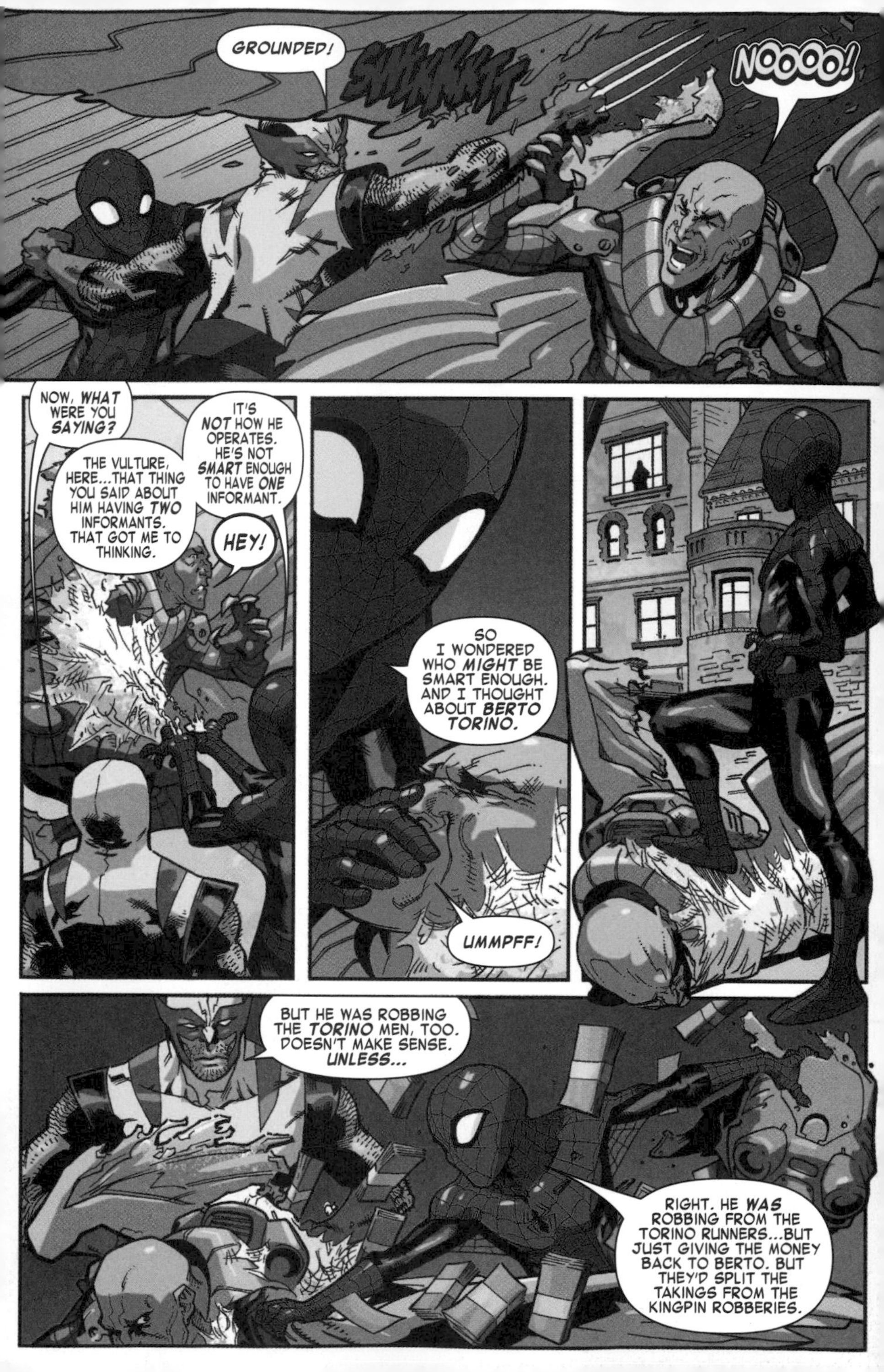
GROUNDED!
SHHNKKT!
NOOOO!
NOW, WHAT WERE YOU SAYING?
THE VULTURE, HERE...THAT THING YOU SAID ABOUT HIM HAVING TWO INFORMANTS. THAT GOT ME TO THINKING.
IT'S NOT HOW HE OPERATES. HE'S NOT SMART ENOUGH TO HAVE ONE INFORMANT.
HEY!
SO I WONDERED WHO MIGHT BE SMART ENOUGH. AND I THOUGHT ABOUT BERTO TORINO.
UMMPFF!
BUT HE WAS ROBBING THE TORINO MEN, TOO. DOESN'T MAKE SENSE. UNLESS...
RIGHT. HE WAS ROBBING FROM THE TORINO RUNNERS...BUT JUST GIVING THE MONEY BACK TO BERTO. BUT THEY'D SPLIT THE TAKINGS FROM THE KINGPIN ROBBERIES.

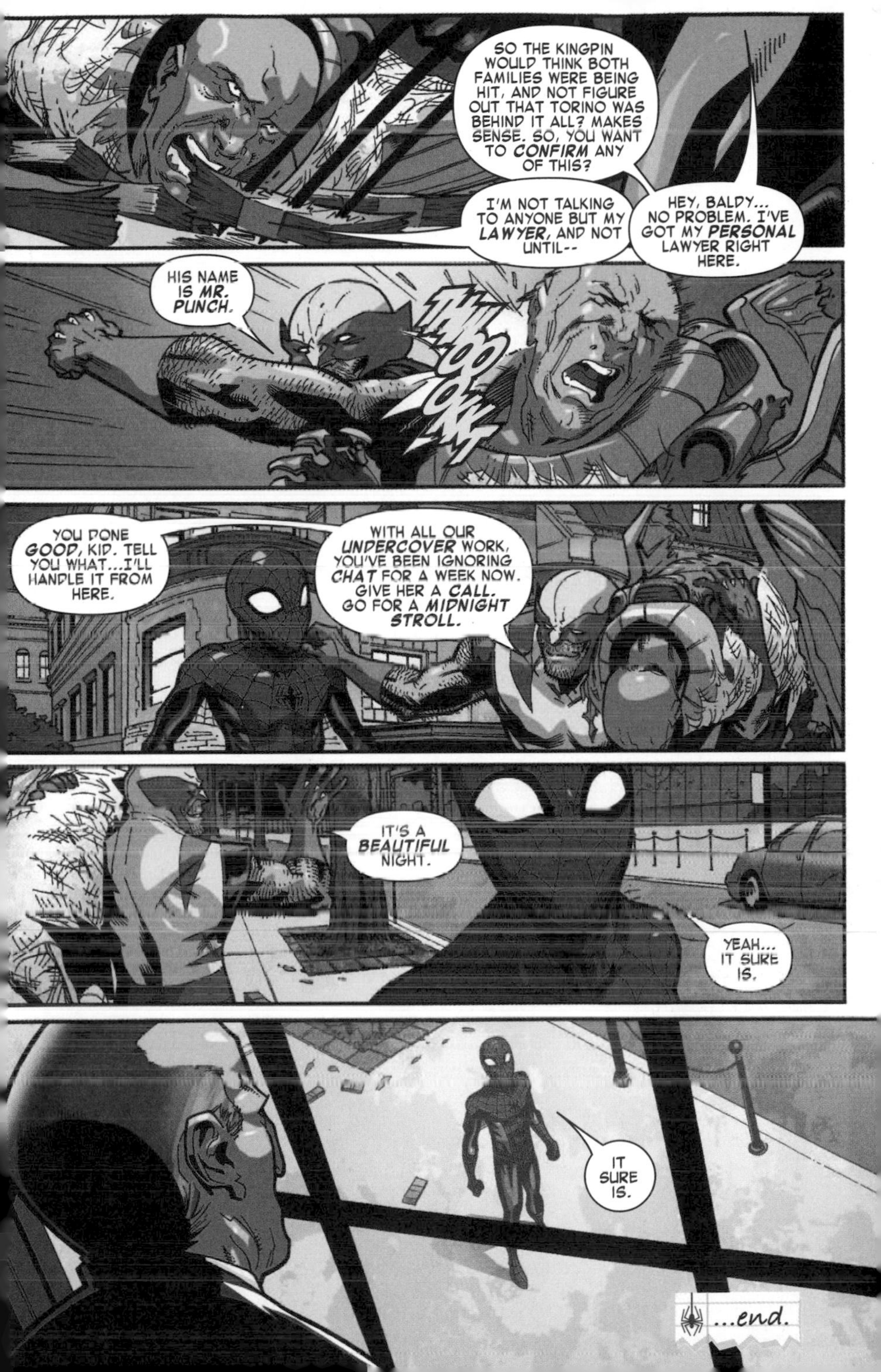
SO THE KINGPIN WOULD THINK BOTH FAMILIES WERE BEING HIT, AND NOT FIGURE OUT THAT TORINO WAS BEHIND IT ALL? MAKES SENSE. SO, YOU WANT TO CONFIRM ANY OF THIS?
I'M NOT TALKING TO ANYONE BUT MY LAWYER, AND NOT UNTIL--
HEY, BALDY... NO PROBLEM. I'VE GOT MY PERSONAL LAWYER RIGHT HERE.
HIS NAME IS MR. PUNCH.
THOOOOMK
YOU DONE GOOD, KID. TELL YOU WHAT...I'LL HANDLE IT FROM HERE.
WITH ALL OUR UNDERCOVER WORK, YOU'VE BEEN IGNORING CHAT FOR A WEEK NOW. GIVE HER A CALL. GO FOR A MIDNIGHT STROLL.
IT'S A BEAUTIFUL NIGHT.
YEAH... IT SURE IS.
IT SURE IS.
...end.

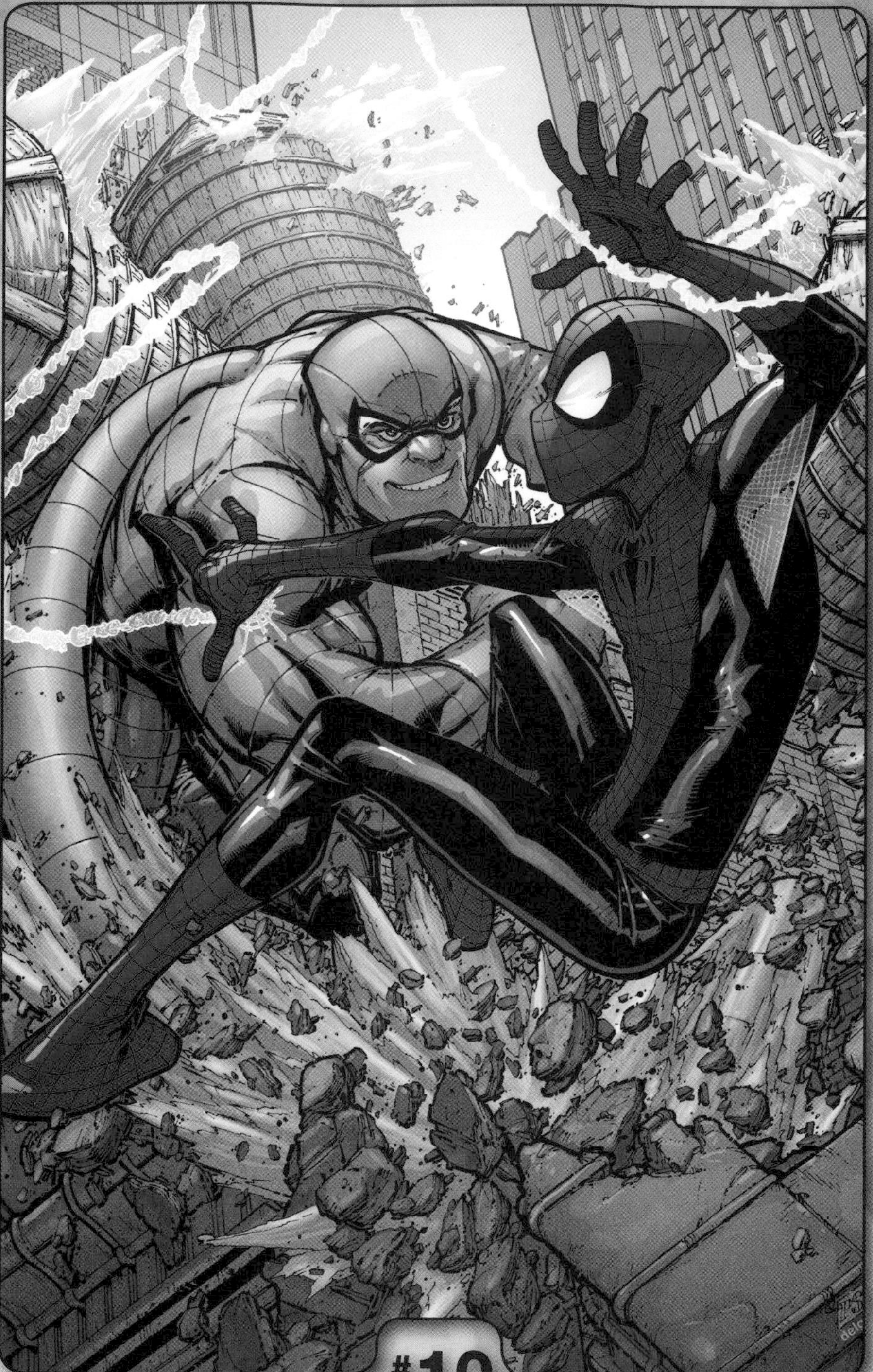

#10

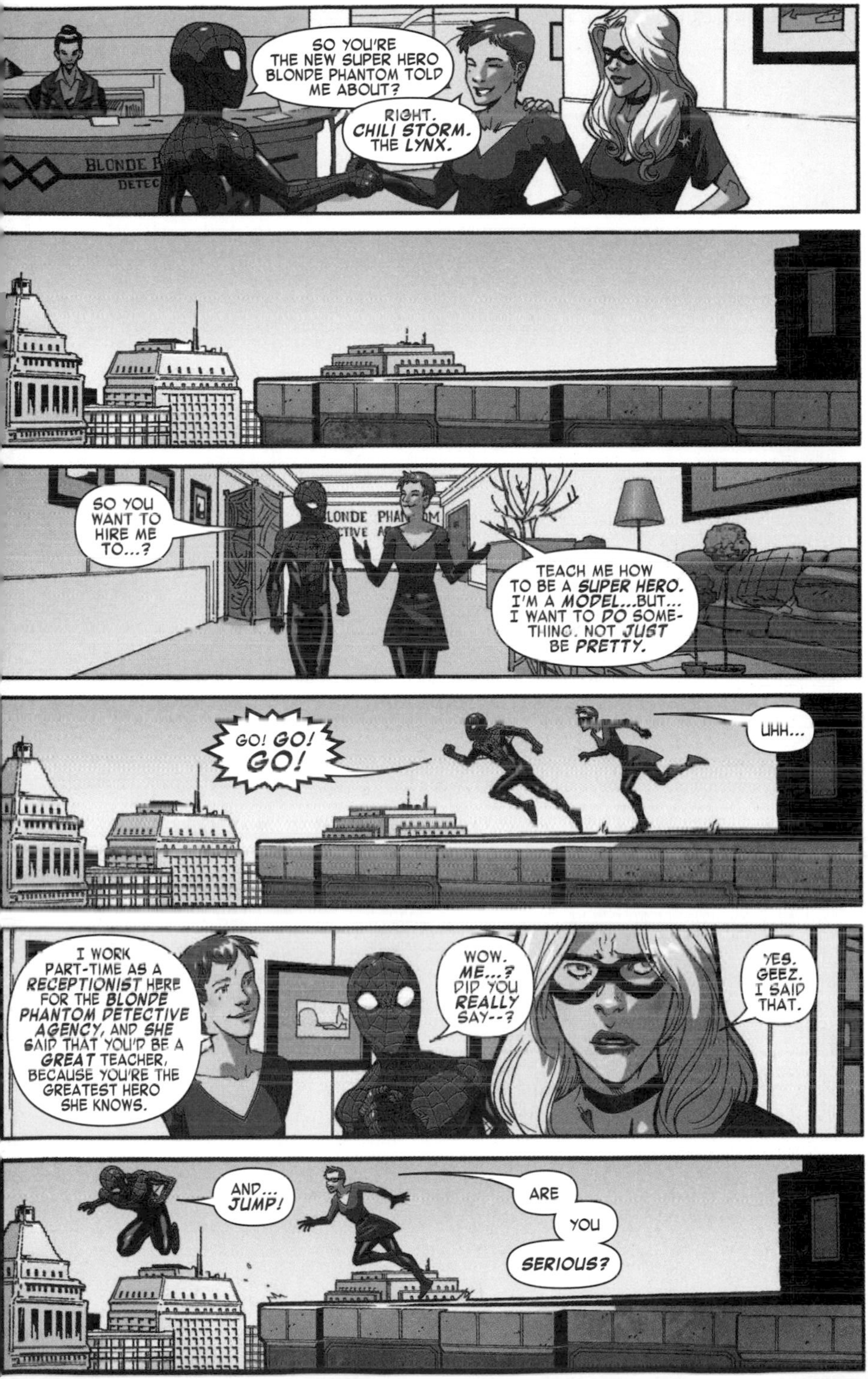
SO YOU'RE THE NEW SUPER HERO BLONDE PHANTOM TOLD ME ABOUT?
RIGHT. CHILI STORM. THE LYNX.
SO YOU WANT TO HIRE ME TO...?
TEACH ME HOW TO BE A SUPER HERO. I'M A MODEL...BUT... I WANT TO DO SOMETHING. NOT JUST BE PRETTY.
GO! GO! GO!
UHH...
I WORK PART-TIME AS A RECEPTIONIST HERE FOR THE BLONDE PHANTOM DETECTIVE AGENCY, AND SHE SAID THAT YOU'D BE A GREAT TEACHER, BECAUSE YOU'RE THE GREATEST HERO SHE KNOWS.
WOW. ME...? DID YOU REALLY SAY--?
YES. GEEZ. I SAID THAT.
AND... JUMP!
ARE YOU SERIOUS?

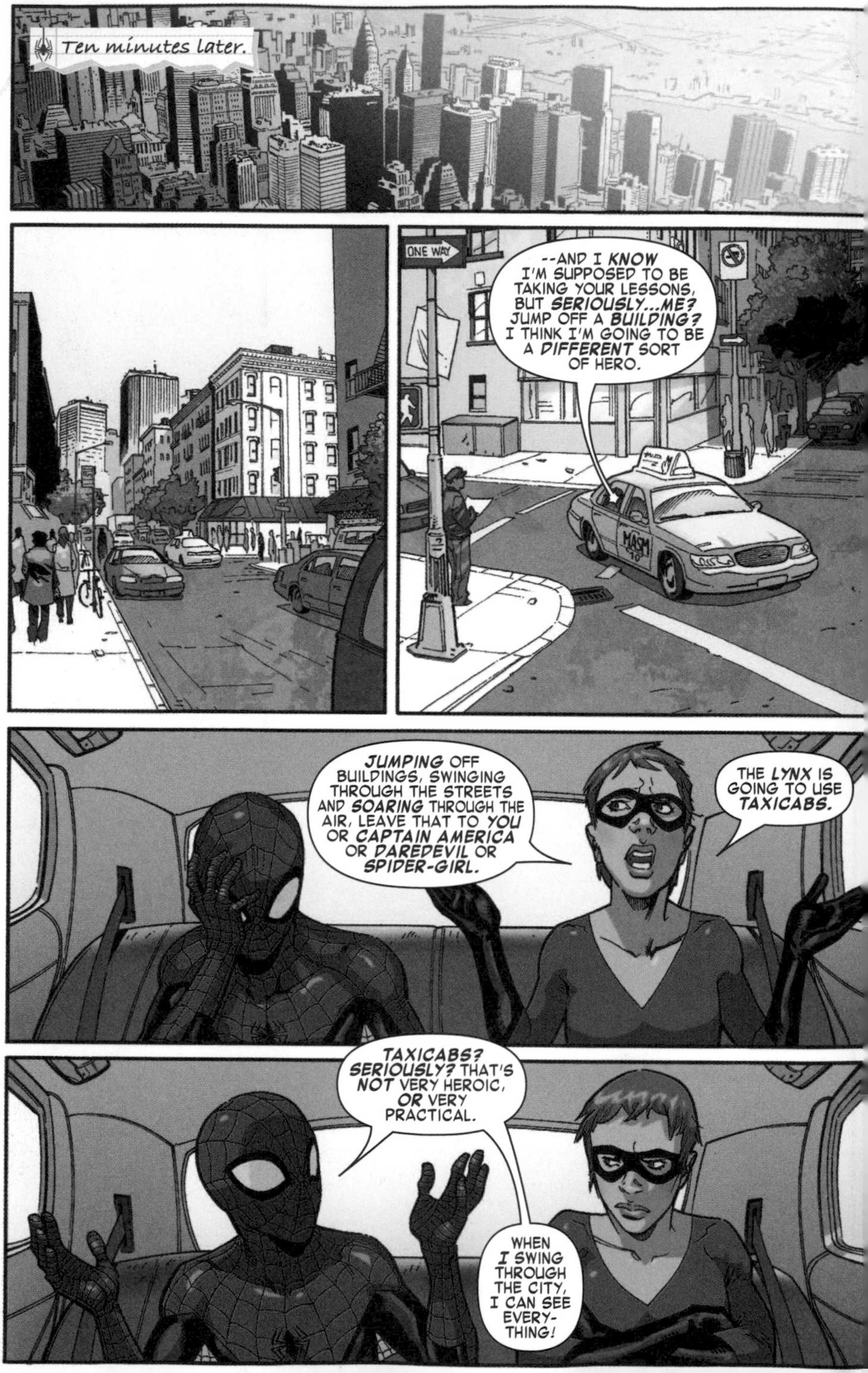

Ten minutes later.
ONE WAY
--AND I KNOW I'M SUPPOSED TO BE TAKING YOUR LESSONS, BUT SERIOUSLY...ME? JUMP OFF A BUILDING? I THINK I'M GOING TO BE A DIFFERENT SORT OF HERO.
JUMPING OFF BUILDINGS, SWINGING THROUGH THE STREETS AND SOARING THROUGH THE AIR, LEAVE THAT TO YOU OR CAPTAIN AMERICA OR DAREDEVIL OR SPIDER-GIRL.
THE LYNX IS GOING TO USE TAXICABS.
TAXICABS? SERIOUSLY? THAT'S NOT VERY HEROIC, OR VERY PRACTICAL.
WHEN I SWING THROUGH THE CITY, I CAN SEE EVERY-THING!

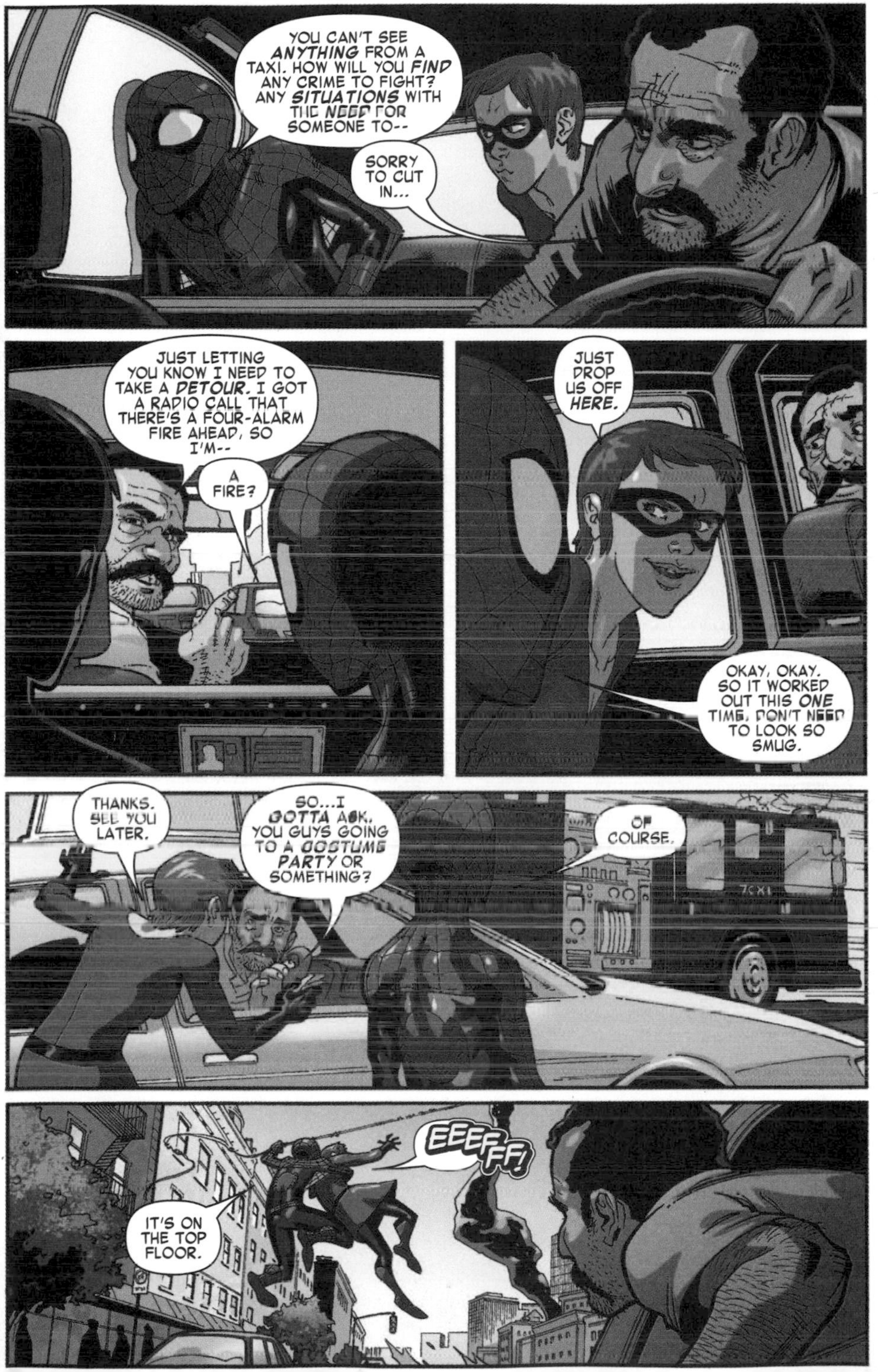

YOU CAN'T SEE ANYTHING FROM A TAXI. HOW WILL YOU FIND ANY CRIME TO FIGHT? ANY SITUATIONS WITH THE NEED FOR SOMEONE TO--
SORRY TO CUT IN...
JUST LETTING YOU KNOW I NEED TO TAKE A DETOUR. I GOT A RADIO CALL THAT THERE'S A FOUR-ALARM FIRE AHEAD, SO I'M--
A FIRE?
JUST DROP US OFF HERE.
OKAY, OKAY. SO IT WORKED OUT THIS ONE TIME. DON'T NEED TO LOOK SO SMUG.
THANKS. SEE YOU LATER.
SO...I GOTTA ASK. YOU GUYS GOING TO A COSTUME PARTY OR SOMETHING?
OF COURSE.
EEEFFF!
IT'S ON THE TOP FLOOR.

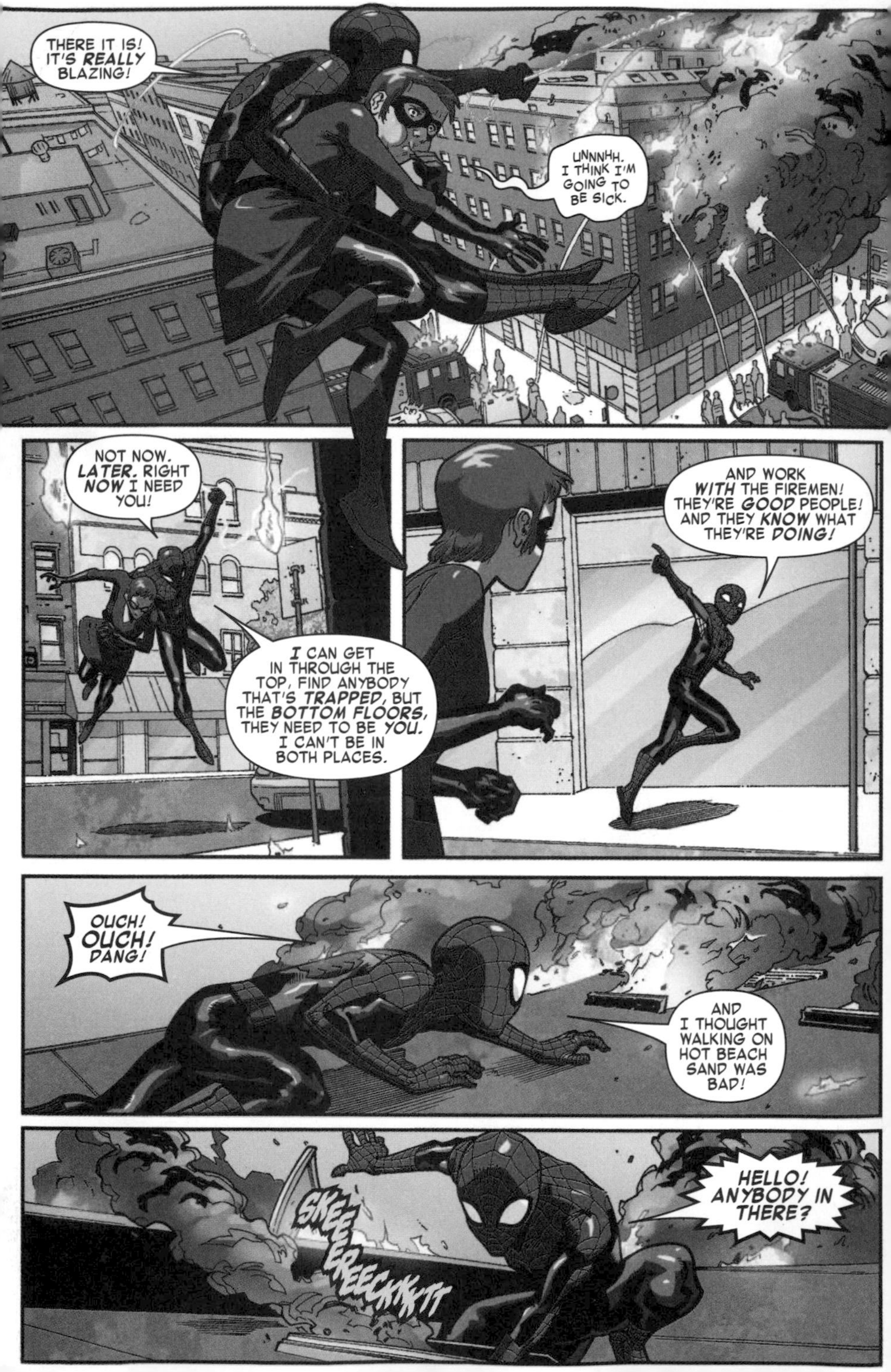
THERE IT IS! IT'S REALLY BLAZING!
UNNNHH. I THINK I'M GOING TO BE SICK.
NOT NOW. LATER. RIGHT NOW I NEED YOU!
I CAN GET IN THROUGH THE TOP, FIND ANYBODY THAT'S TRAPPED, BUT THE BOTTOM FLOORS, THEY NEED TO BE YOU. I CAN'T BE IN BOTH PLACES.
AND WORK WITH THE FIREMEN! THEY'RE GOOD PEOPLE! AND THEY KNOW WHAT THEY'RE DOING!
OUCH! OUCH! DANG!
AND I THOUGHT WALKING ON HOT BEACH SAND WAS BAD!
SKREEEREECKKKTT
HELLO! ANYBODY IN THERE?

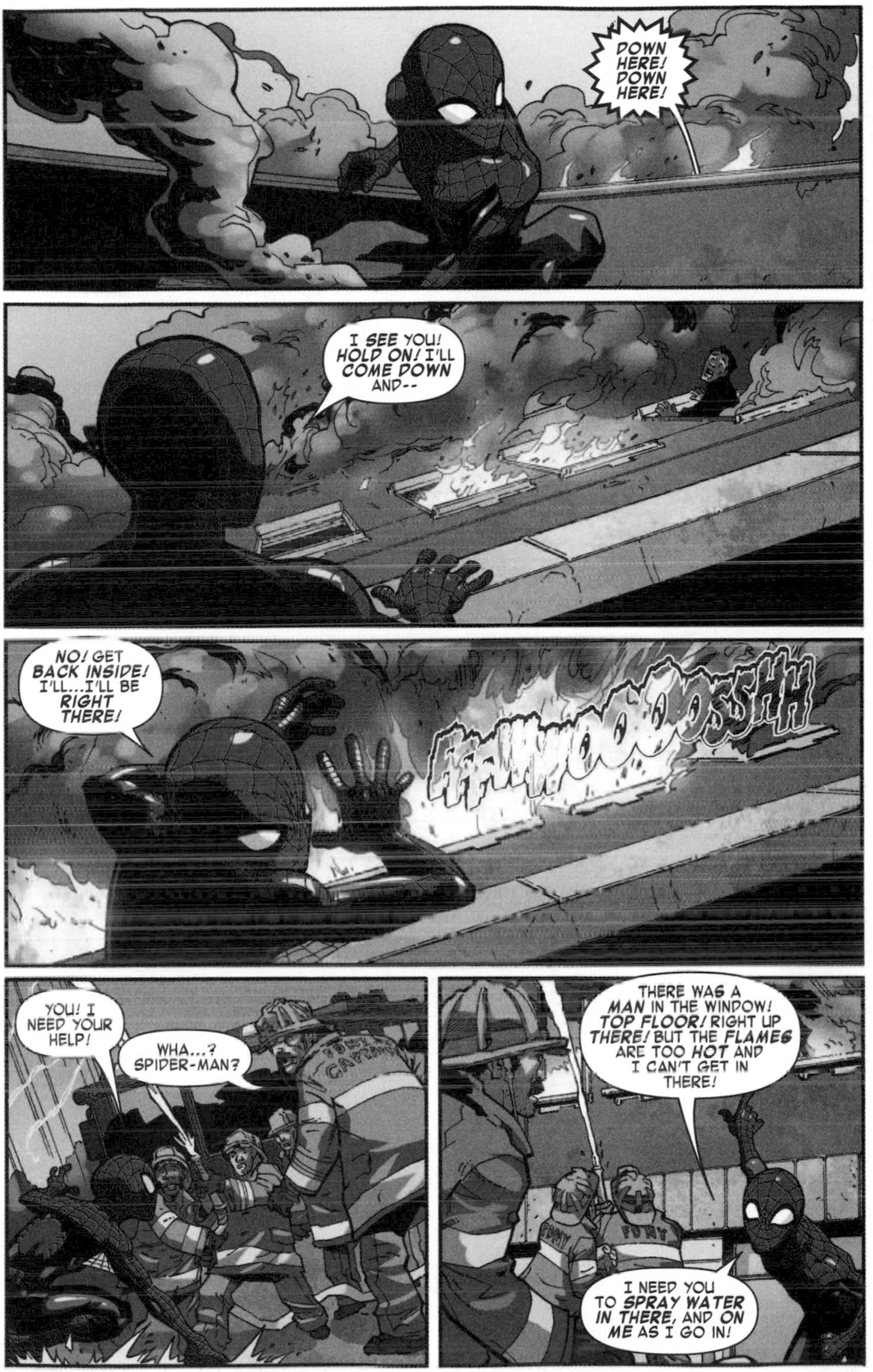
DOWN HERE! DOWN HERE!
I SEE YOU! HOLD ON! I'LL COME DOWN AND--
NO! GET BACK INSIDE! I'LL...I'LL BE RIGHT THERE!
FFWOOOOSSHH
YOU! I NEED YOUR HELP!
WHA...? SPIDER-MAN?
THERE WAS A MAN IN THE WINDOW! TOP FLOOR! RIGHT UP THERE! BUT THE FLAMES ARE TOO HOT AND I CAN'T GET IN THERE!
I NEED YOU TO SPRAY WATER IN THERE, AND ON ME AS I GO IN!

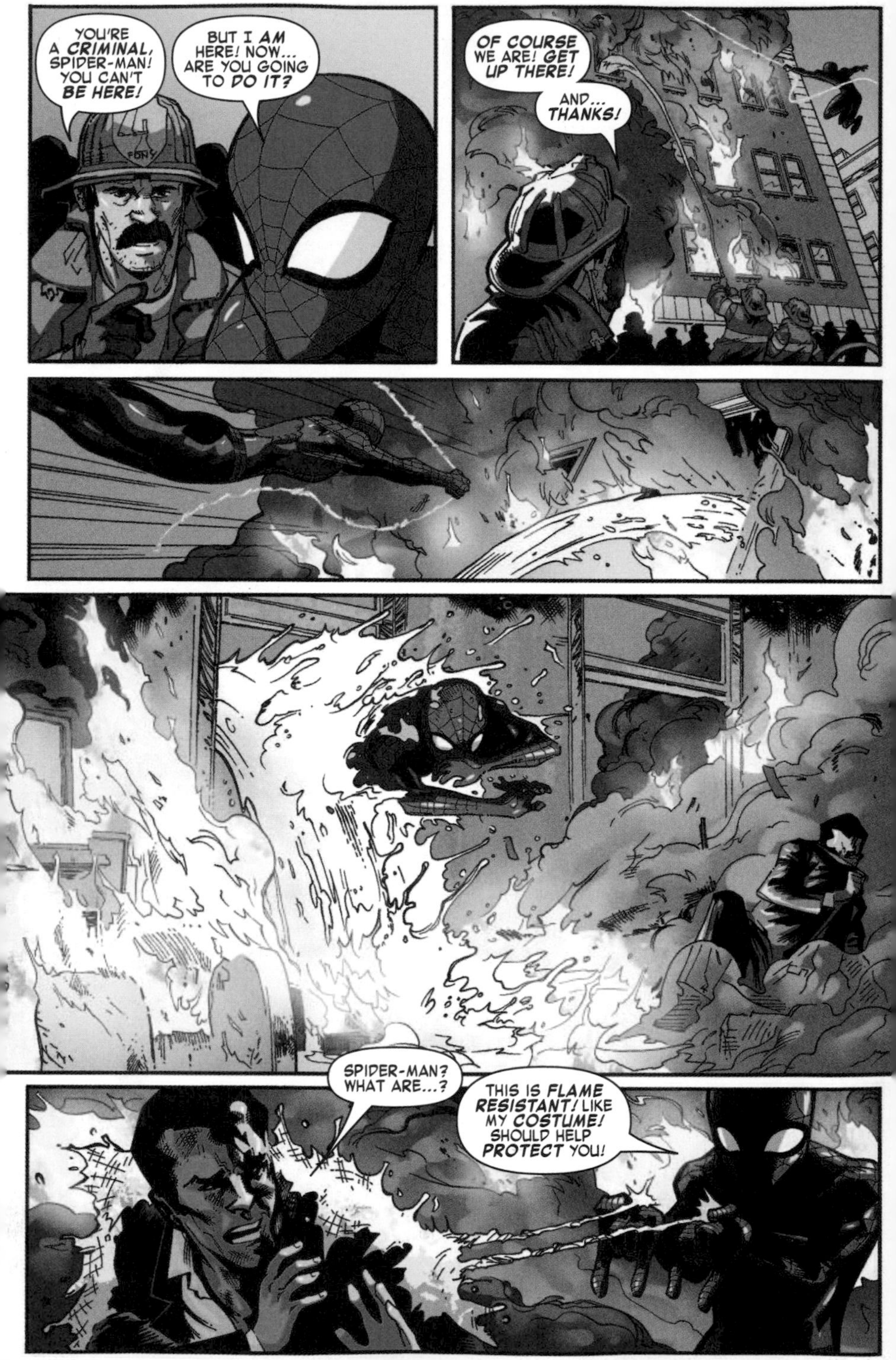
YOU'RE A CRIMINAL, SPIDER-MAN! YOU CAN'T BE HERE!
BUT I AM HERE! NOW... ARE YOU GOING TO DO IT?
OF COURSE WE ARE! GET UP THERE!
AND... THANKS!
SPIDER-MAN? WHAT ARE...?
THIS IS FLAME RESISTANT! LIKE MY COSTUME! SHOULD HELP PROTECT YOU!

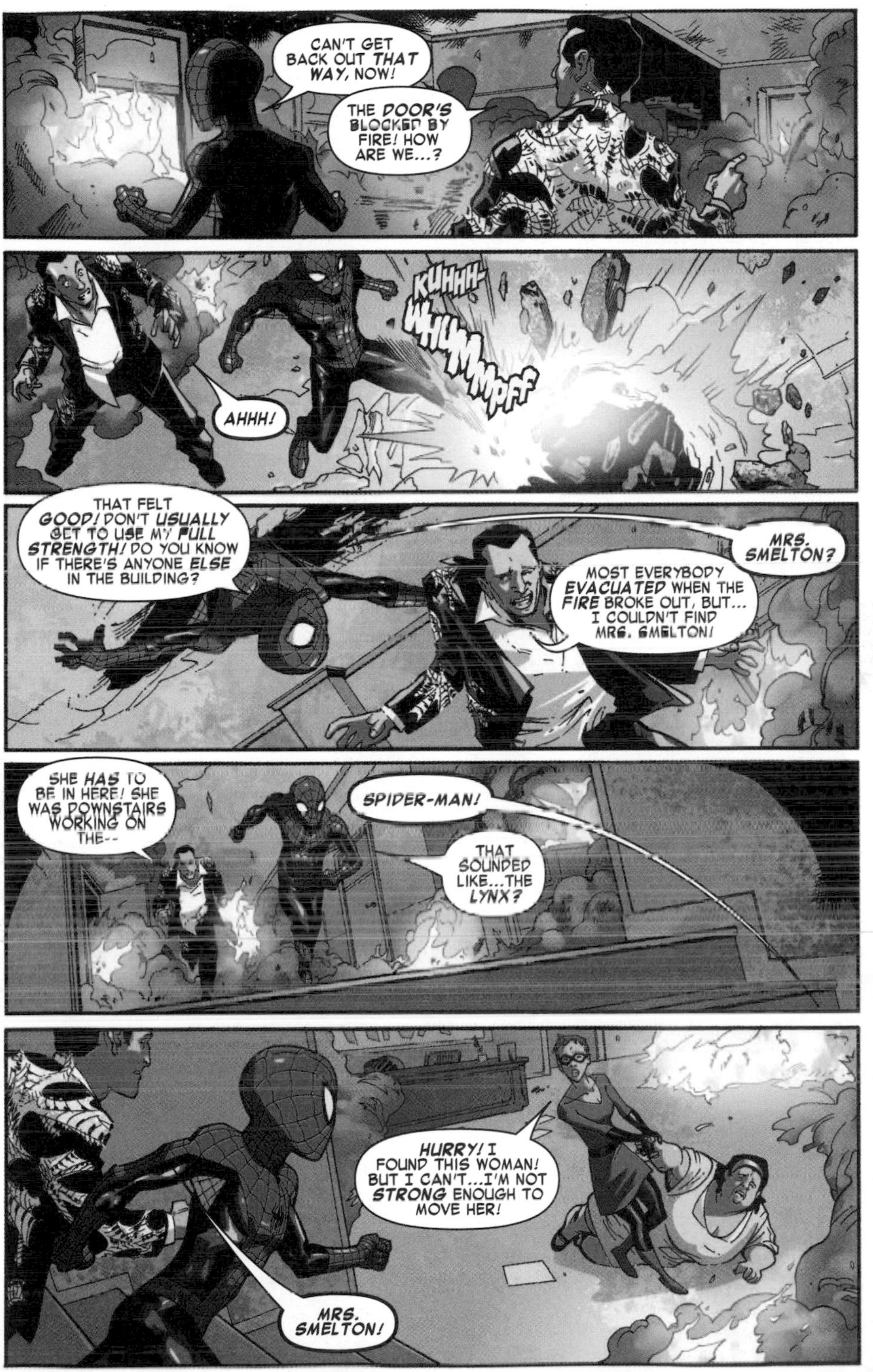
CAN'T GET BACK OUT THAT WAY, NOW!
THE DOOR'S BLOCKED BY FIRE! HOW ARE WE...?
KUHHH-WHUMMMPFF
AHHH!
THAT FELT GOOD! DON'T USUALLY GET TO USE MY FULL STRENGTH! DO YOU KNOW IF THERE'S ANYONE ELSE IN THE BUILDING?
MOST EVERYBODY EVACUATED WHEN THE FIRE BROKE OUT, BUT... I COULDN'T FIND MRS. SMELTON!
MRS. SMELTON?
SHE HAS TO BE IN HERE! SHE WAS DOWNSTAIRS WORKING ON THE--
SPIDER-MAN!
THAT SOUNDED LIKE...THE LYNX?
HURRY! I FOUND THIS WOMAN! BUT I CAN'T...I'M NOT STRONG ENOUGH TO MOVE HER!
MRS. SMELTON!

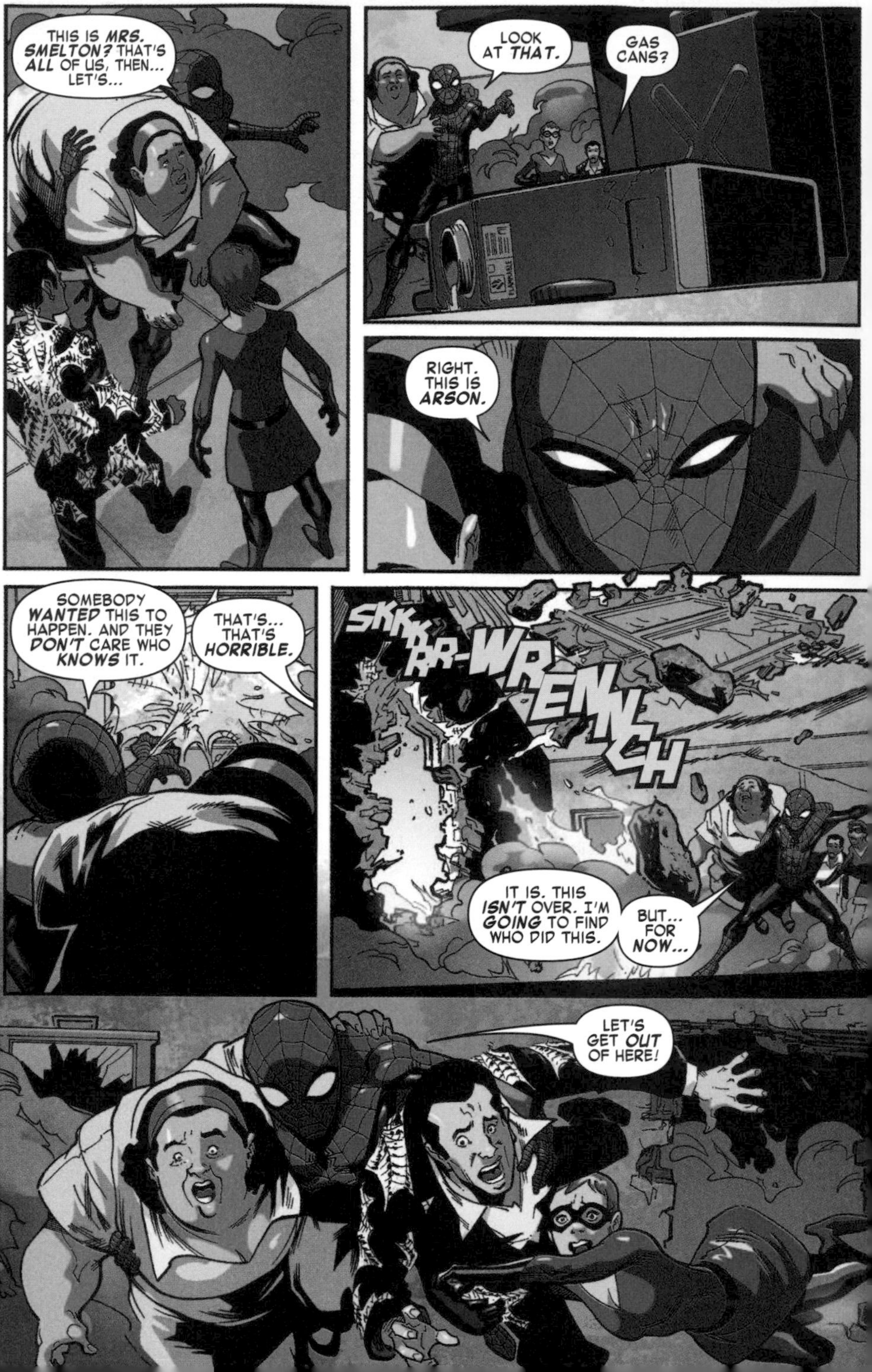
THIS IS MRS. SMELTON? THAT'S ALL OF US, THEN... LET'S...
LOOK AT THAT.
GAS CANS?
RIGHT. THIS IS ARSON.
SOMEBODY WANTED THIS TO HAPPEN. AND THEY DON'T CARE WHO KNOWS IT.
THAT'S... THAT'S HORRIBLE.
SKKRR-WRENNCH
IT IS. THIS ISN'T OVER. I'M GOING TO FIND WHO DID THIS.
BUT... FOR NOW...
LET'S GET OUT OF HERE!

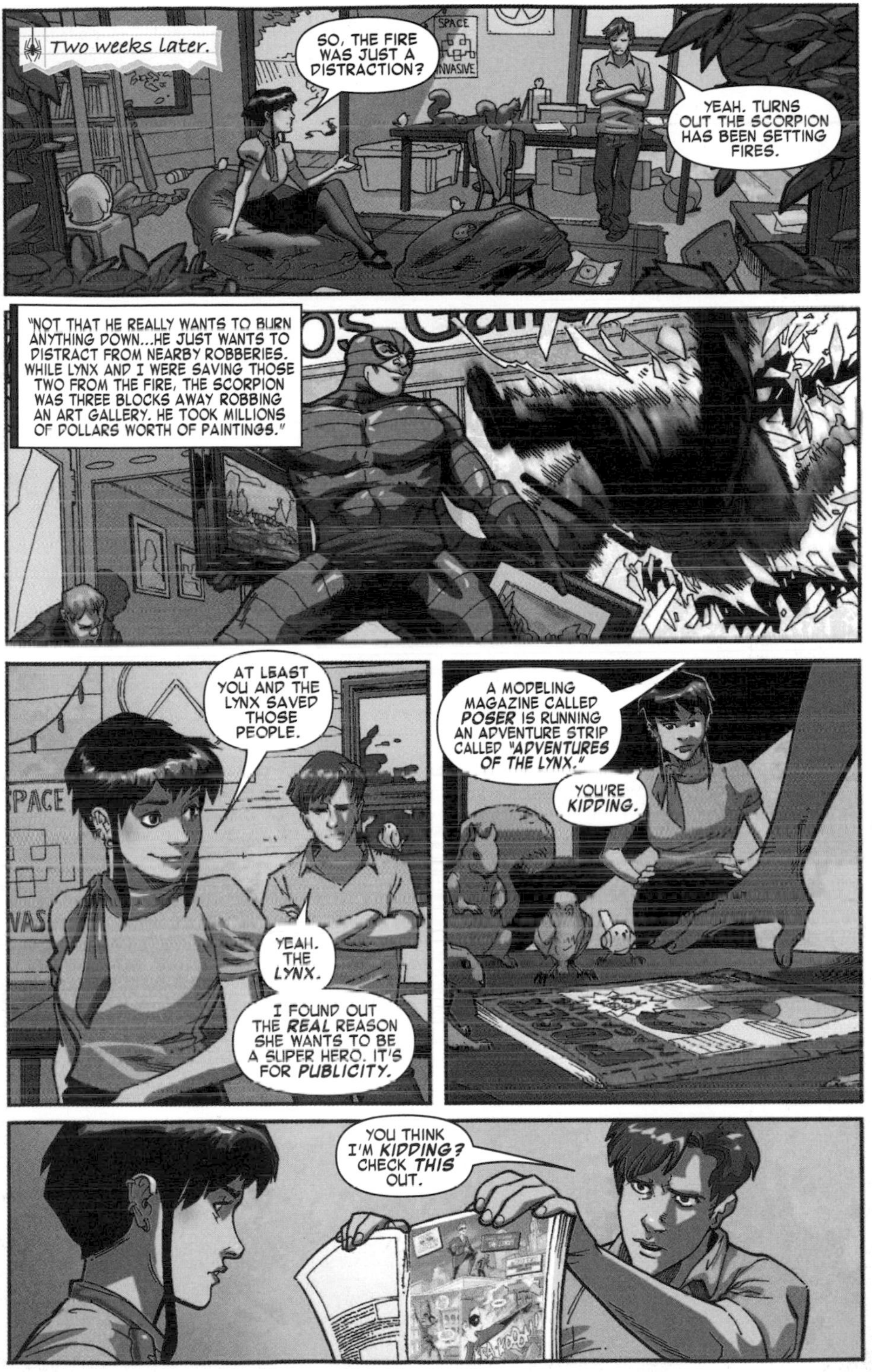

Two weeks later.
SO, THE FIRE WAS JUST A DISTRACTION?
YEAH. TURNS OUT THE SCORPION HAS BEEN SETTING FIRES.
"NOT THAT HE REALLY WANTS TO BURN ANYTHING DOWN...HE JUST WANTS TO DISTRACT FROM NEARBY ROBBERIES. WHILE LYNX AND I WERE SAVING THOSE TWO FROM THE FIRE, THE SCORPION WAS THREE BLOCKS AWAY ROBBING AN ART GALLERY. HE TOOK MILLIONS OF DOLLARS WORTH OF PAINTINGS."
AT LEAST YOU AND THE LYNX SAVED THOSE PEOPLE.
YEAH. THE *LYNX*.
I FOUND OUT THE *REAL* REASON SHE WANTS TO BE A SUPER HERO. IT'S FOR *PUBLICITY*.
A MODELING MAGAZINE CALLED *POSER* IS RUNNING AN ADVENTURE STRIP CALLED *"ADVENTURES OF THE LYNX."*
YOU'RE *KIDDING*.
YOU THINK I'M *KIDDING?* CHECK *THIS* OUT.

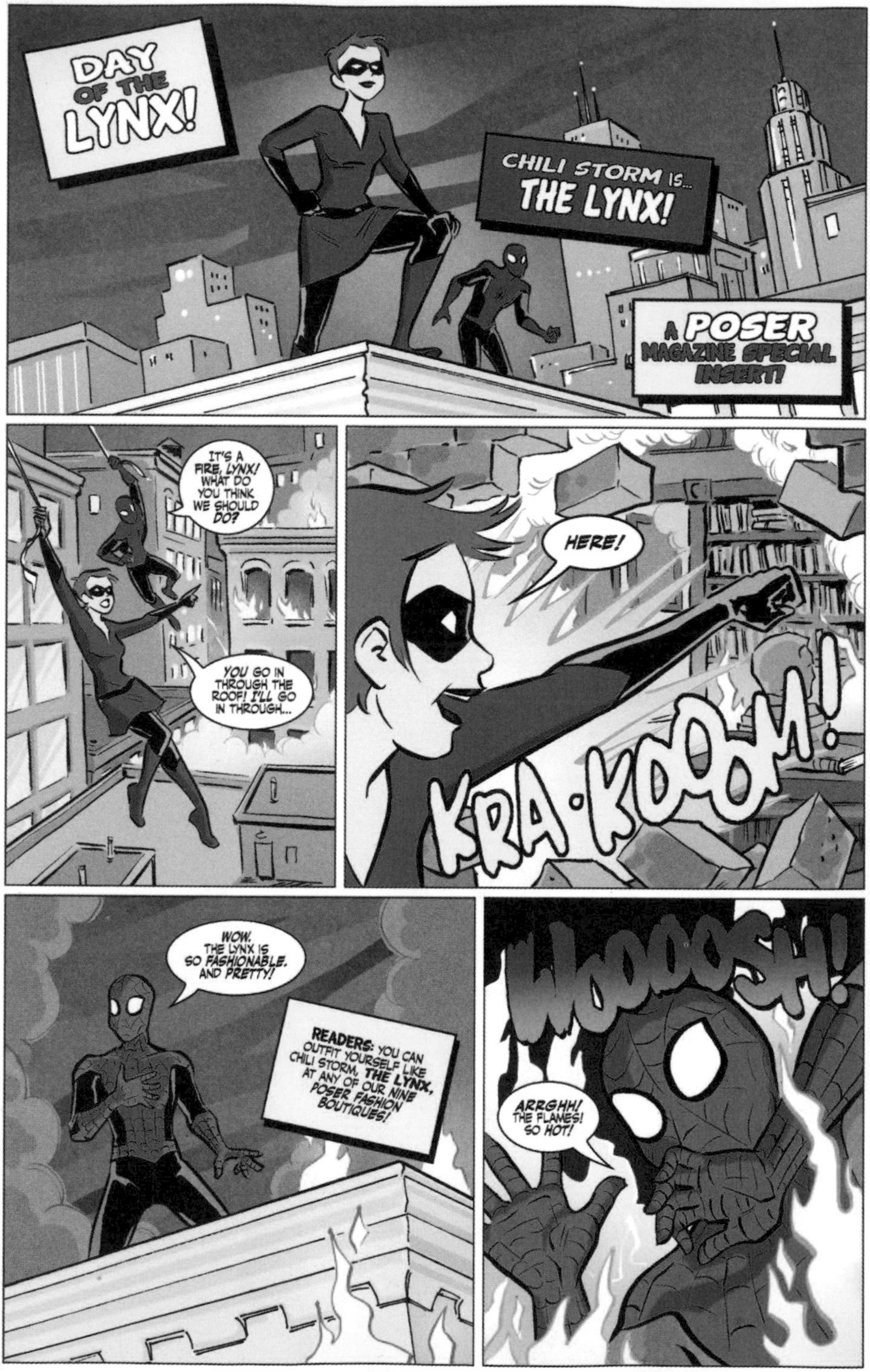
DAY OF THE LYNX!
CHILI STORM IS... THE LYNX!
A POSER MAGAZINE SPECIAL INSERT!
IT'S A FIRE, LYNX! WHAT DO YOU THINK WE SHOULD DO?
YOU GO IN THROUGH THE ROOF! I'LL GO IN THROUGH...
HERE!
KRA-KOOOM!
WOW. THE LYNX IS SO FASHIONABLE. AND PRETTY!
READERS: YOU CAN OUTFIT YOURSELF LIKE CHILI STORM, THE LYNX, AT ANY OF OUR NINE POSER FASHION BOUTIQUES!
WOOOOSH!
ARRGHH! THE FLAMES! SO HOT!

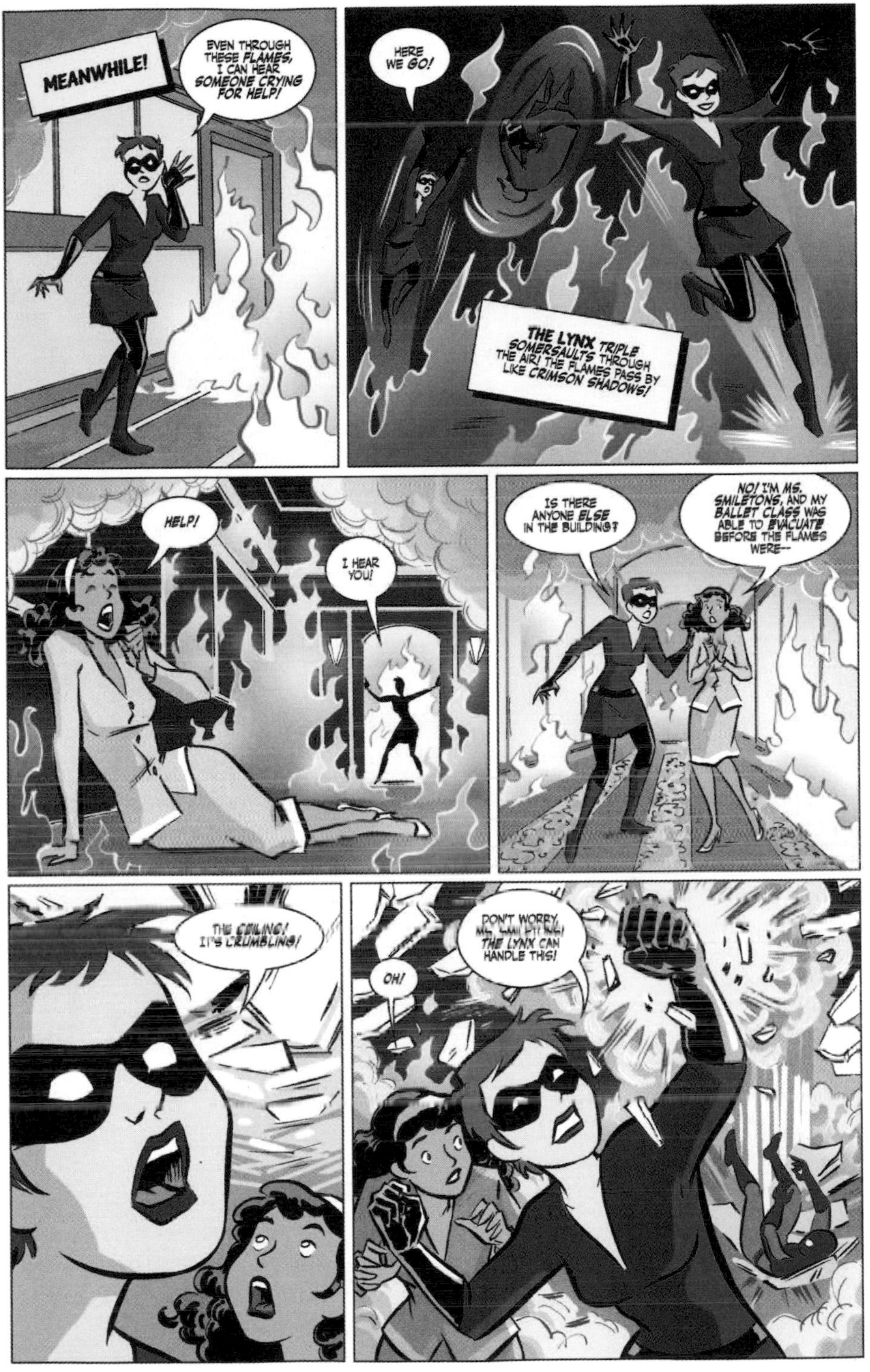
MEANWHILE!
EVEN THROUGH THESE FLAMES, I CAN HEAR SOMEONE CRYING FOR HELP!
HERE WE GO!
THE LYNX TRIPLE SOMERSAULTS THROUGH THE AIR! THE FLAMES PASS BY LIKE CRIMSON SHADOWS!
HELP!
I HEAR YOU!
IS THERE ANYONE ELSE IN THE BUILDING?
NO! I'M MS. SMILETONS, AND MY BALLET CLASS WAS ABLE TO EVACUATE BEFORE THE FLAMES WERE--
THE CEILING! IT'S CRUMBLING!
OH!
DON'T WORRY, THE LYNX CAN HANDLE THIS!

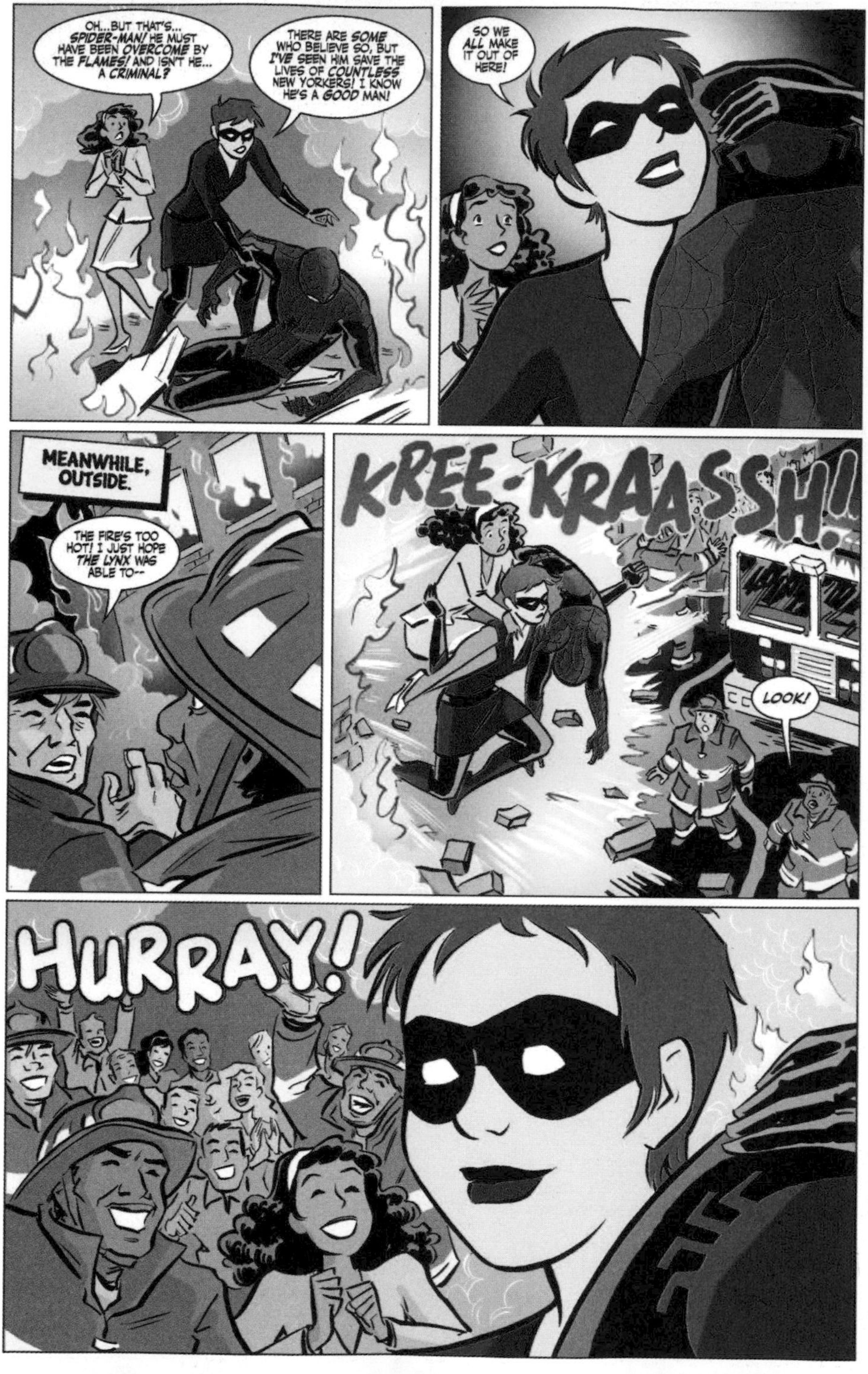
OH...BUT THAT'S... SPIDER-MAN! HE MUST HAVE BEEN OVERCOME BY THE FLAMES! AND ISN'T HE... A CRIMINAL?
THERE ARE SOME WHO BELIEVE SO, BUT I'VE SEEN HIM SAVE THE LIVES OF COUNTLESS NEW YORKERS! I KNOW HE'S A GOOD MAN!
SO WE ALL MAKE IT OUT OF HERE!
MEANWHILE, OUTSIDE.
THE FIRE'S TOO HOT! I JUST HOPE THE LYNX WAS ABLE TO--
KREE-KRAASSH!!
LOOK!
HURRAY!

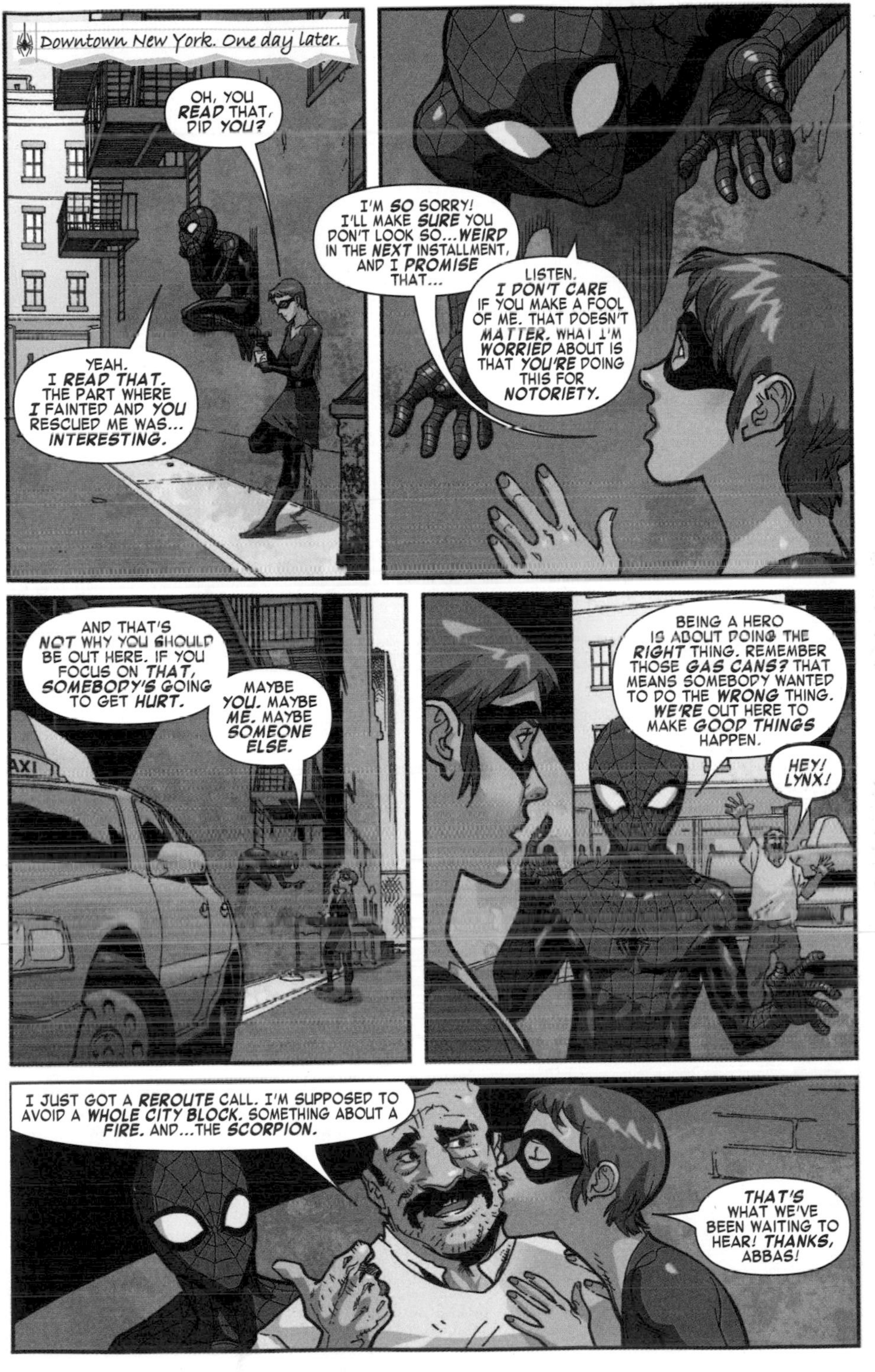
Downtown New York. One day later.
OH, YOU READ THAT, DID YOU?
YEAH. I READ THAT. THE PART WHERE I FAINTED AND YOU RESCUED ME WAS... INTERESTING.
I'M SO SORRY! I'LL MAKE SURE YOU DON'T LOOK SO...WEIRD IN THE NEXT INSTALLMENT, AND I PROMISE THAT...
LISTEN. I DON'T CARE IF YOU MAKE A FOOL OF ME. THAT DOESN'T MATTER. WHAT I'M WORRIED ABOUT IS THAT YOU'RE DOING THIS FOR NOTORIETY.
AND THAT'S NOT WHY YOU SHOULD BE OUT HERE. IF YOU FOCUS ON THAT, SOMEBODY'S GOING TO GET HURT.
MAYBE YOU. MAYBE ME. MAYBE SOMEONE ELSE.
TAXI
BEING A HERO IS ABOUT DOING THE RIGHT THING. REMEMBER THOSE GAS CANS? THAT MEANS SOMEBODY WANTED TO DO THE WRONG THING. WE'RE OUT HERE TO MAKE GOOD THINGS HAPPEN.
HEY! LYNX!
I JUST GOT A REROUTE CALL. I'M SUPPOSED TO AVOID A WHOLE CITY BLOCK. SOMETHING ABOUT A FIRE. AND...THE SCORPION.
THAT'S WHAT WE'VE BEEN WAITING TO HEAR! THANKS, ABBAS!

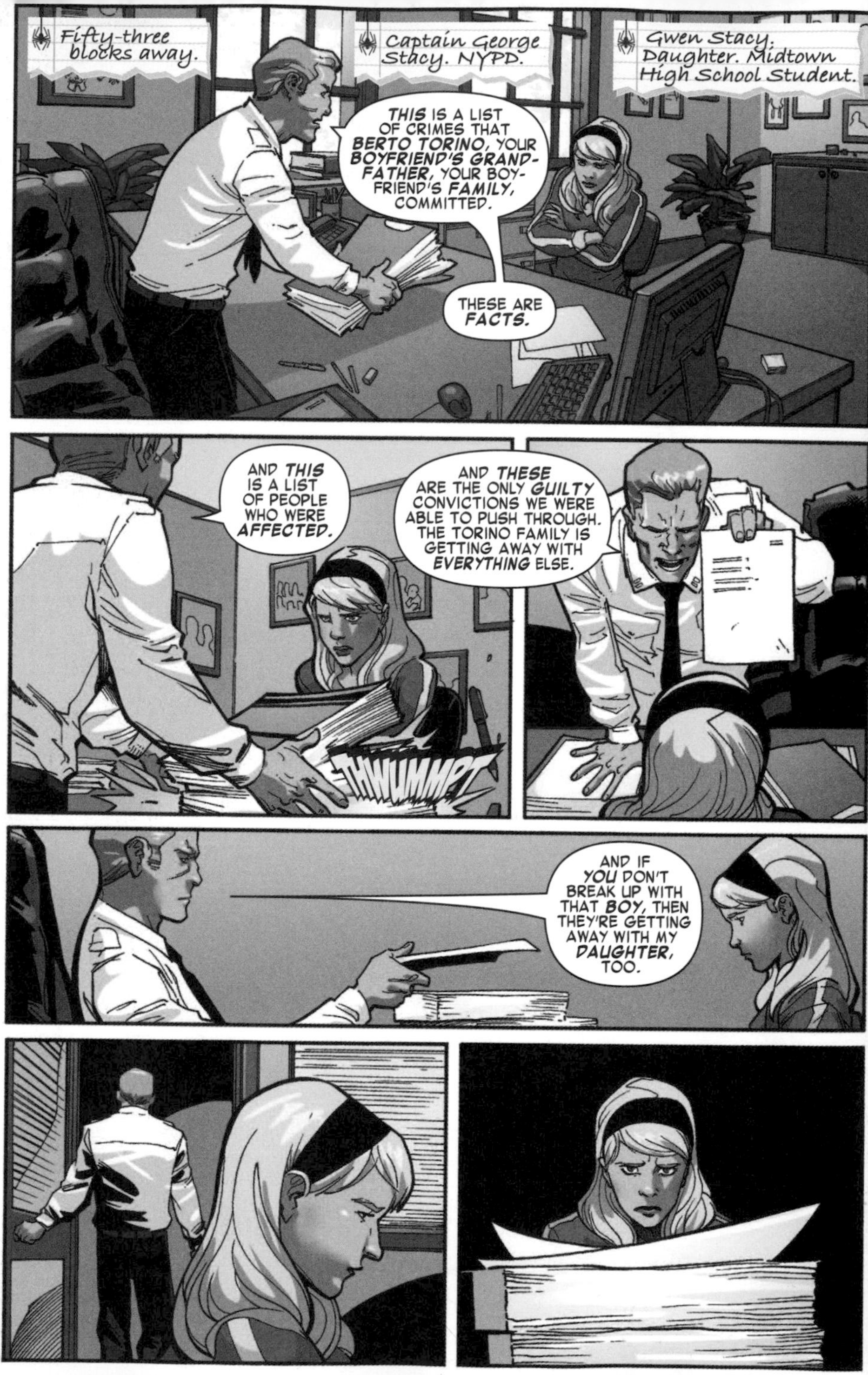
Fifty-three blocks away.
Captain George Stacy. NYPD.
Gwen Stacy. Daughter. Midtown High School Student.
THIS IS A LIST OF CRIMES THAT BERTO TORINO, YOUR BOYFRIEND'S GRANDFATHER, YOUR BOYFRIEND'S FAMILY, COMMITTED.
THESE ARE FACTS.
AND THIS IS A LIST OF PEOPLE WHO WERE AFFECTED.
THWUMMP!
AND THESE ARE THE ONLY GUILTY CONVICTIONS WE WERE ABLE TO PUSH THROUGH. THE TORINO FAMILY IS GETTING AWAY WITH EVERYTHING ELSE.
AND IF YOU DON'T BREAK UP WITH THAT BOY, THEN THEY'RE GETTING AWAY WITH MY DAUGHTER, TOO.

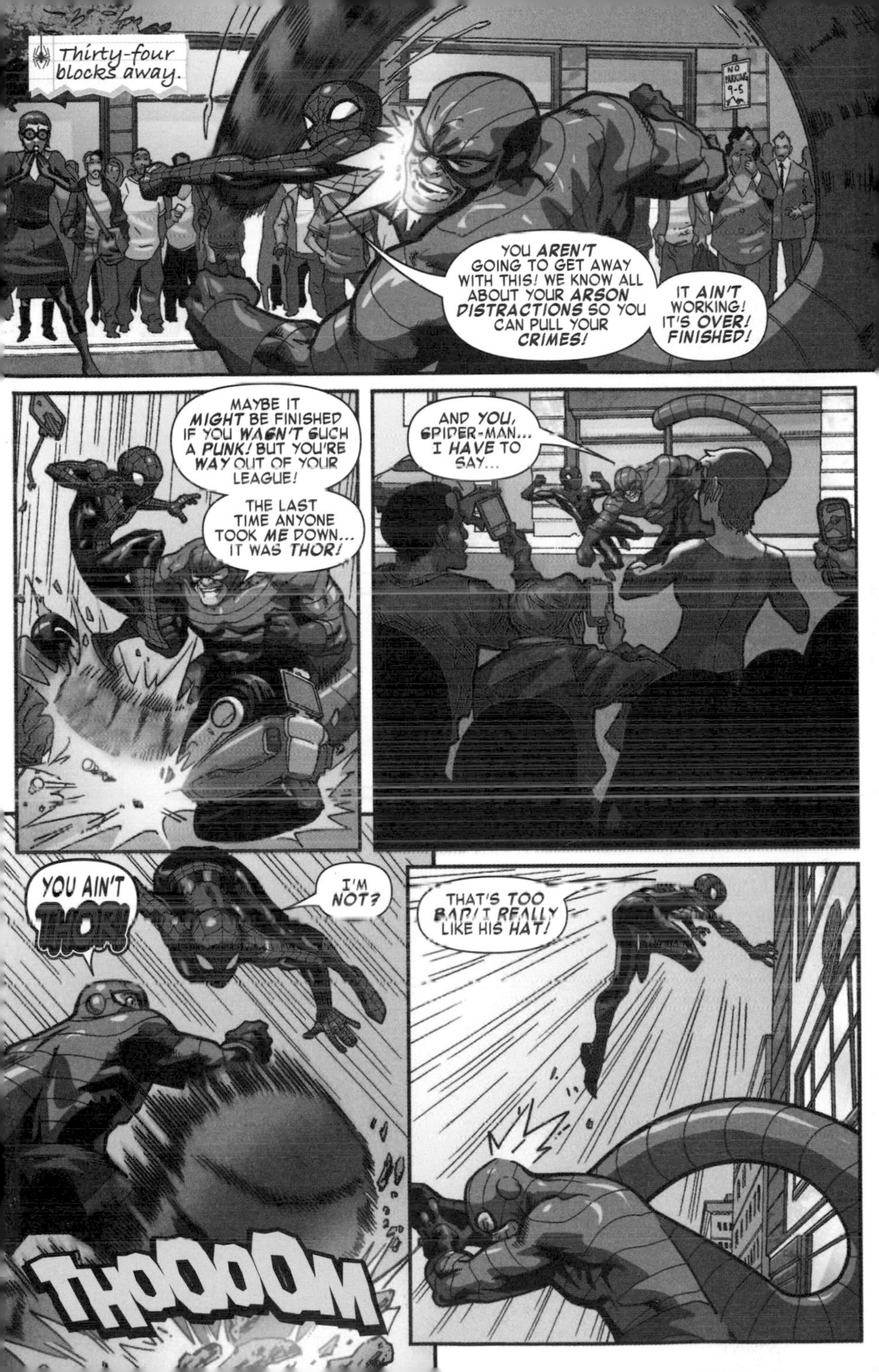
Thirty-four blocks away.
NO PARKING 9-5
YOU AREN'T GOING TO GET AWAY WITH THIS! WE KNOW ALL ABOUT YOUR ARSON DISTRACTIONS SO YOU CAN PULL YOUR CRIMES!
IT AIN'T WORKING! IT'S OVER! FINISHED!
MAYBE IT MIGHT BE FINISHED IF YOU WASN'T SUCH A PUNK! BUT YOU'RE WAY OUT OF YOUR LEAGUE!
THE LAST TIME ANYONE TOOK ME DOWN... IT WAS THOR!
AND YOU, SPIDER-MAN... I HAVE TO SAY...
YOU AIN'T THOR!
I'M NOT?
THOOOOM
THAT'S TOO BAD! I REALLY LIKE HIS HAT!

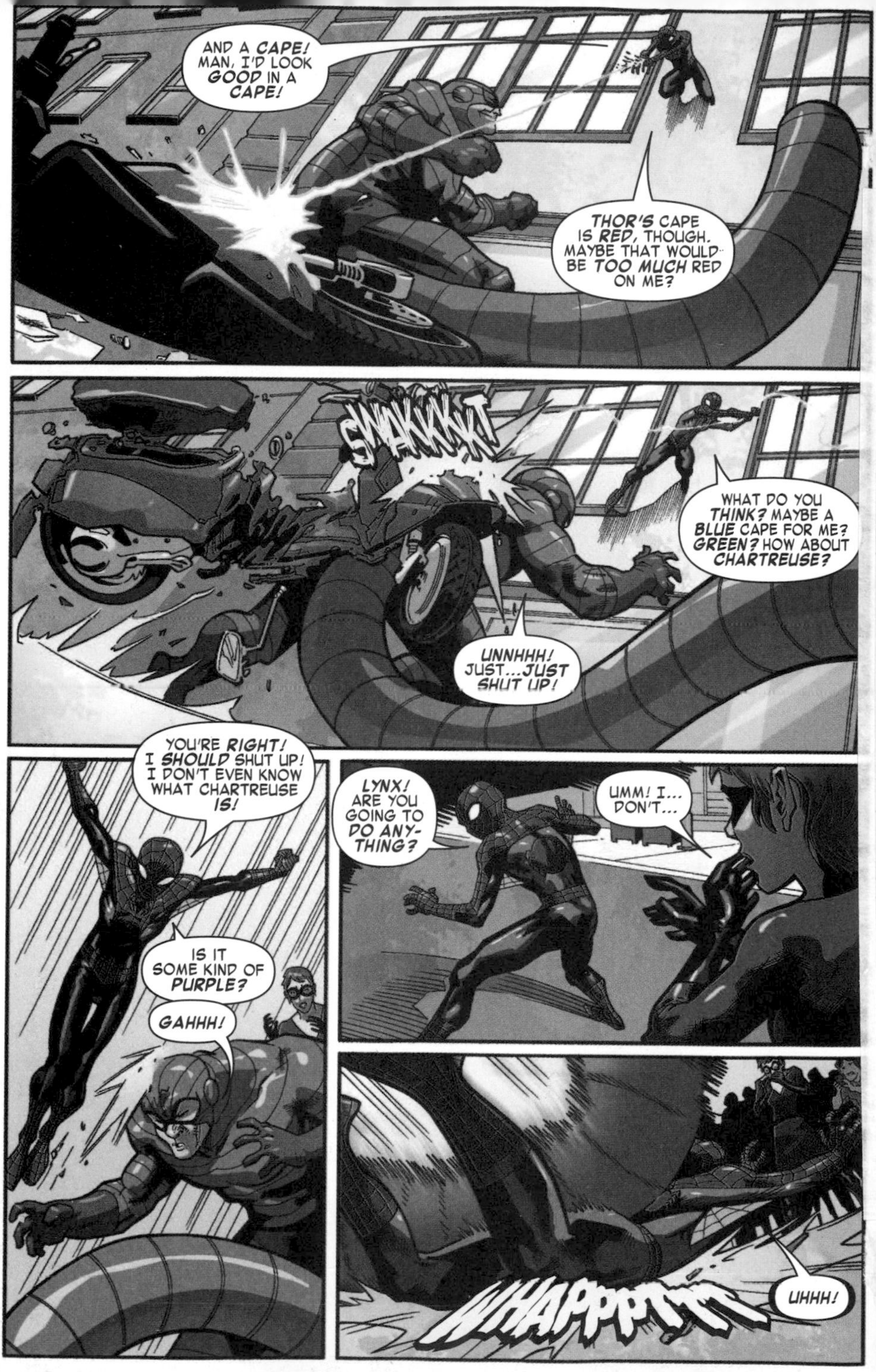
AND A CAPE! MAN, I'D LOOK GOOD IN A CAPE!
THOR'S CAPE IS RED, THOUGH. MAYBE THAT WOULD.. BE TOO MUCH RED ON ME?
SWAKKKT!
WHAT DO YOU THINK? MAYBE A BLUE CAPE FOR ME? GREEN? HOW ABOUT CHARTREUSE?
UNNHHH! JUST...JUST SHUT UP!
YOU'RE RIGHT! I SHOULD SHUT UP! I DON'T EVEN KNOW WHAT CHARTREUSE IS!
IS IT SOME KIND OF PURPLE?
GAHHH!
LYNX! ARE YOU GOING TO DO ANY-THING?
UMM! I... DON'T...
UHHH!

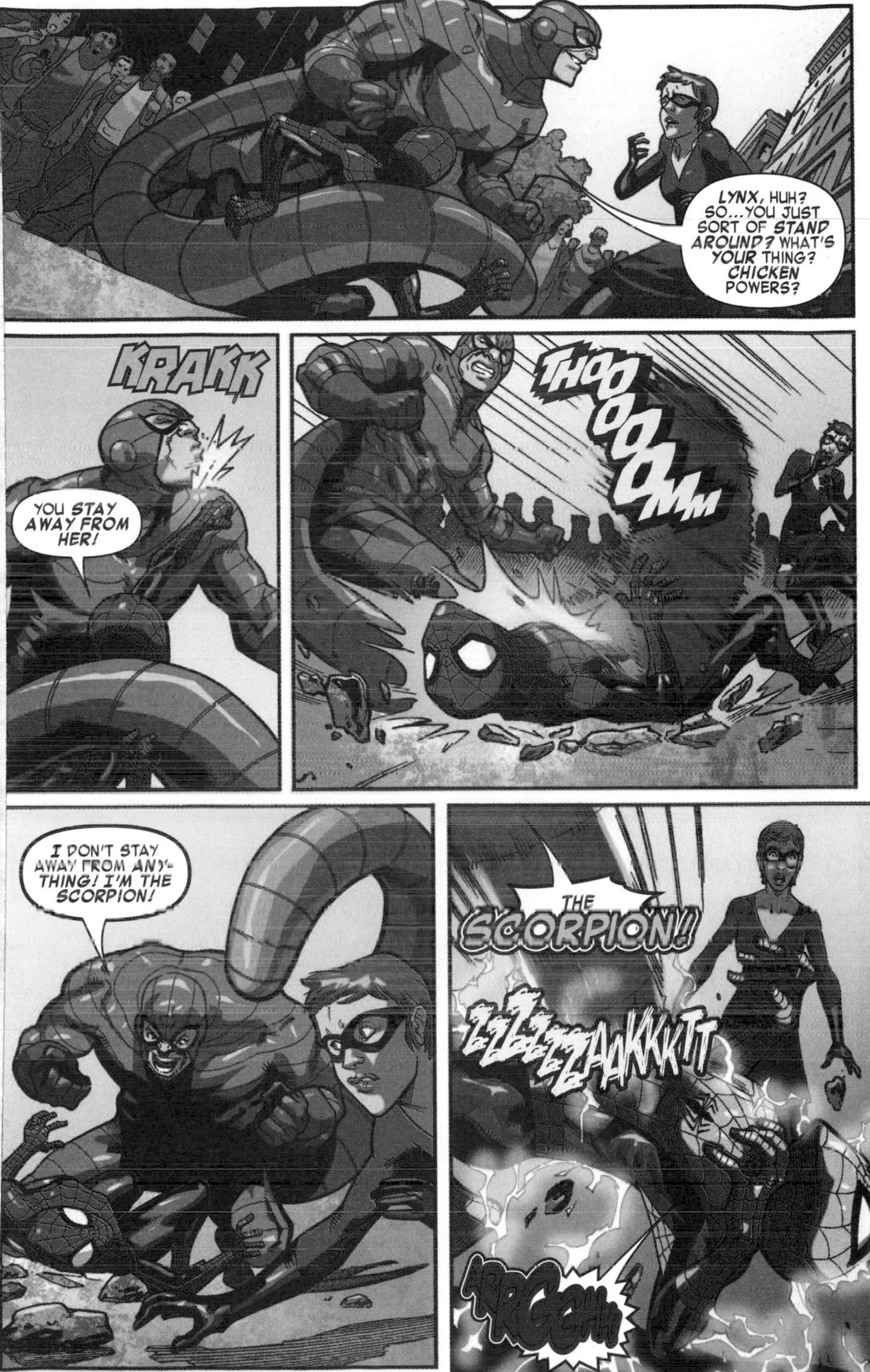
LYNX, HUH? SO...YOU JUST SORT OF STAND AROUND? WHAT'S YOUR THING? CHICKEN POWERS?
KRAKK
YOU STAY AWAY FROM HER!
THOOOOOMM
I DON'T STAY AWAY FROM ANY-THING! I'M THE SCORPION!
THE SCORPION!!
ZZZZZZAKKKTT

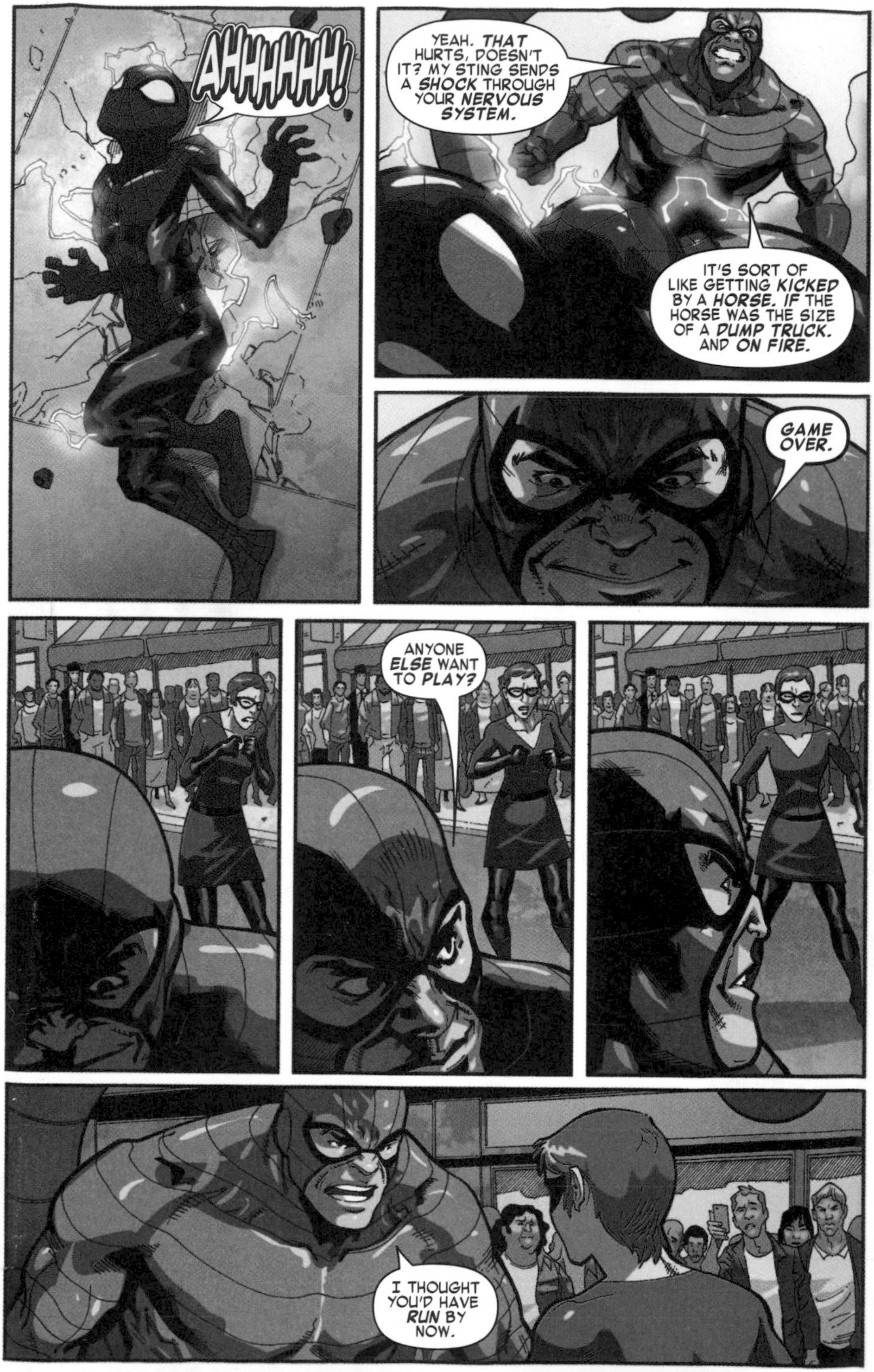

AHHHHHH!
YEAH. THAT HURTS, DOESN'T IT? MY STING SENDS A SHOCK THROUGH YOUR NERVOUS SYSTEM.
IT'S SORT OF LIKE GETTING KICKED BY A HORSE. IF THE HORSE WAS THE SIZE OF A DUMP TRUCK. AND ON FIRE.
GAME OVER.
ANYONE ELSE WANT TO PLAY?
I THOUGHT YOU'D HAVE RUN BY NOW.

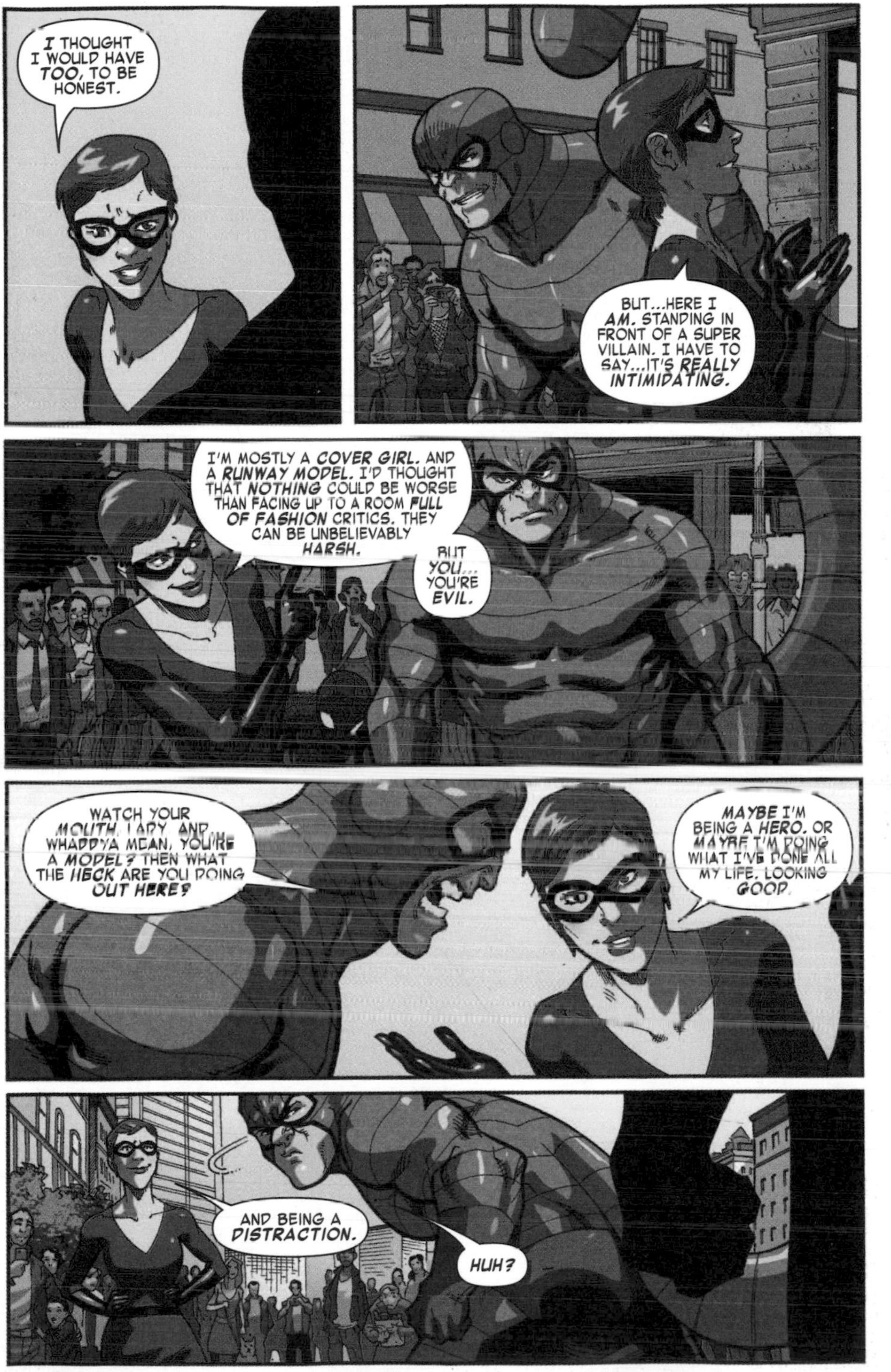
I THOUGHT I WOULD HAVE TOO, TO BE HONEST.
BUT...HERE I AM. STANDING IN FRONT OF A SUPER VILLAIN. I HAVE TO SAY...IT'S REALLY INTIMIDATING.
I'M MOSTLY A COVER GIRL. AND A RUNWAY MODEL. I'D THOUGHT THAT NOTHING COULD BE WORSE THAN FACING UP TO A ROOM FULL OF FASHION CRITICS. THEY CAN BE UNBELIEVABLY HARSH.
BUT YOU... YOU'RE EVIL.
WATCH YOUR MOUTH, LADY. AND UH, WHADD'YA MEAN, YOU'RE A MODEL? THEN WHAT THE HECK ARE YOU DOING OUT HERE?
MAYBE I'M BEING A HERO. OR MAYBE I'M DOING WHAT I'VE DONE ALL MY LIFE. LOOKING GOOD.
AND BEING A DISTRACTION.
HUH?

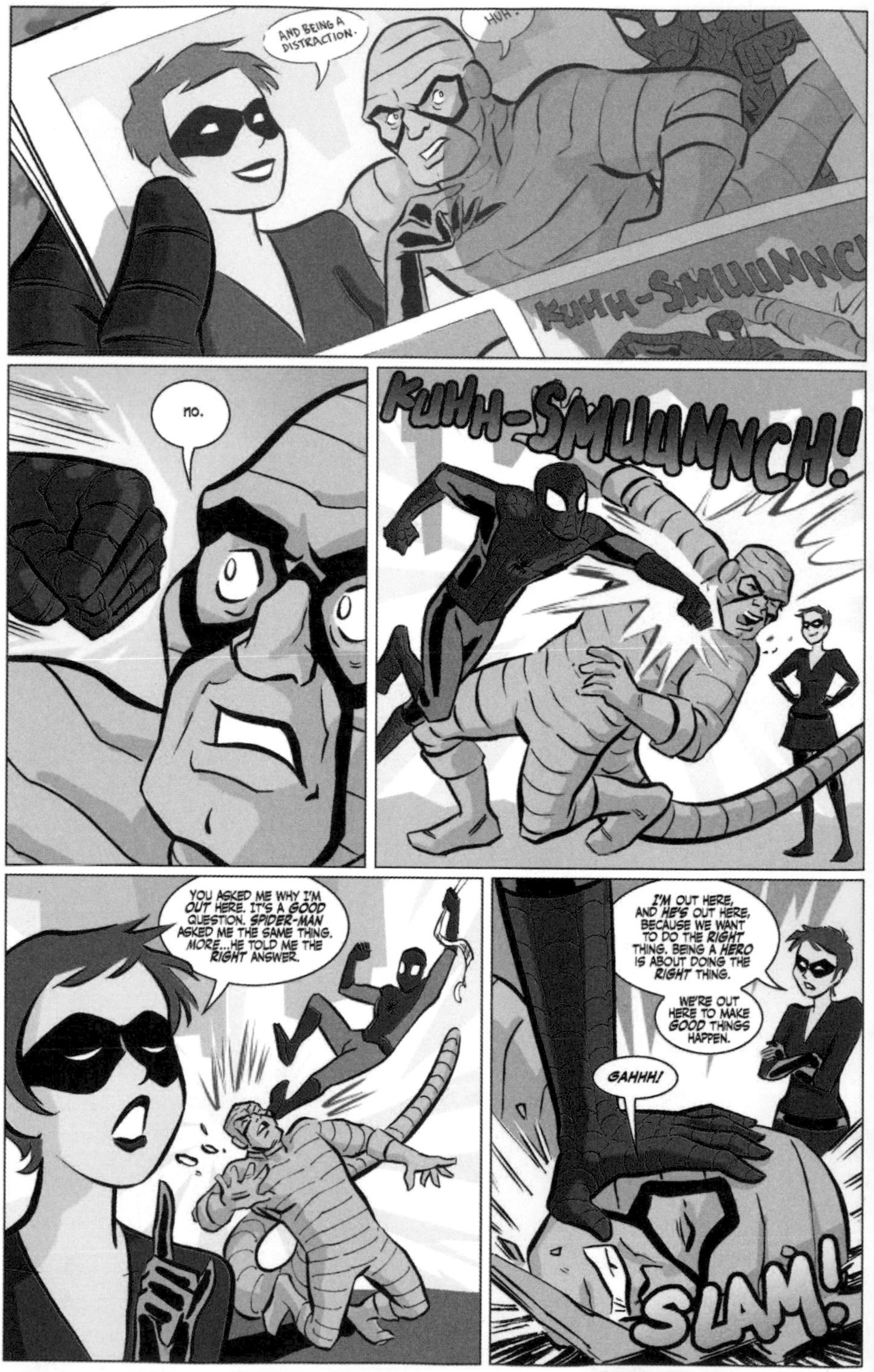
AND BEING A DISTRACTION.
HUH?
KUHH-SMUUNNCH
NO.
KUHH-SMUUNNCH!
YOU ASKED ME WHY I'M OUT HERE. IT'S A GOOD QUESTION. SPIDER-MAN ASKED ME THE SAME THING. MORE...HE TOLD ME THE RIGHT ANSWER.
I'M OUT HERE, AND HE'S OUT HERE, BECAUSE WE WANT TO DO THE RIGHT THING. BEING A HERO IS ABOUT DOING THE RIGHT THING.
WE'RE OUT HERE TO MAKE GOOD THINGS HAPPEN.
GAHHH!
SLAM!

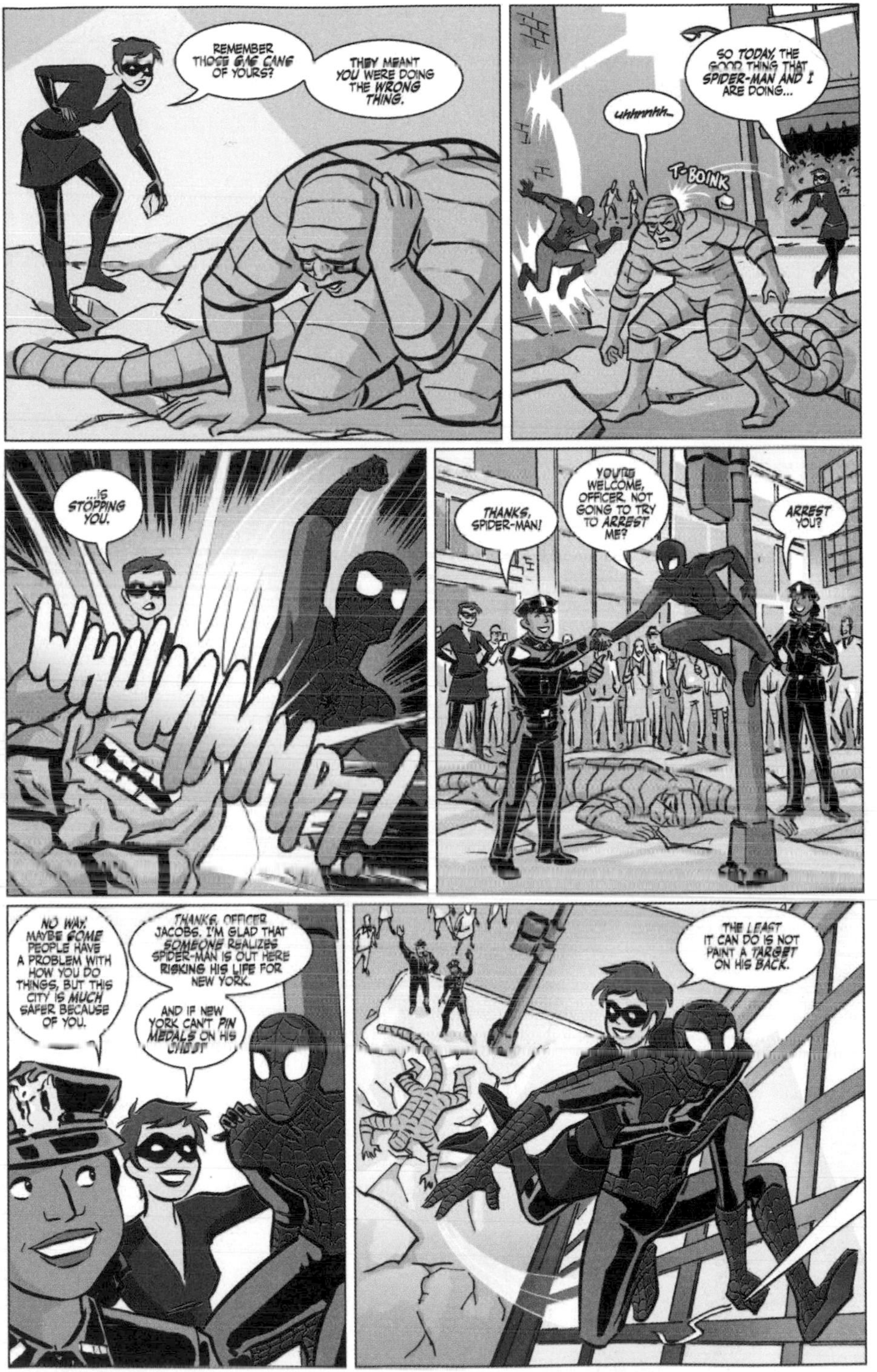
REMEMBER THOSE GAG CANS OF YOURS?
THEY MEANT YOU WERE DOING THE WRONG THING.
SO TODAY, THE GOOD THING THAT SPIDER-MAN AND I ARE DOING...
uhhhnnhh...
T-BOINK
...IS STOPPING YOU.
WHUMMMMPT!
THANKS, SPIDER-MAN!
YOU'RE WELCOME, OFFICER. NOT GOING TO TRY TO ARREST ME?
ARREST YOU?
NO WAY. MAYBE SOME PEOPLE HAVE A PROBLEM WITH HOW YOU DO THINGS, BUT THIS CITY IS MUCH SAFER BECAUSE OF YOU.
THANKS, OFFICER JACOBS. I'M GLAD THAT SOMEONE REALIZES SPIDER-MAN IS OUT HERE RISKING HIS LIFE FOR NEW YORK.
AND IF NEW YORK CAN'T PIN MEDALS ON HIS CHEST
THE LEAST IT CAN DO IS NOT PAINT A TARGET ON HIS BACK.

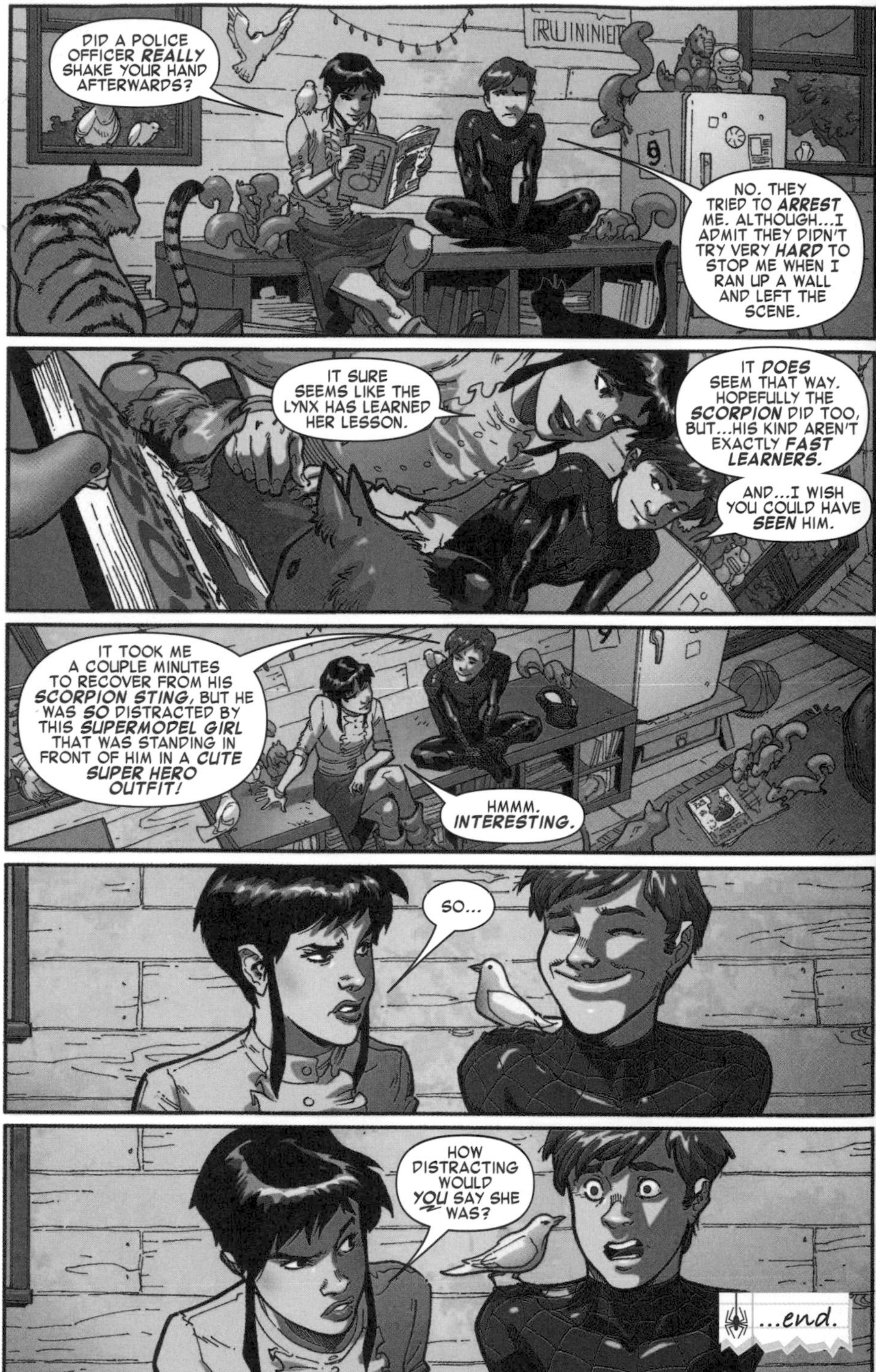
DID A POLICE OFFICER REALLY SHAKE YOUR HAND AFTERWARDS?
NO. THEY TRIED TO ARREST ME. ALTHOUGH...I ADMIT THEY DIDN'T TRY VERY HARD TO STOP ME WHEN I RAN UP A WALL AND LEFT THE SCENE.
RUINIE
IT SURE SEEMS LIKE THE LYNX HAS LEARNED HER LESSON.
IT DOES SEEM THAT WAY. HOPEFULLY THE SCORPION DID TOO, BUT...HIS KIND AREN'T EXACTLY FAST LEARNERS.
AND...I WISH YOU COULD HAVE SEEN HIM.
IT TOOK ME A COUPLE MINUTES TO RECOVER FROM HIS SCORPION STING, BUT HE WAS SO DISTRACTED BY THIS SUPERMODEL GIRL THAT WAS STANDING IN FRONT OF HIM IN A CUTE SUPER HERO OUTFIT!
HMMM. INTERESTING.
SO...
HOW DISTRACTING WOULD YOU SAY SHE WAS?
...end.

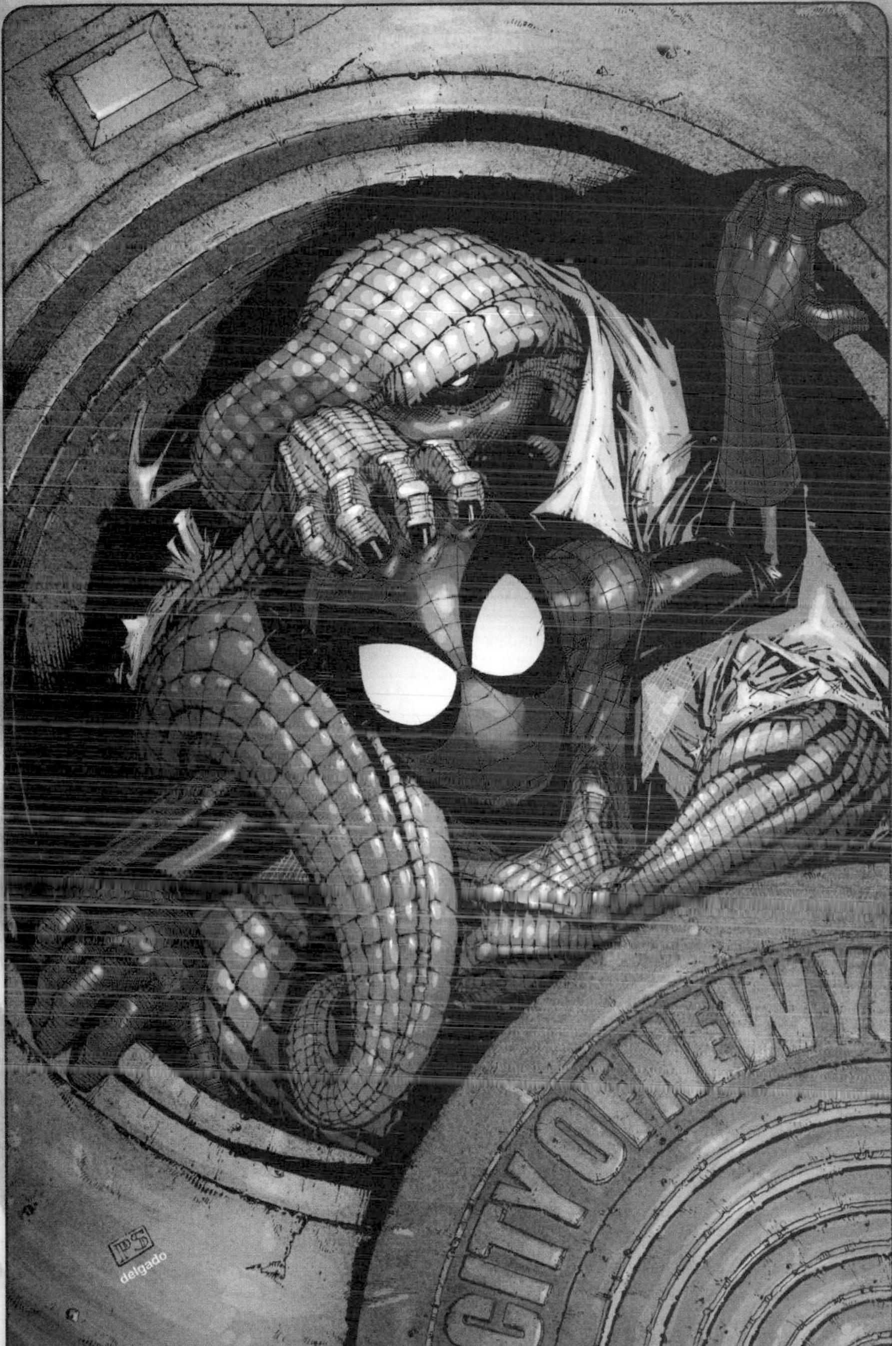
CITYOFNEWYO
delgado

#11

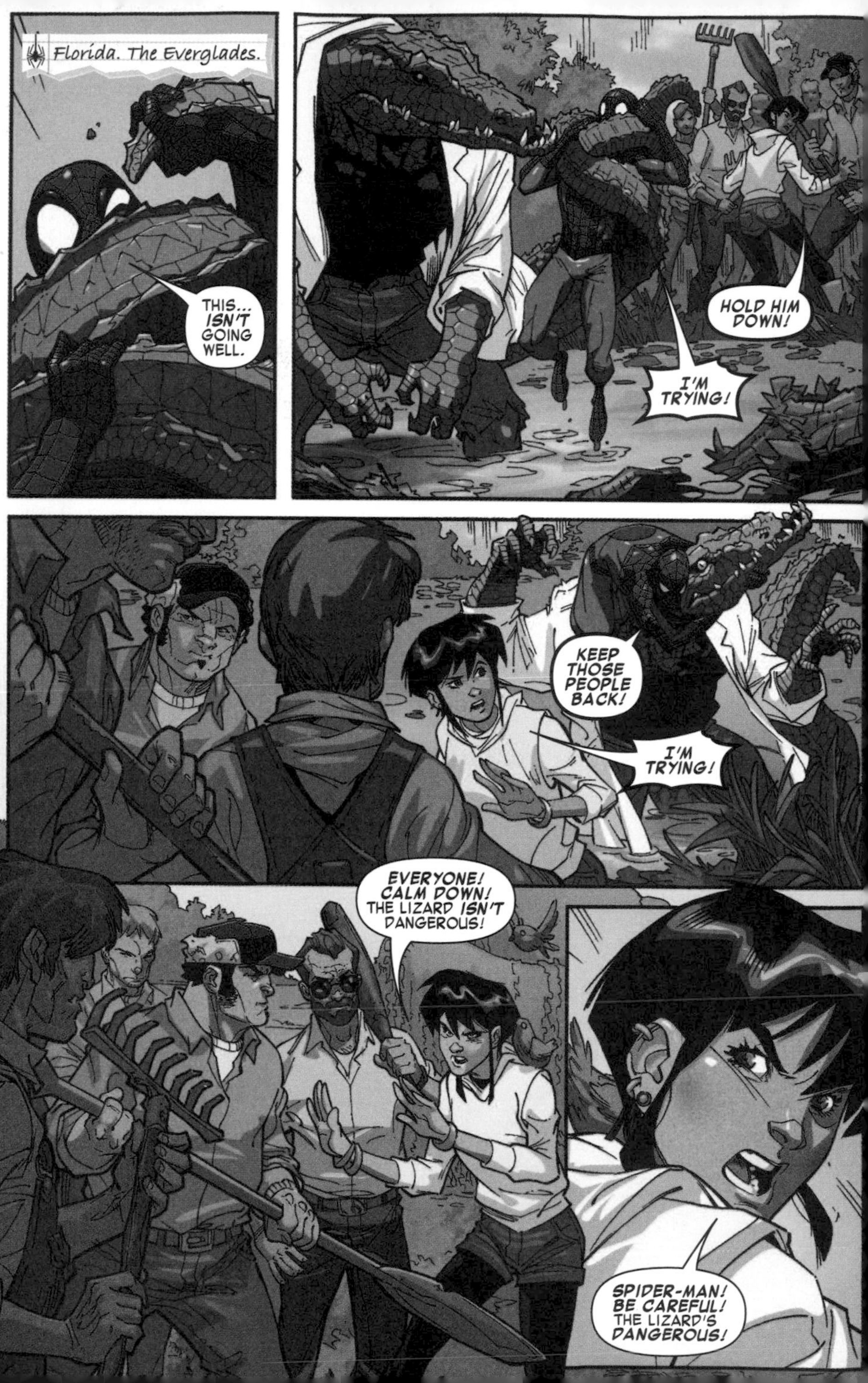
Florida. The Everglades.
THIS... ISN'T GOING WELL.
HOLD HIM DOWN!
I'M TRYING!
KEEP THOSE PEOPLE BACK!
I'M TRYING!
EVERYONE! CALM DOWN! THE LIZARD ISN'T DANGEROUS!
SPIDER-MAN! BE CAREFUL! THE LIZARD'S DANGEROUS!

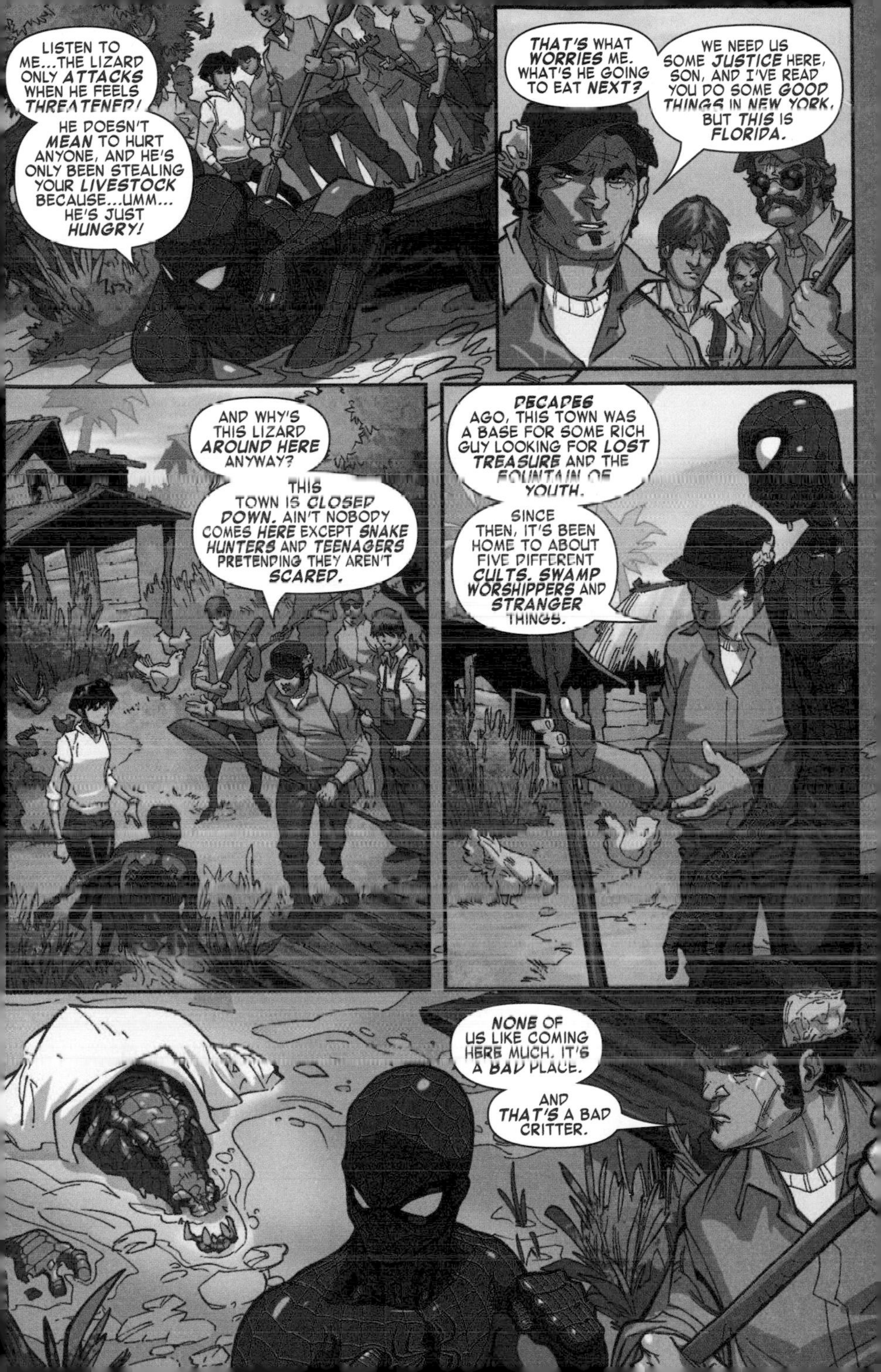
LISTEN TO ME...THE LIZARD ONLY ATTACKS WHEN HE FEELS THREATENED!
HE DOESN'T MEAN TO HURT ANYONE, AND HE'S ONLY BEEN STEALING YOUR LIVESTOCK BECAUSE...UMM... HE'S JUST HUNGRY!
THAT'S WHAT WORRIES ME. WHAT'S HE GOING TO EAT NEXT?
WE NEED US SOME JUSTICE HERE, SON, AND I'VE READ YOU DO SOME GOOD THINGS IN NEW YORK. BUT THIS IS FLORIDA.
AND WHY'S THIS LIZARD AROUND HERE ANYWAY?
THIS TOWN IS CLOSED DOWN. AIN'T NOBODY COMES HERE EXCEPT SNAKE HUNTERS AND TEENAGERS PRETENDING THEY AREN'T SCARED.
DECADES AGO, THIS TOWN WAS A BASE FOR SOME RICH GUY LOOKING FOR LOST TREASURE AND THE FOUNTAIN OF YOUTH.
SINCE THEN, IT'S BEEN HOME TO ABOUT FIVE DIFFERENT CULTS. SWAMP WORSHIPPERS AND STRANGER THINGS.
NONE OF US LIKE COMING HERE MUCH. IT'S A BAD PLACE.
AND THAT'S A BAD CRITTER.

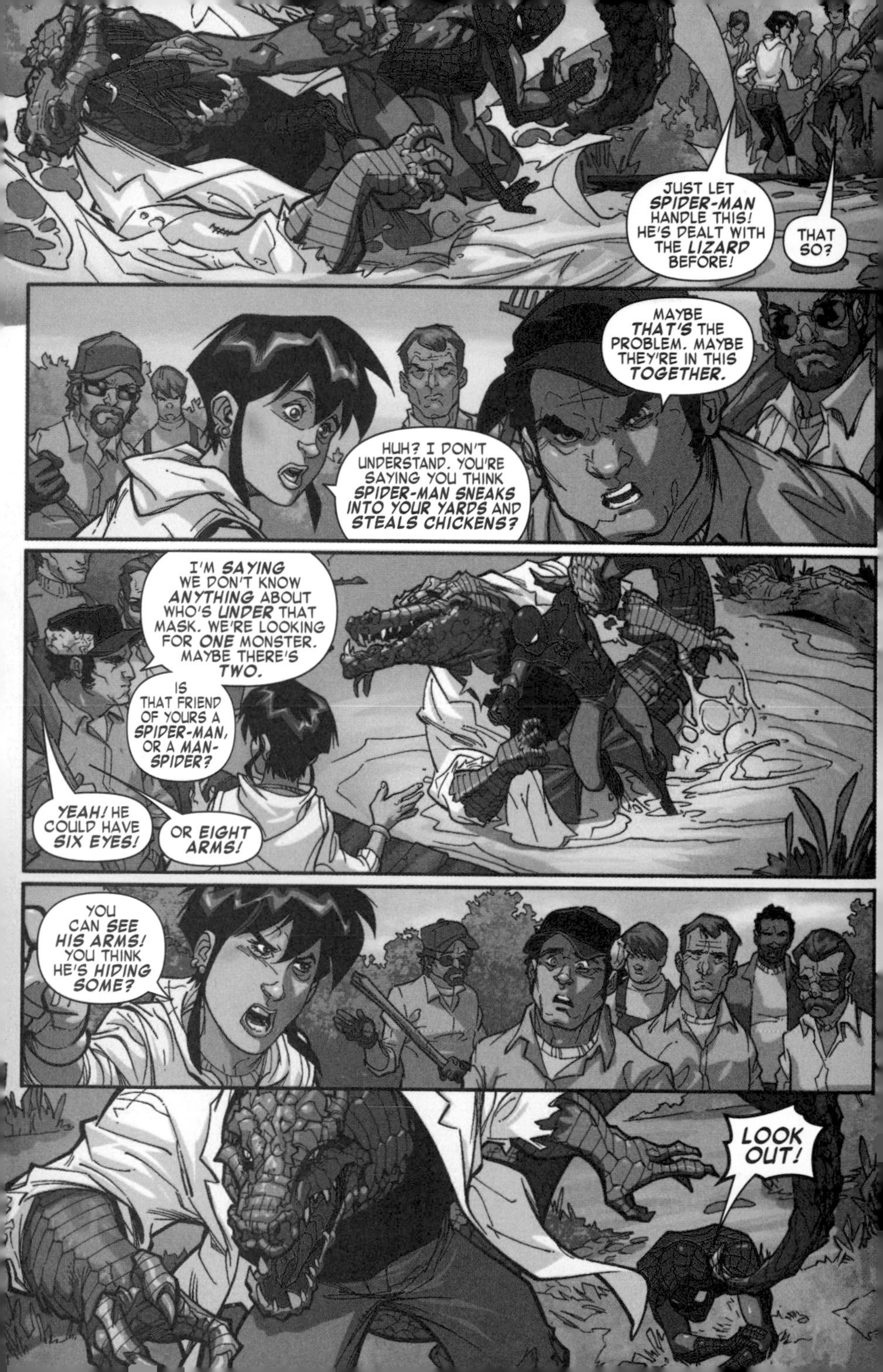
JUST LET SPIDER-MAN HANDLE THIS! HE'S DEALT WITH THE LIZARD BEFORE!
THAT SO?
MAYBE THAT'S THE PROBLEM. MAYBE THEY'RE IN THIS TOGETHER.
HUH? I DON'T UNDERSTAND. YOU'RE SAYING YOU THINK SPIDER-MAN SNEAKS INTO YOUR YARDS AND STEALS CHICKENS?
I'M SAYING WE DON'T KNOW ANYTHING ABOUT WHO'S UNDER THAT MASK. WE'RE LOOKING FOR ONE MONSTER. MAYBE THERE'S TWO.
IS THAT FRIEND OF YOURS A SPIDER-MAN, OR A MAN-SPIDER?
YEAH! HE COULD HAVE SIX EYES!
OR EIGHT ARMS!
YOU CAN SEE HIS ARMS! YOU THINK HE'S HIDING SOME?
LOOK OUT!

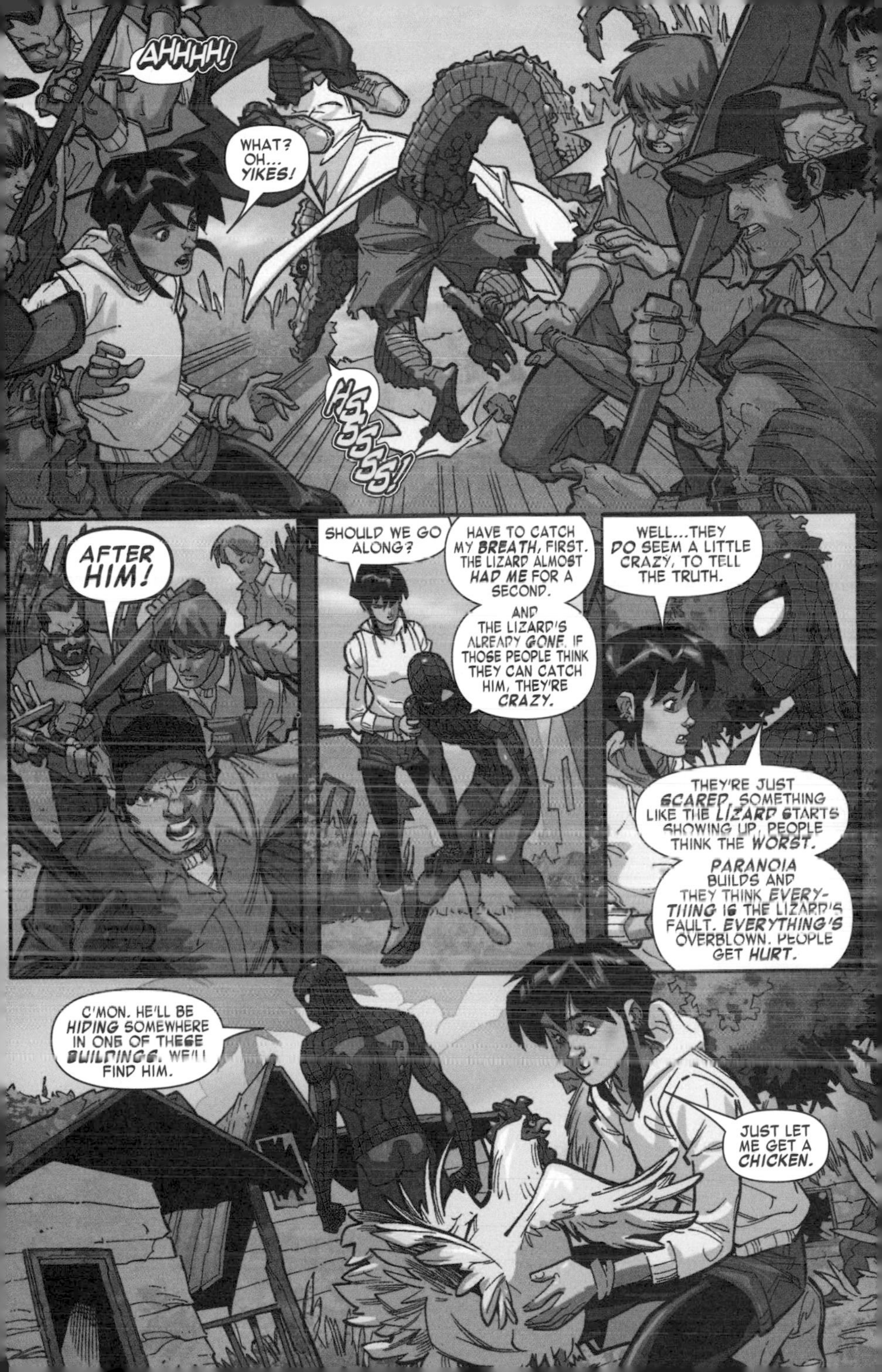
AHHHH!
WHAT? OH... YIKES!
HSSSSS!
AFTER HIM!
SHOULD WE GO ALONG?
HAVE TO CATCH MY BREATH, FIRST. THE LIZARD ALMOST HAD ME FOR A SECOND.
AND THE LIZARD'S ALREADY GONE. IF THOSE PEOPLE THINK THEY CAN CATCH HIM, THEY'RE CRAZY.
WELL...THEY DO SEEM A LITTLE CRAZY, TO TELL THE TRUTH.
THEY'RE JUST SCARED. SOMETHING LIKE THE LIZARD STARTS SHOWING UP, PEOPLE THINK THE WORST.
PARANOIA BUILDS AND THEY THINK EVERYTHING IS THE LIZARD'S FAULT. EVERYTHING'S OVERBLOWN. PEOPLE GET HURT.
C'MON. HE'LL BE HIDING SOMEWHERE IN ONE OF THESE BUILDINGS. WE'LL FIND HIM.
JUST LET ME GET A CHICKEN.

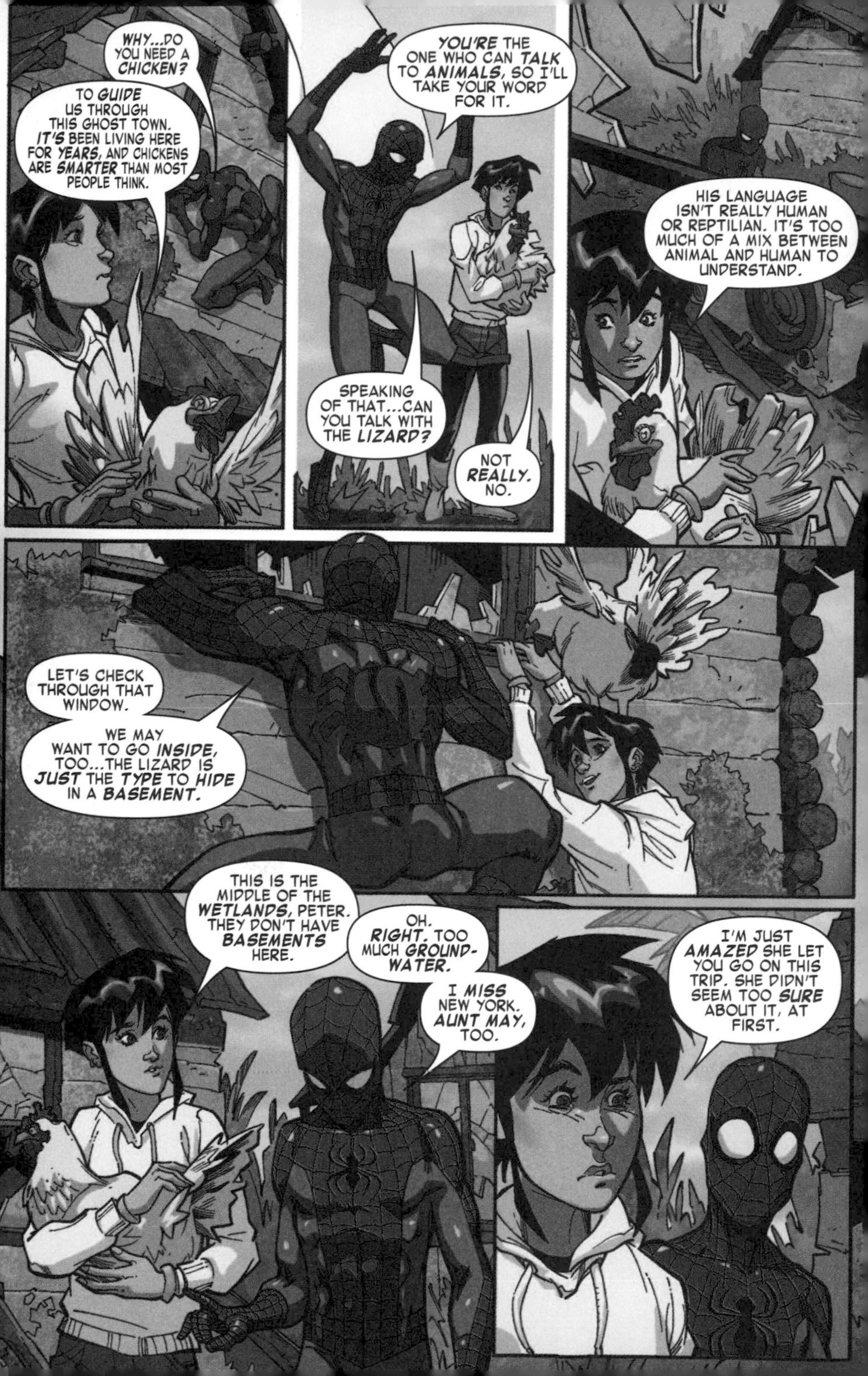
WHY...DO YOU NEED A CHICKEN?
TO GUIDE US THROUGH THIS GHOST TOWN. IT'S BEEN LIVING HERE FOR YEARS, AND CHICKENS ARE SMARTER THAN MOST PEOPLE THINK.
YOU'RE THE ONE WHO CAN TALK TO ANIMALS, SO I'LL TAKE YOUR WORD FOR IT.
SPEAKING OF THAT...CAN YOU TALK WITH THE LIZARD?
NOT REALLY. NO.
HIS LANGUAGE ISN'T REALLY HUMAN OR REPTILIAN. IT'S TOO MUCH OF A MIX BETWEEN ANIMAL AND HUMAN TO UNDERSTAND.
LET'S CHECK THROUGH THAT WINDOW.
WE MAY WANT TO GO INSIDE, TOO...THE LIZARD IS JUST THE TYPE TO HIDE IN A BASEMENT.
THIS IS THE MIDDLE OF THE WETLANDS, PETER. THEY DON'T HAVE BASEMENTS HERE.
OH. RIGHT. TOO MUCH GROUND-WATER.
I MISS NEW YORK. AUNT MAY, TOO.
I'M JUST AMAZED SHE LET YOU GO ON THIS TRIP. SHE DIDN'T SEEM TOO SURE ABOUT IT, AT FIRST.

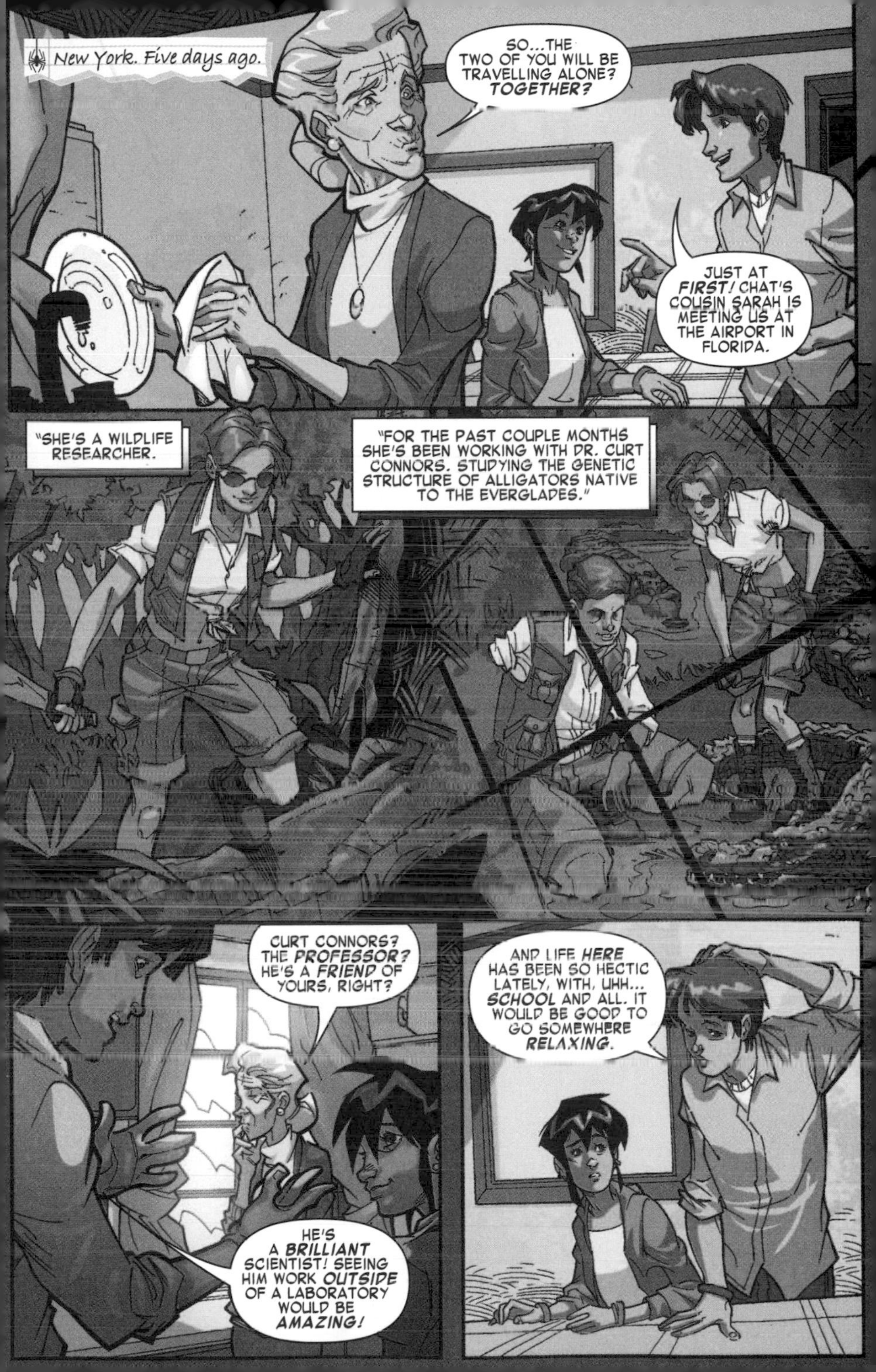
New York. Five days ago.
SO...THE TWO OF YOU WILL BE TRAVELLING ALONE? TOGETHER?
JUST AT FIRST! CHAT'S COUSIN SARAH IS MEETING US AT THE AIRPORT IN FLORIDA.
"SHE'S A WILDLIFE RESEARCHER.
"FOR THE PAST COUPLE MONTHS SHE'S BEEN WORKING WITH DR. CURT CONNORS. STUDYING THE GENETIC STRUCTURE OF ALLIGATORS NATIVE TO THE EVERGLADES."
CURT CONNORS? THE PROFESSOR? HE'S A FRIEND OF YOURS, RIGHT?
HE'S A BRILLIANT SCIENTIST! SEEING HIM WORK OUTSIDE OF A LABORATORY WOULD BE AMAZING!
AND LIFE HERE HAS BEEN SO HECTIC LATELY, WITH, UHH... SCHOOL AND ALL. IT WOULD BE GOOD TO GO SOMEWHERE RELAXING.

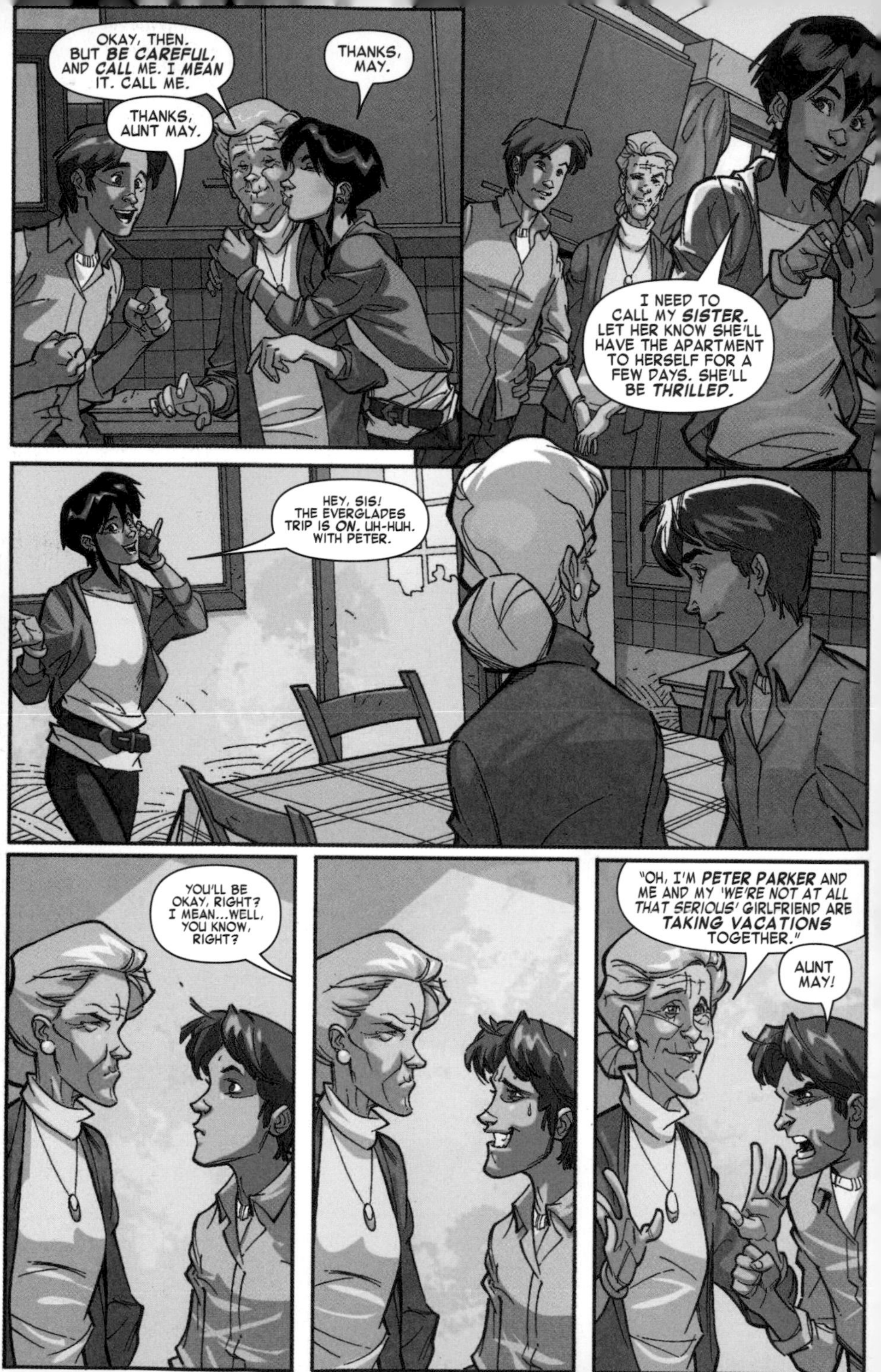
OKAY, THEN. BUT BE CAREFUL, AND CALL ME. I MEAN IT. CALL ME.
THANKS, AUNT MAY.
THANKS, MAY.
I NEED TO CALL MY SISTER. LET HER KNOW SHE'LL HAVE THE APARTMENT TO HERSELF FOR A FEW DAYS. SHE'LL BE THRILLED.
HEY, SIS! THE EVERGLADES TRIP IS ON. UH-HUH. WITH PETER.
YOU'LL BE OKAY, RIGHT? I MEAN...WELL, YOU KNOW, RIGHT?
"OH, I'M PETER PARKER AND ME AND MY 'WE'RE NOT AT ALL THAT SERIOUS' GIRLFRIEND ARE TAKING VACATIONS TOGETHER."
AUNT MAY!

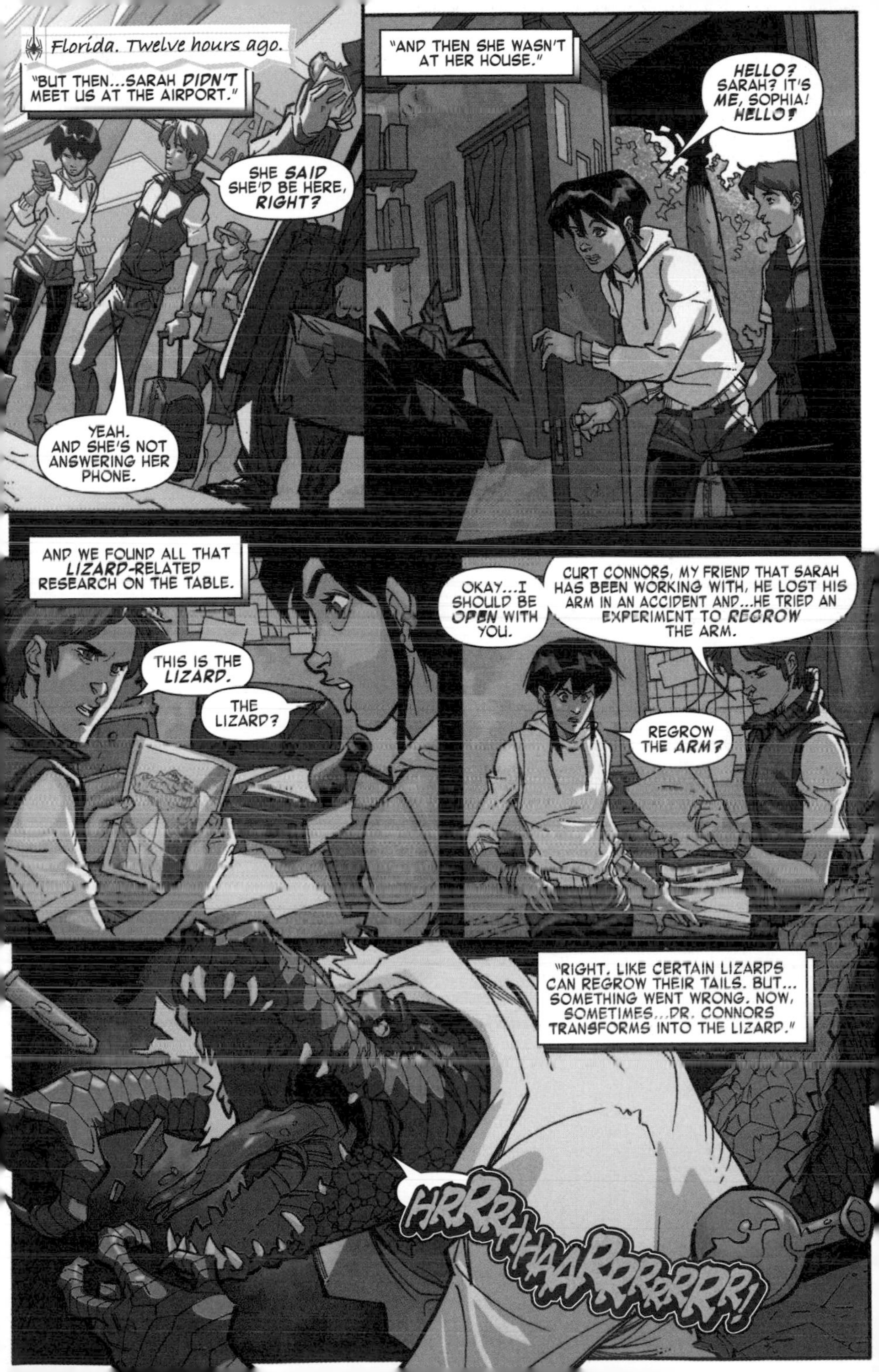
Florida. Twelve hours ago.
"BUT THEN...SARAH DIDN'T MEET US AT THE AIRPORT."
SHE SAID SHE'D BE HERE, RIGHT?
YEAH. AND SHE'S NOT ANSWERING HER PHONE.
"AND THEN SHE WASN'T AT HER HOUSE."
HELLO? SARAH? IT'S ME, SOPHIA! HELLO?
AND WE FOUND ALL THAT LIZARD-RELATED RESEARCH ON THE TABLE.
THIS IS THE LIZARD.
THE LIZARD?
OKAY...I SHOULD BE OPEN WITH YOU.
CURT CONNORS, MY FRIEND THAT SARAH HAS BEEN WORKING WITH, HE LOST HIS ARM IN AN ACCIDENT AND...HE TRIED AN EXPERIMENT TO REGROW THE ARM.
REGROW THE ARM?
"RIGHT. LIKE CERTAIN LIZARDS CAN REGROW THEIR TAILS. BUT... SOMETHING WENT WRONG. NOW, SOMETIMES...DR. CONNORS TRANSFORMS INTO THE LIZARD."
HRRRHAARRRRRRR!

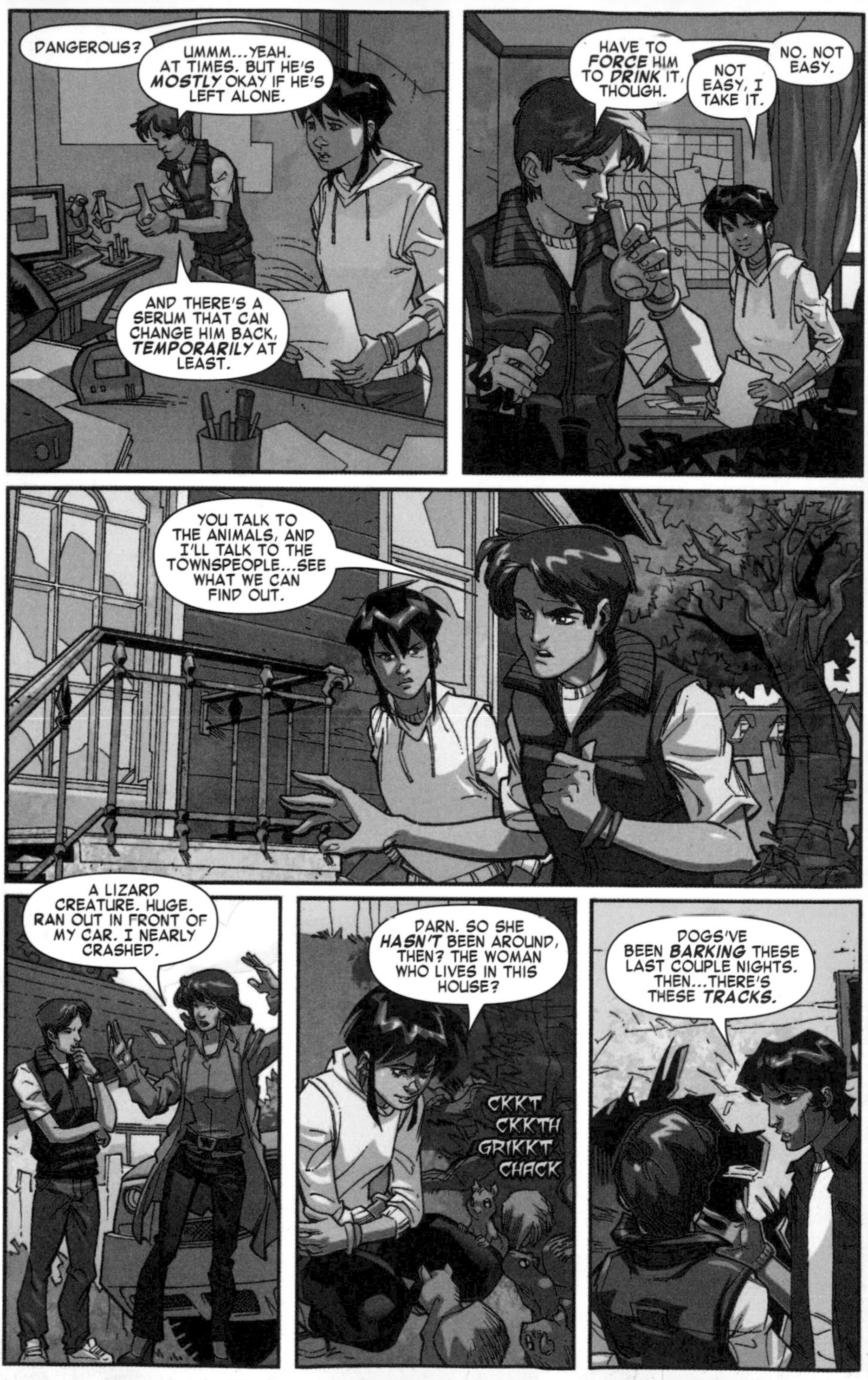
DANGEROUS?
UMMM...YEAH. AT TIMES. BUT HE'S MOSTLY OKAY IF HE'S LEFT ALONE.
AND THERE'S A SERUM THAT CAN CHANGE HIM BACK, TEMPORARILY AT LEAST.
HAVE TO FORCE HIM TO DRINK IT, THOUGH.
NOT EASY, I TAKE IT.
NO. NOT EASY.
YOU TALK TO THE ANIMALS, AND I'LL TALK TO THE TOWNSPEOPLE...SEE WHAT WE CAN FIND OUT.
A LIZARD CREATURE. HUGE. RAN OUT IN FRONT OF MY CAR. I NEARLY CRASHED.
DARN. SO SHE HASN'T BEEN AROUND, THEN? THE WOMAN WHO LIVES IN THIS HOUSE?
CKKT
CKKTH
GRIKKT
CHACK
DOGS'VE BEEN BARKING THESE LAST COUPLE NIGHTS. THEN...THERE'S THESE TRACKS.

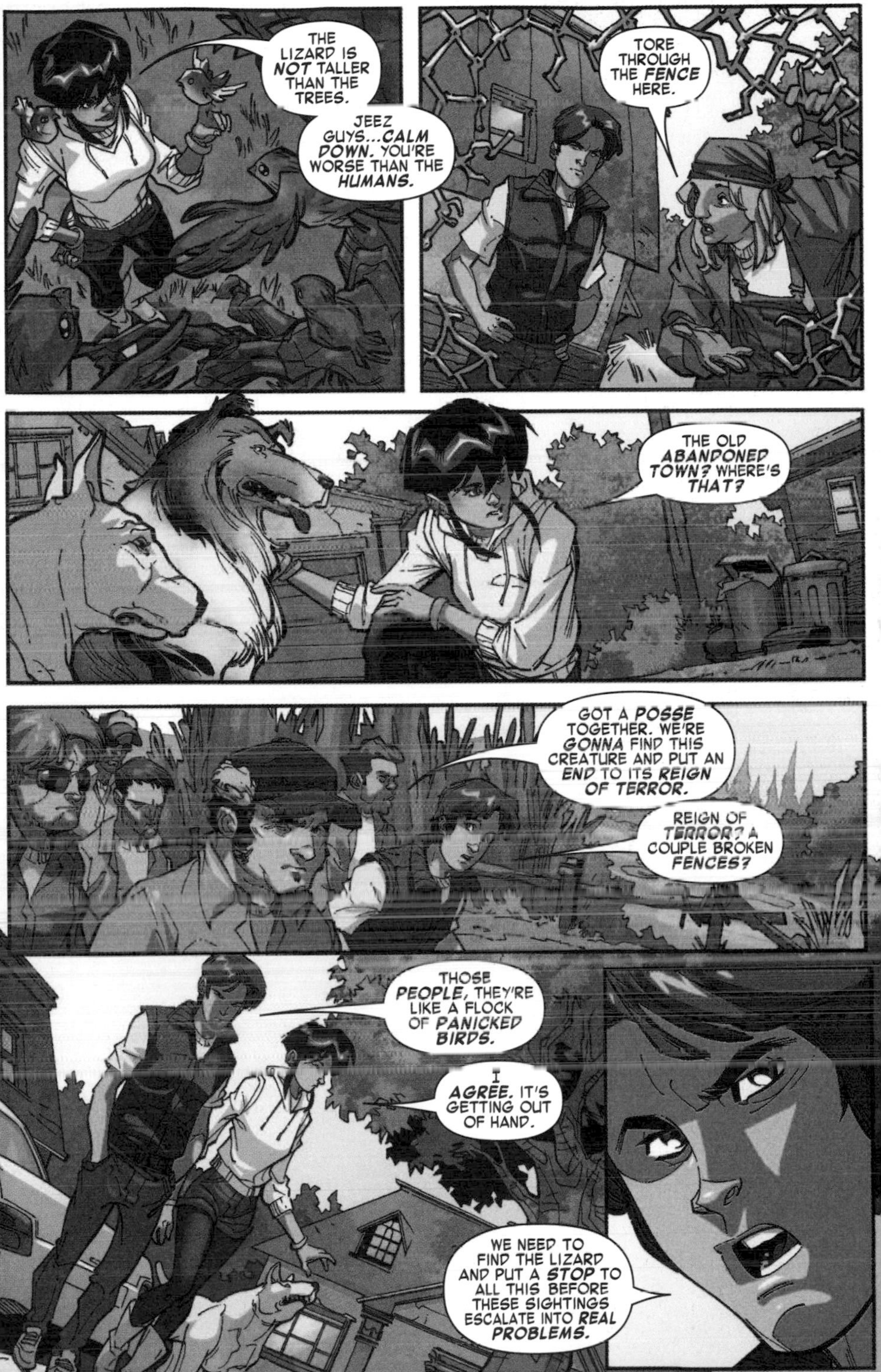
THE LIZARD IS NOT TALLER THAN THE TREES.
JEEZ GUYS...CALM DOWN. YOU'RE WORSE THAN THE HUMANS.
TORE THROUGH THE FENCE HERE.
THE OLD ABANDONED TOWN? WHERE'S THAT?
GOT A POSSE TOGETHER. WE'RE GONNA FIND THIS CREATURE AND PUT AN END TO ITS REIGN OF TERROR.
REIGN OF TERROR? A COUPLE BROKEN FENCES?
THOSE PEOPLE, THEY'RE LIKE A FLOCK OF PANICKED BIRDS.
I AGREE. IT'S GETTING OUT OF HAND.
WE NEED TO FIND THE LIZARD AND PUT A STOP TO ALL THIS BEFORE THESE SIGHTINGS ESCALATE INTO REAL PROBLEMS.

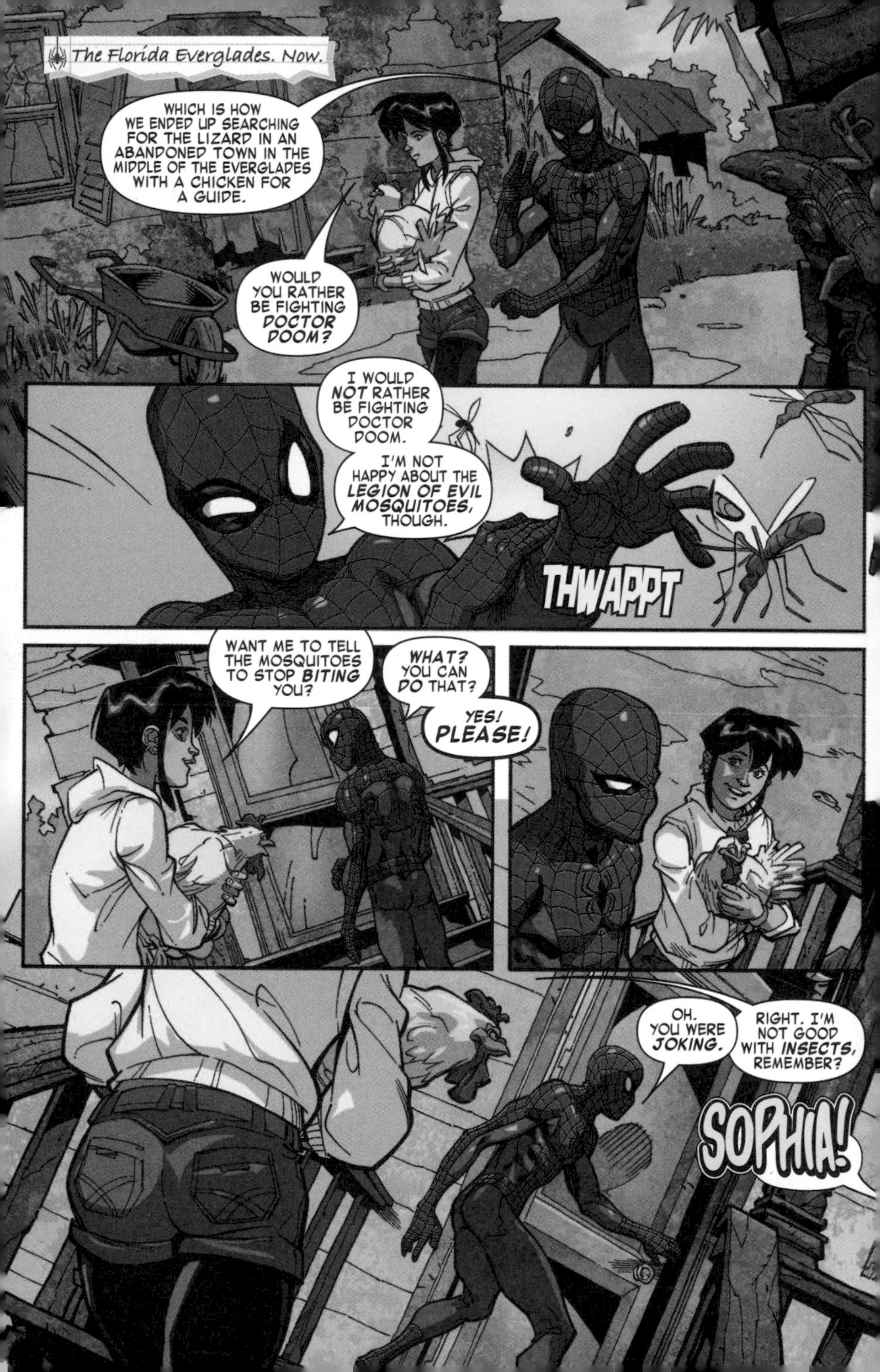
The Florida Everglades. Now.
WHICH IS HOW WE ENDED UP SEARCHING FOR THE LIZARD IN AN ABANDONED TOWN IN THE MIDDLE OF THE EVERGLADES WITH A CHICKEN FOR A GUIDE.
WOULD YOU RATHER BE FIGHTING DOCTOR DOOM?
I WOULD NOT RATHER BE FIGHTING DOCTOR DOOM.
I'M NOT HAPPY ABOUT THE LEGION OF EVIL MOSQUITOES, THOUGH.
THWAPPT
WANT ME TO TELL THE MOSQUITOES TO STOP BITING YOU?
WHAT? YOU CAN DO THAT?
YES! PLEASE!
OH. YOU WERE JOKING.
RIGHT. I'M NOT GOOD WITH INSECTS, REMEMBER?
SOPHIA!

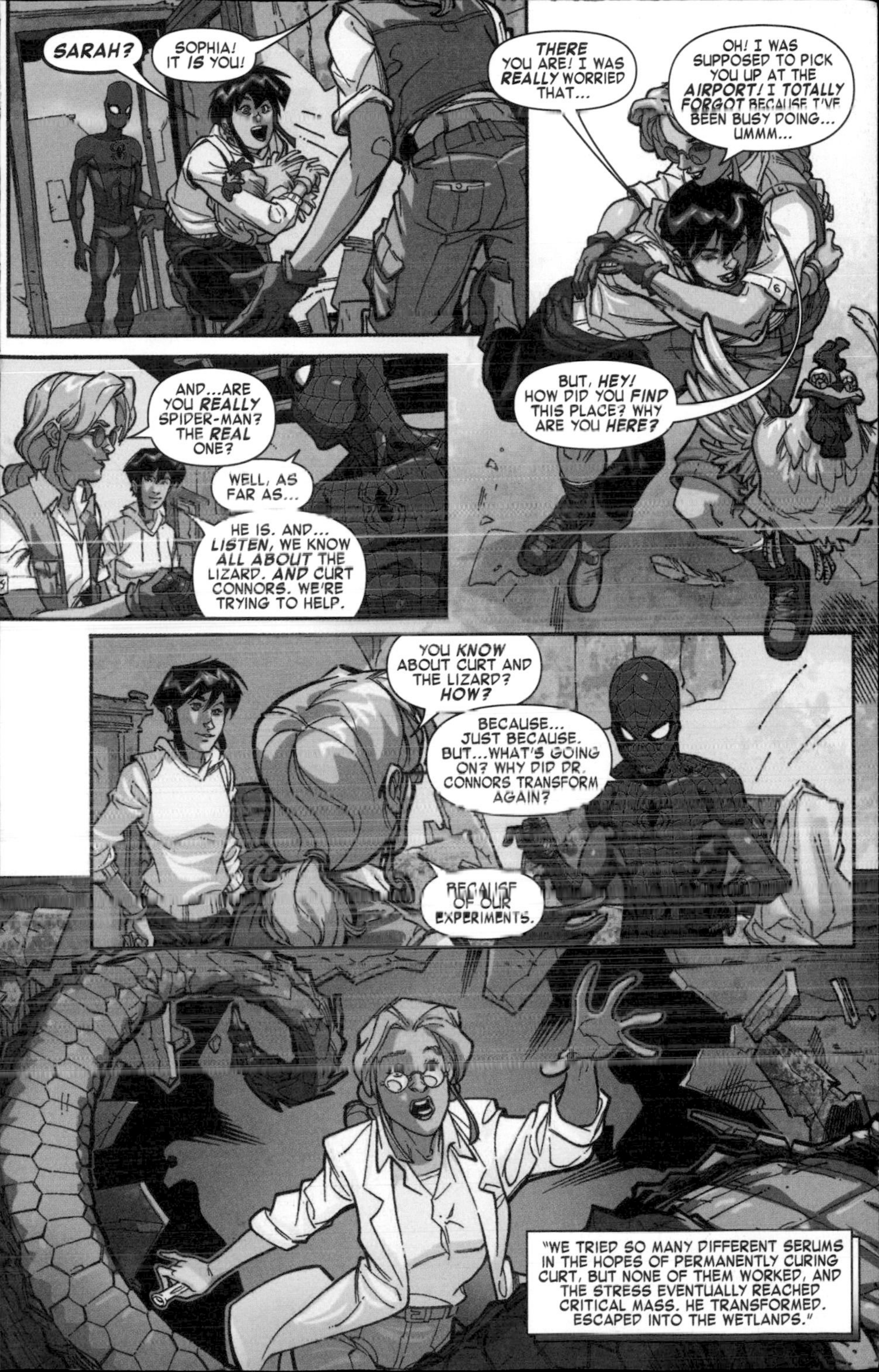
SARAH?
SOPHIA! IT IS YOU!
THERE YOU ARE! I WAS REALLY WORRIED THAT...
OH! I WAS SUPPOSED TO PICK YOU UP AT THE AIRPORT! I TOTALLY FORGOT BECAUSE I'VE BEEN BUSY DOING... UMMM...
BUT, HEY! HOW DID YOU FIND THIS PLACE? WHY ARE YOU HERE?
AND...ARE YOU REALLY SPIDER-MAN? THE REAL ONE?
WELL, AS FAR AS...
HE IS. AND... LISTEN, WE KNOW ALL ABOUT THE LIZARD. AND CURT CONNORS. WE'RE TRYING TO HELP.
YOU KNOW ABOUT CURT AND THE LIZARD? HOW?
BECAUSE... JUST BECAUSE. BUT...WHAT'S GOING ON? WHY DID DR. CONNORS TRANSFORM AGAIN?
BECAUSE OF OUR EXPERIMENTS.
"WE TRIED SO MANY DIFFERENT SERUMS IN THE HOPES OF PERMANENTLY CURING CURT, BUT NONE OF THEM WORKED, AND THE STRESS EVENTUALLY REACHED CRITICAL MASS. HE TRANSFORMED. ESCAPED INTO THE WETLANDS."

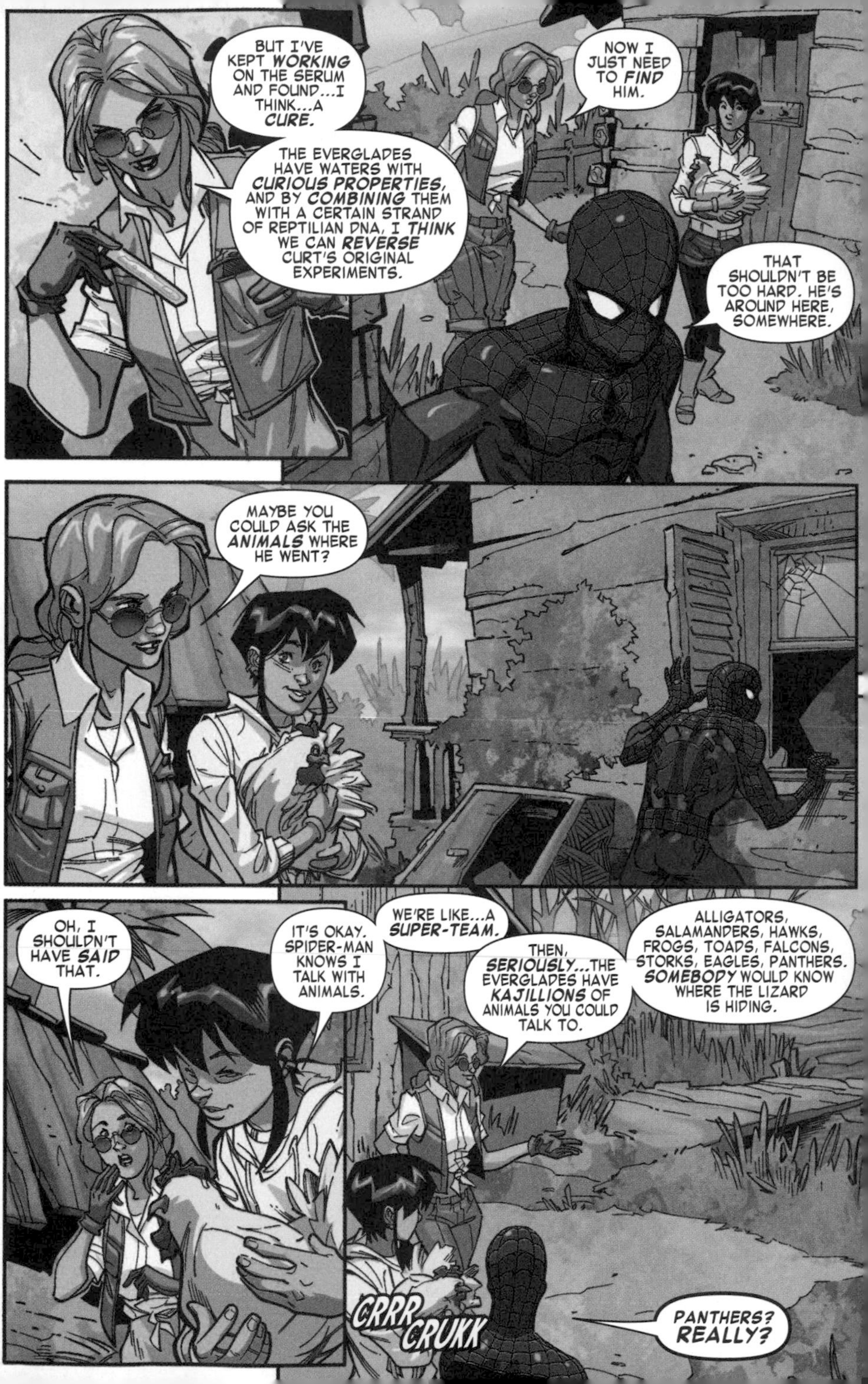
BUT I'VE KEPT WORKING ON THE SERUM AND FOUND...I THINK...A CURE.
THE EVERGLADES HAVE WATERS WITH CURIOUS PROPERTIES, AND BY COMBINING THEM WITH A CERTAIN STRAND OF REPTILIAN DNA, I THINK WE CAN REVERSE CURT'S ORIGINAL EXPERIMENTS.
NOW I JUST NEED TO FIND HIM.
THAT SHOULDN'T BE TOO HARD. HE'S AROUND HERE, SOMEWHERE.
MAYBE YOU COULD ASK THE ANIMALS WHERE HE WENT?
OH, I SHOULDN'T HAVE SAID THAT.
IT'S OKAY. SPIDER-MAN KNOWS I TALK WITH ANIMALS.
WE'RE LIKE...A SUPER-TEAM.
THEN, SERIOUSLY...THE EVERGLADES HAVE KAJILLIONS OF ANIMALS YOU COULD TALK TO.
ALLIGATORS, SALAMANDERS, HAWKS, FROGS, TOADS, FALCONS, STORKS, EAGLES, PANTHERS. SOMEBODY WOULD KNOW WHERE THE LIZARD IS HIDING.
CRRR CRUKK
PANTHERS? REALLY?

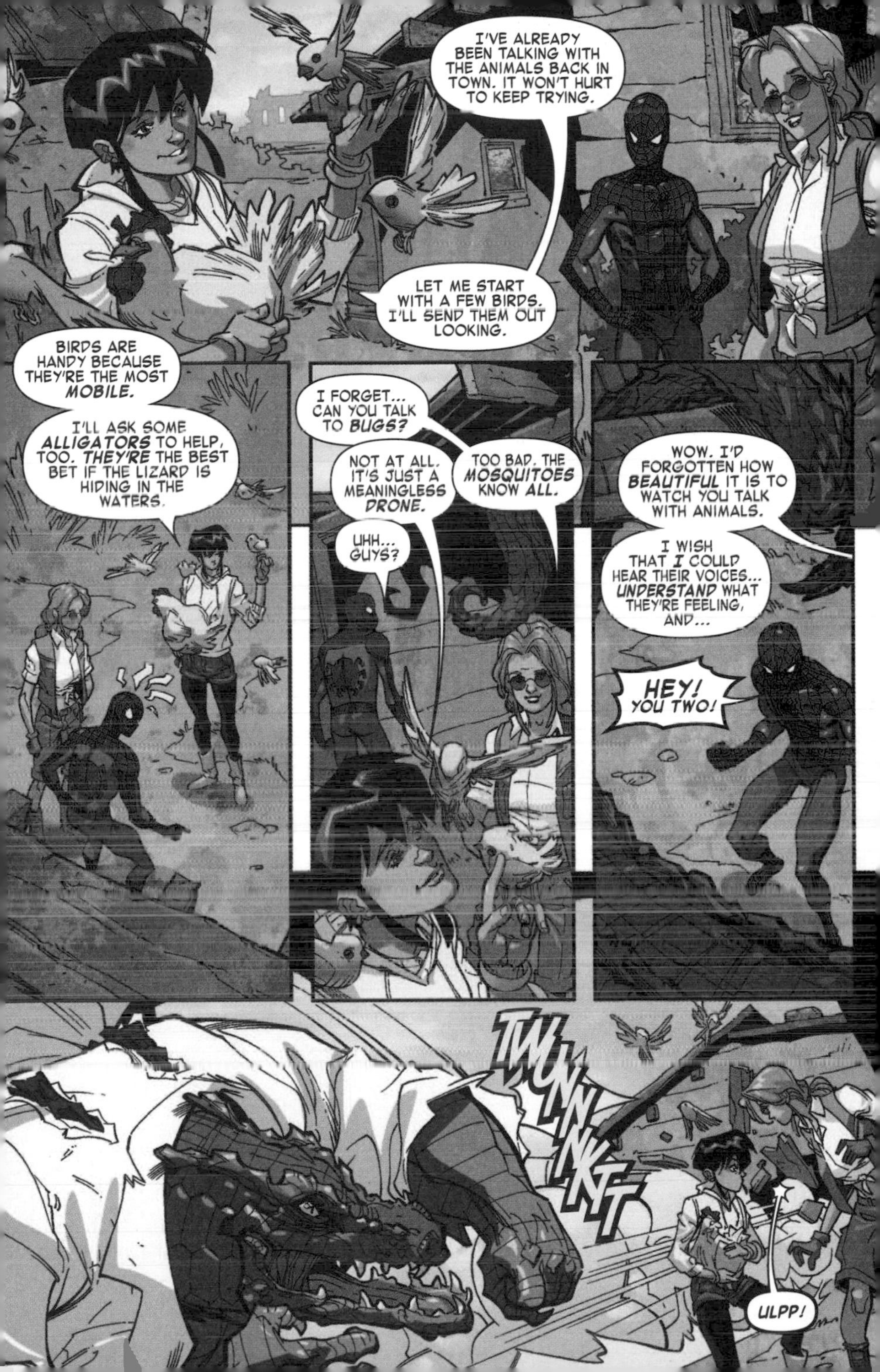
I'VE ALREADY BEEN TALKING WITH THE ANIMALS BACK IN TOWN. IT WON'T HURT TO KEEP TRYING.
LET ME START WITH A FEW BIRDS. I'LL SEND THEM OUT LOOKING.
BIRDS ARE HANDY BECAUSE THEY'RE THE MOST MOBILE.
I'LL ASK SOME ALLIGATORS TO HELP, TOO. THEY'RE THE BEST BET IF THE LIZARD IS HIDING IN THE WATERS.
I FORGET... CAN YOU TALK TO BUGS?
NOT AT ALL. IT'S JUST A MEANINGLESS DRONE.
TOO BAD. THE MOSQUITOES KNOW ALL.
UHH... GUYS?
WOW. I'D FORGOTTEN HOW BEAUTIFUL IT IS TO WATCH YOU TALK WITH ANIMALS.
I WISH THAT I COULD HEAR THEIR VOICES... UNDERSTAND WHAT THEY'RE FEELING, AND...
HEY! YOU TWO!
TWUNNKTT
ULPP!

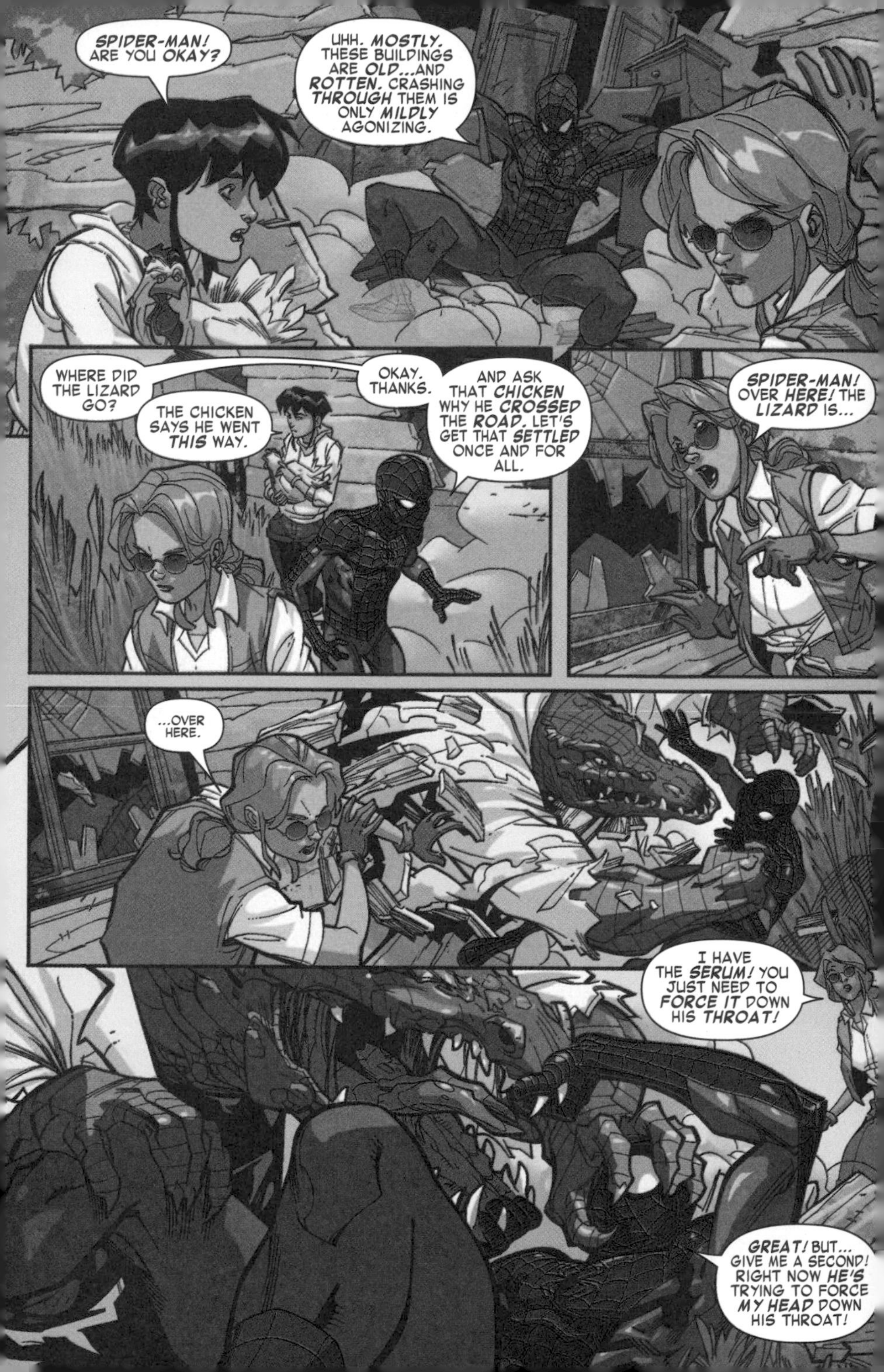
SPIDER-MAN! ARE YOU OKAY?
UHH. MOSTLY. THESE BUILDINGS ARE OLD...AND ROTTEN. CRASHING THROUGH THEM IS ONLY MILDLY AGONIZING.
WHERE DID THE LIZARD GO?
THE CHICKEN SAYS HE WENT THIS WAY.
OKAY. THANKS.
AND ASK THAT CHICKEN WHY HE CROSSED THE ROAD. LET'S GET THAT SETTLED ONCE AND FOR ALL.
SPIDER-MAN! OVER HERE! THE LIZARD IS...
...OVER HERE.
I HAVE THE SERUM! YOU JUST NEED TO FORCE IT DOWN HIS THROAT!
GREAT! BUT... GIVE ME A SECOND! RIGHT NOW HE'S TRYING TO FORCE MY HEAD DOWN HIS THROAT!

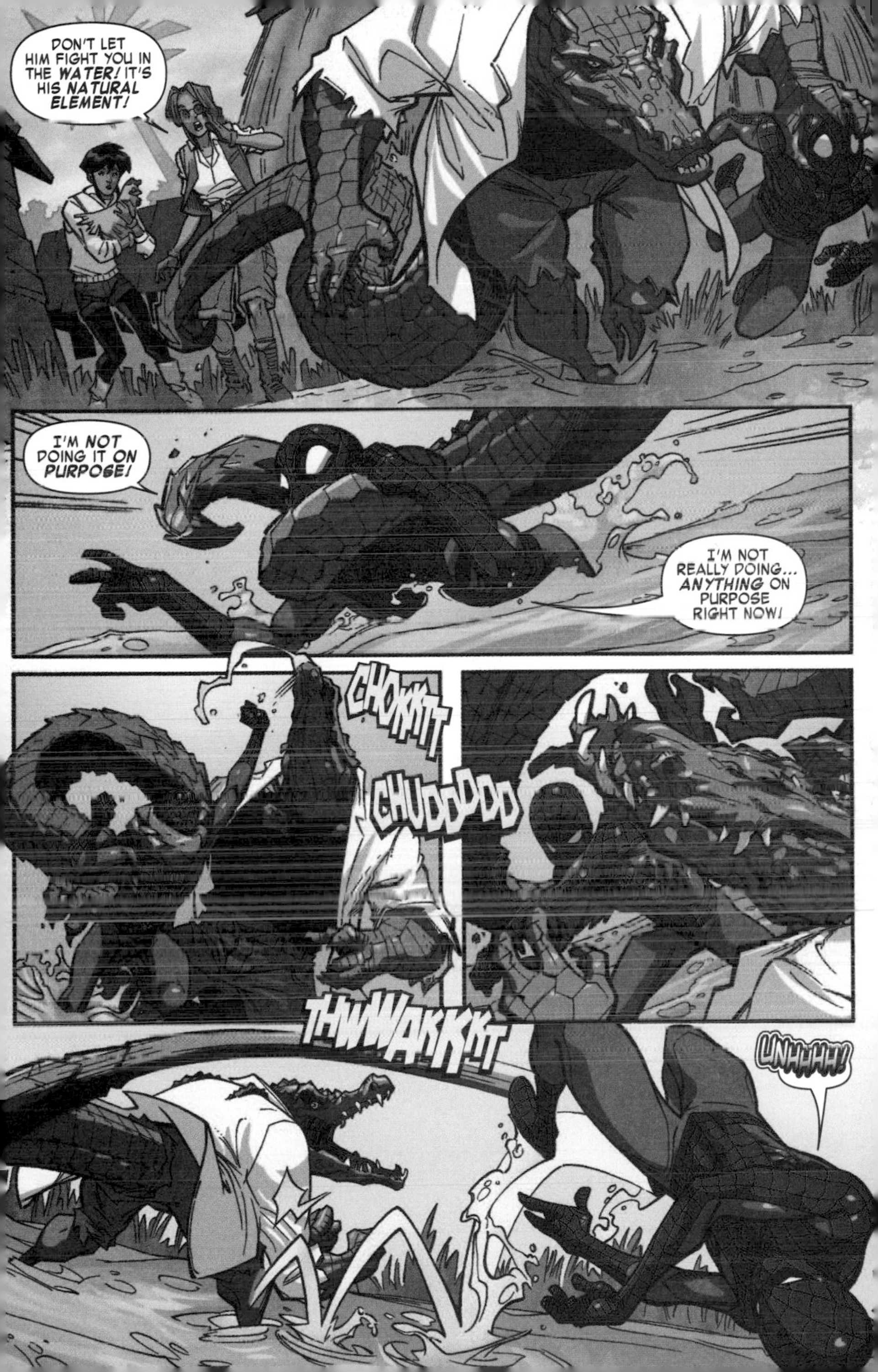
DON'T LET HIM FIGHT YOU IN THE WATER! IT'S HIS NATURAL ELEMENT!
I'M NOT DOING IT ON PURPOSE!
I'M NOT REALLY DOING... ANYTHING ON PURPOSE RIGHT NOW!
CHOKKTT
CHUDDDDD
THWWAKKKT
UNHHHH!

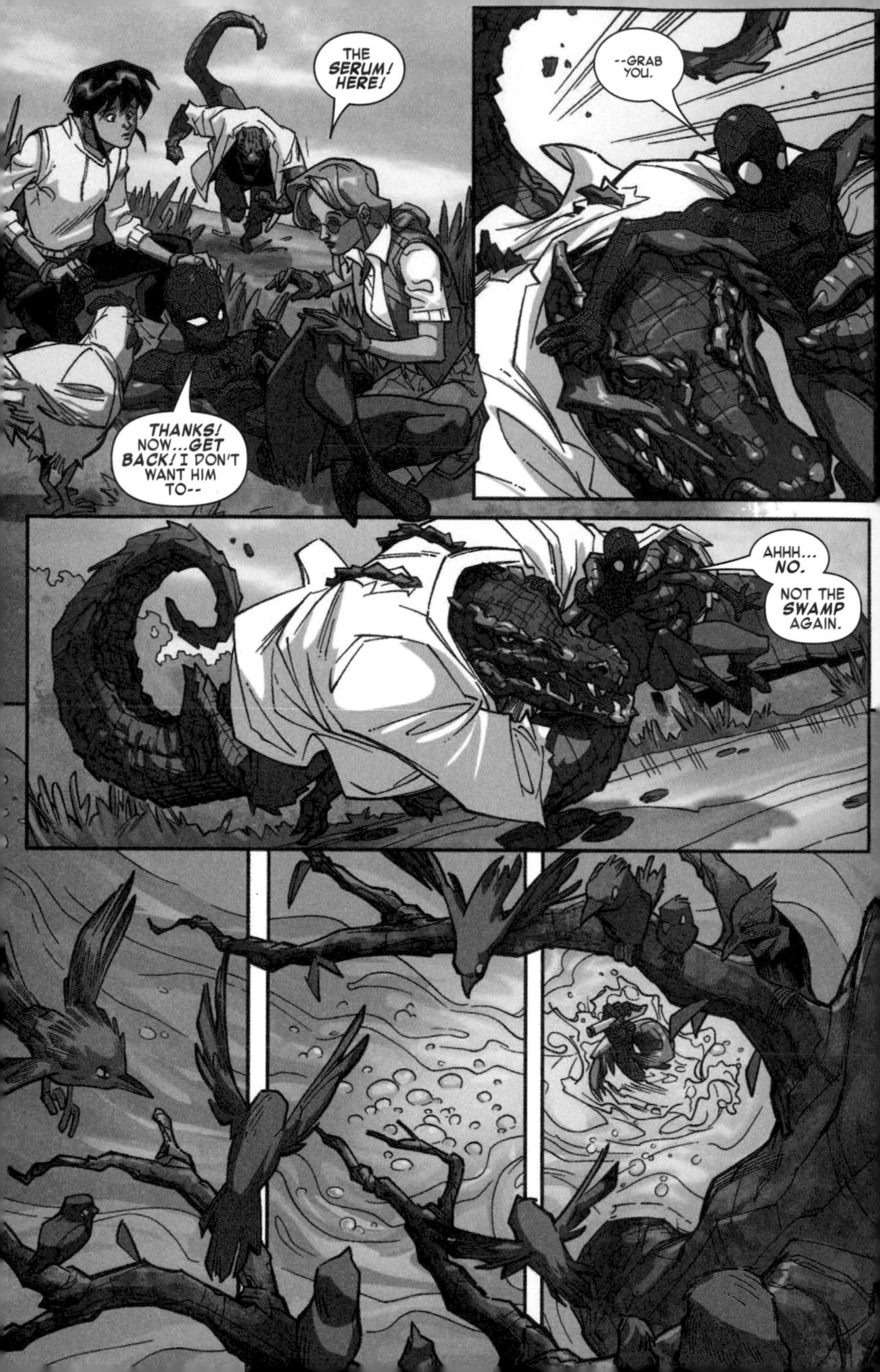
THE SERUM! HERE!
THANKS! NOW...GET BACK! I DON'T WANT HIM TO--
--GRAB YOU.
AHHH... NO.
NOT THE SWAMP AGAIN.

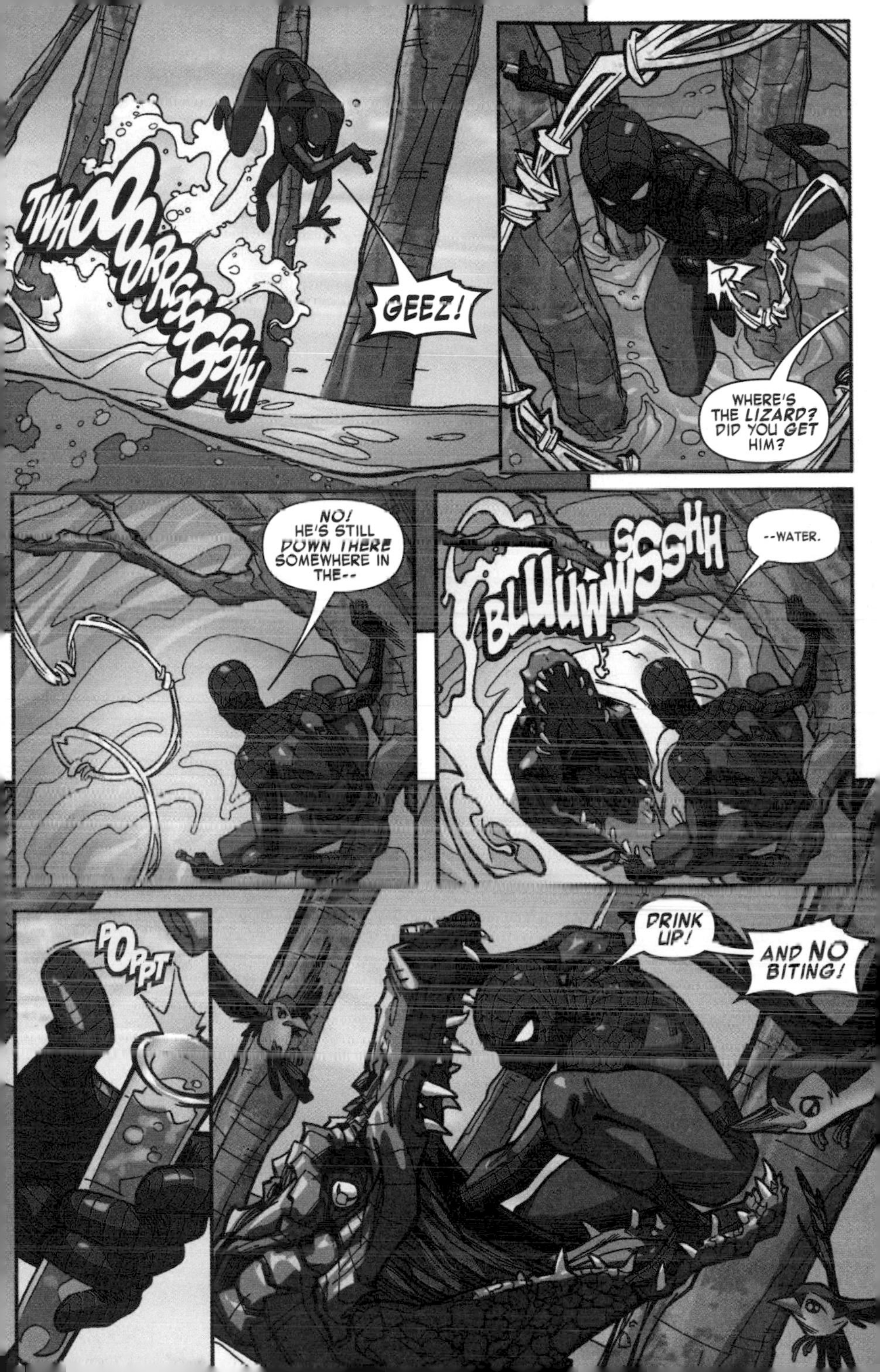
TWHOOOORRSSSSHH
GEEZ!
WHERE'S THE LIZARD? DID YOU GET HIM?
NO! HE'S STILL DOWN THERE SOMEWHERE IN THE--
BLUUWWSSHH
--WATER.
POPPT
DRINK UP!
AND NO BITING!

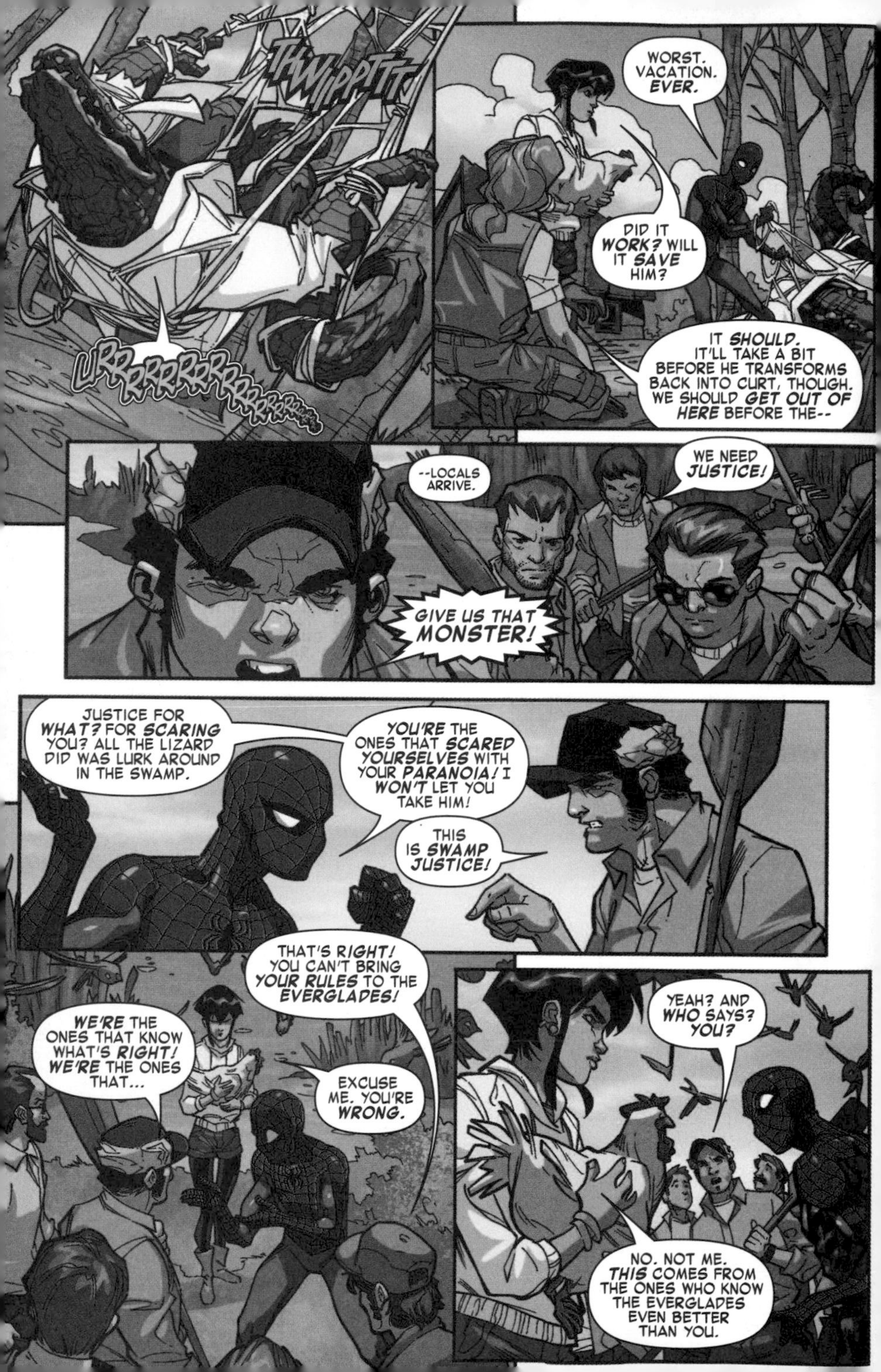
THWIIPPTTT
URRRRRRRRRRRRRRRR
WORST. VACATION. EVER.
DID IT WORK? WILL IT SAVE HIM?
IT SHOULD. IT'LL TAKE A BIT BEFORE HE TRANSFORMS BACK INTO CURT, THOUGH. WE SHOULD GET OUT OF HERE BEFORE THE--
--LOCALS ARRIVE.
WE NEED JUSTICE!
GIVE US THAT MONSTER!
JUSTICE FOR WHAT? FOR SCARING YOU? ALL THE LIZARD DID WAS LURK AROUND IN THE SWAMP.
YOU'RE THE ONES THAT SCARED YOURSELVES WITH YOUR PARANOIA! I WON'T LET YOU TAKE HIM!
THIS IS SWAMP JUSTICE!
THAT'S RIGHT! YOU CAN'T BRING YOUR RULES TO THE EVERGLADES!
WE'RE THE ONES THAT KNOW WHAT'S RIGHT! WE'RE THE ONES THAT...
EXCUSE ME. YOU'RE WRONG.
YEAH? AND WHO SAYS? YOU?
NO. NOT ME. THIS COMES FROM THE ONES WHO KNOW THE EVERGLADES EVEN BETTER THAN YOU.

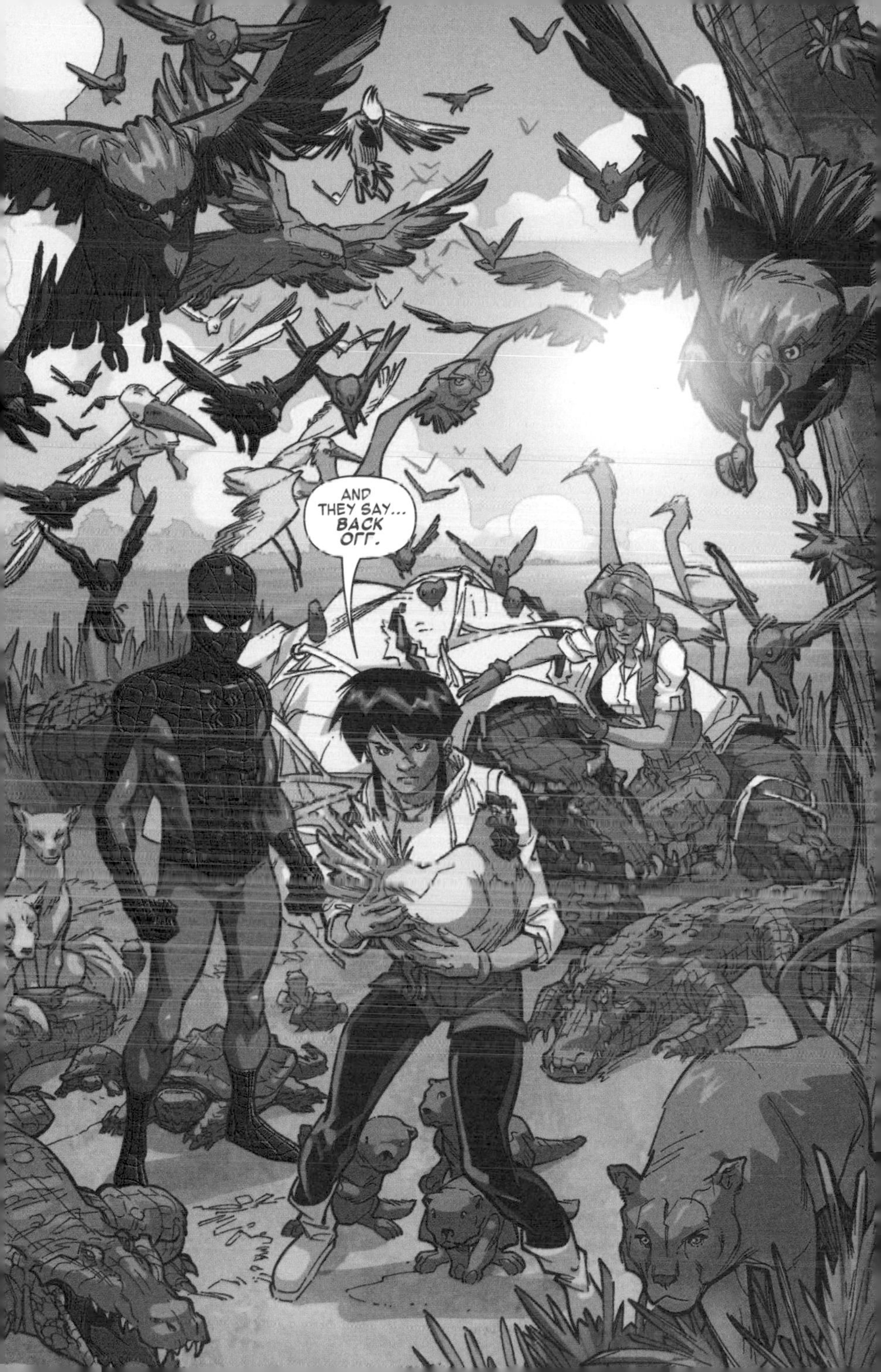
AND THEY SAY... BACK OFF.

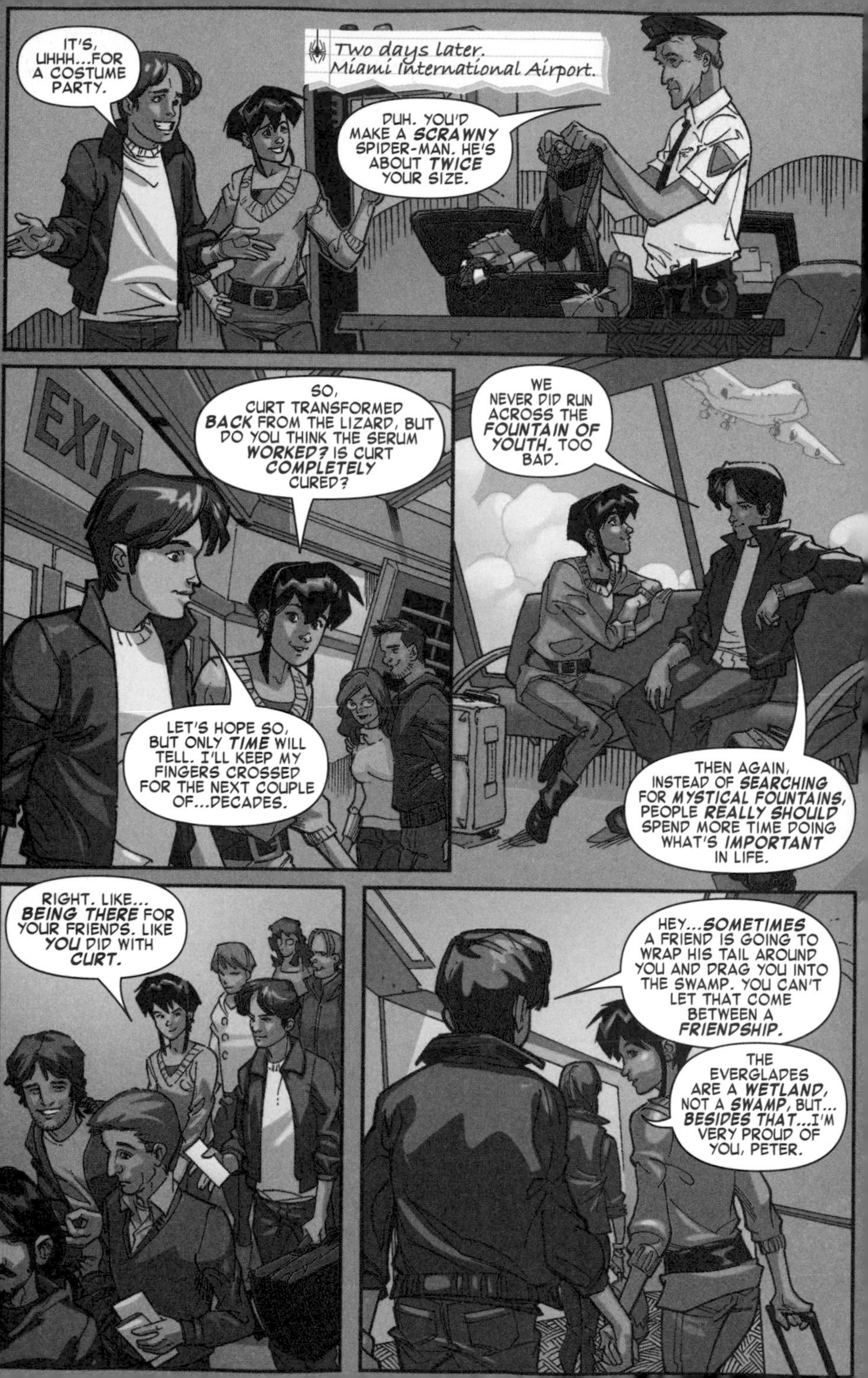
Two days later.
Miami International Airport.
IT'S, UHHH...FOR A COSTUME PARTY.
DUH. YOU'D MAKE A SCRAWNY SPIDER-MAN. HE'S ABOUT TWICE YOUR SIZE.
EXIT
SO, CURT TRANSFORMED BACK FROM THE LIZARD, BUT DO YOU THINK THE SERUM WORKED? IS CURT COMPLETELY CURED?
LET'S HOPE SO, BUT ONLY TIME WILL TELL. I'LL KEEP MY FINGERS CROSSED FOR THE NEXT COUPLE OF...DECADES.
WE NEVER DID RUN ACROSS THE FOUNTAIN OF YOUTH. TOO BAD.
THEN AGAIN, INSTEAD OF SEARCHING FOR MYSTICAL FOUNTAINS, PEOPLE REALLY SHOULD SPEND MORE TIME DOING WHAT'S IMPORTANT IN LIFE.
RIGHT. LIKE... BEING THERE FOR YOUR FRIENDS. LIKE YOU DID WITH CURT.
HEY...SOMETIMES A FRIEND IS GOING TO WRAP HIS TAIL AROUND YOU AND DRAG YOU INTO THE SWAMP. YOU CAN'T LET THAT COME BETWEEN A FRIENDSHIP.
THE EVERGLADES ARE A WETLAND, NOT A SWAMP, BUT... BESIDES THAT...I'M VERY PROUD OF YOU, PETER.

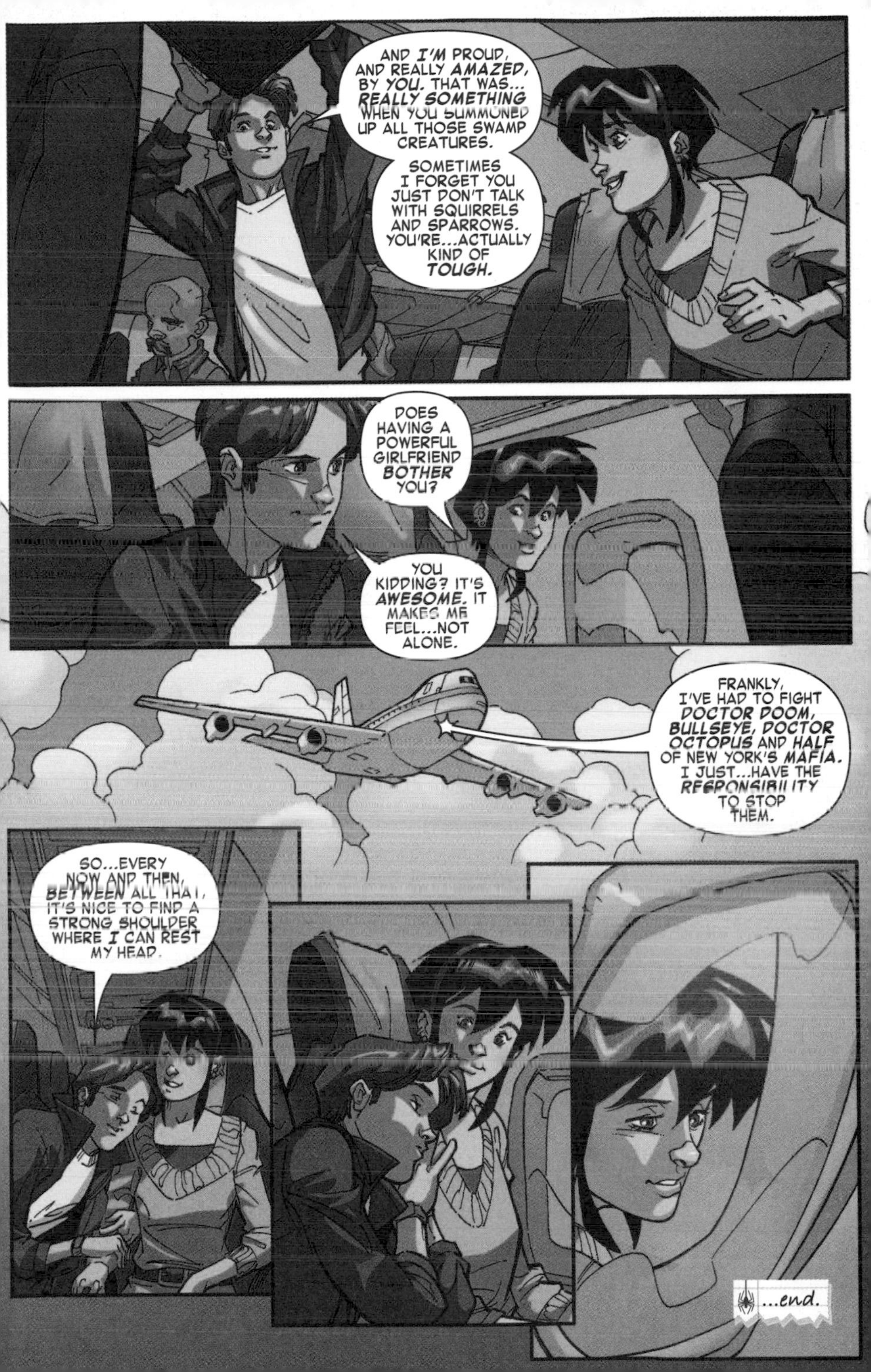
AND I'M PROUD, AND REALLY AMAZED, BY YOU. THAT WAS... REALLY SOMETHING WHEN YOU SUMMONED UP ALL THOSE SWAMP CREATURES.
SOMETIMES I FORGET YOU JUST DON'T TALK WITH SQUIRRELS AND SPARROWS. YOU'RE...ACTUALLY KIND OF TOUGH.
DOES HAVING A POWERFUL GIRLFRIEND BOTHER YOU?
YOU KIDDING? IT'S AWESOME. IT MAKES ME FEEL...NOT ALONE.
FRANKLY, I'VE HAD TO FIGHT DOCTOR DOOM, BULLSEYE, DOCTOR OCTOPUS AND HALF OF NEW YORK'S MAFIA. I JUST...HAVE THE RESPONSIBILITY TO STOP THEM.
SO...EVERY NOW AND THEN, BETWEEN ALL THAT, IT'S NICE TO FIND A STRONG SHOULDER WHERE I CAN REST MY HEAD.
...end.

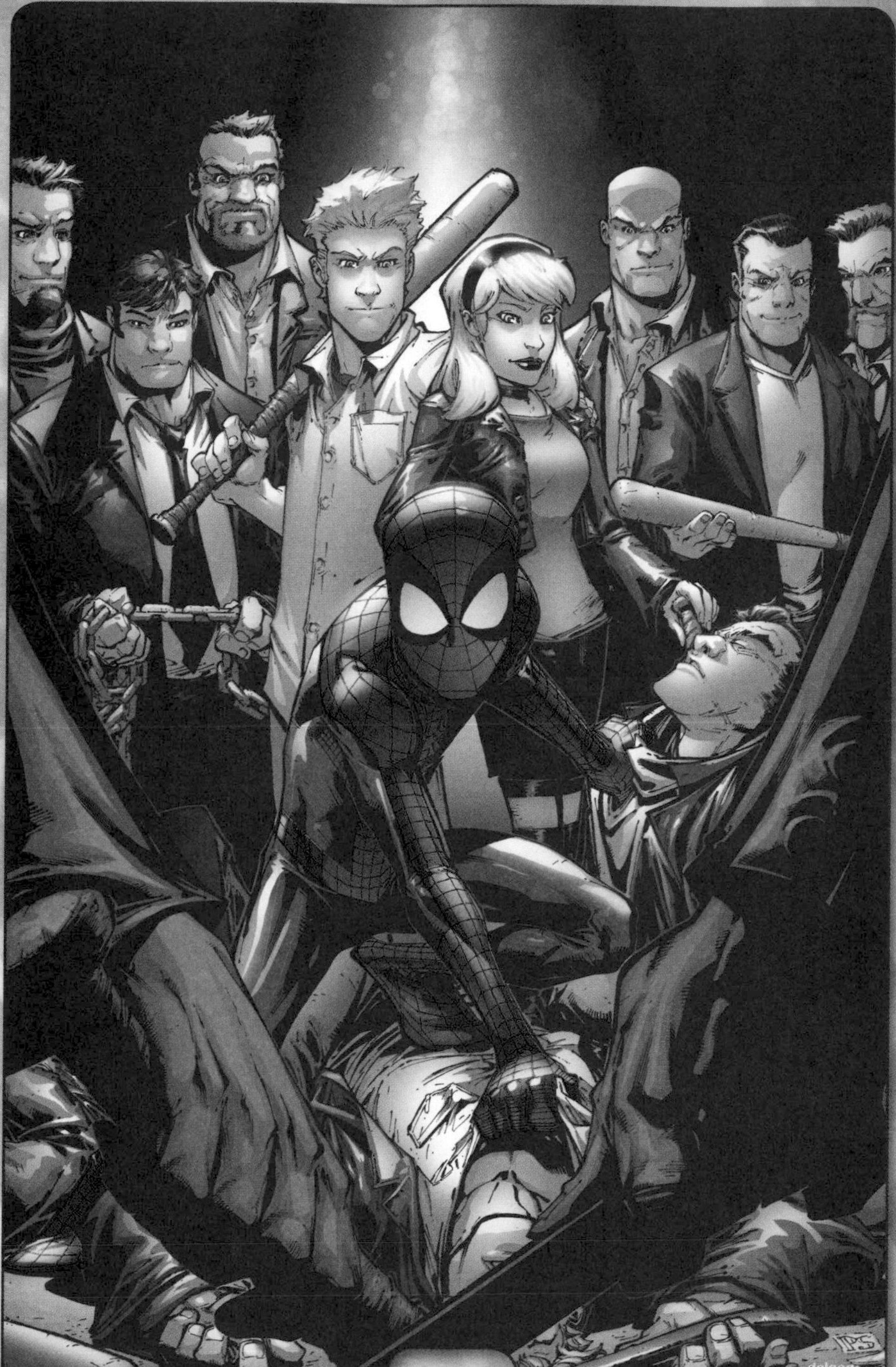

delgado
#12

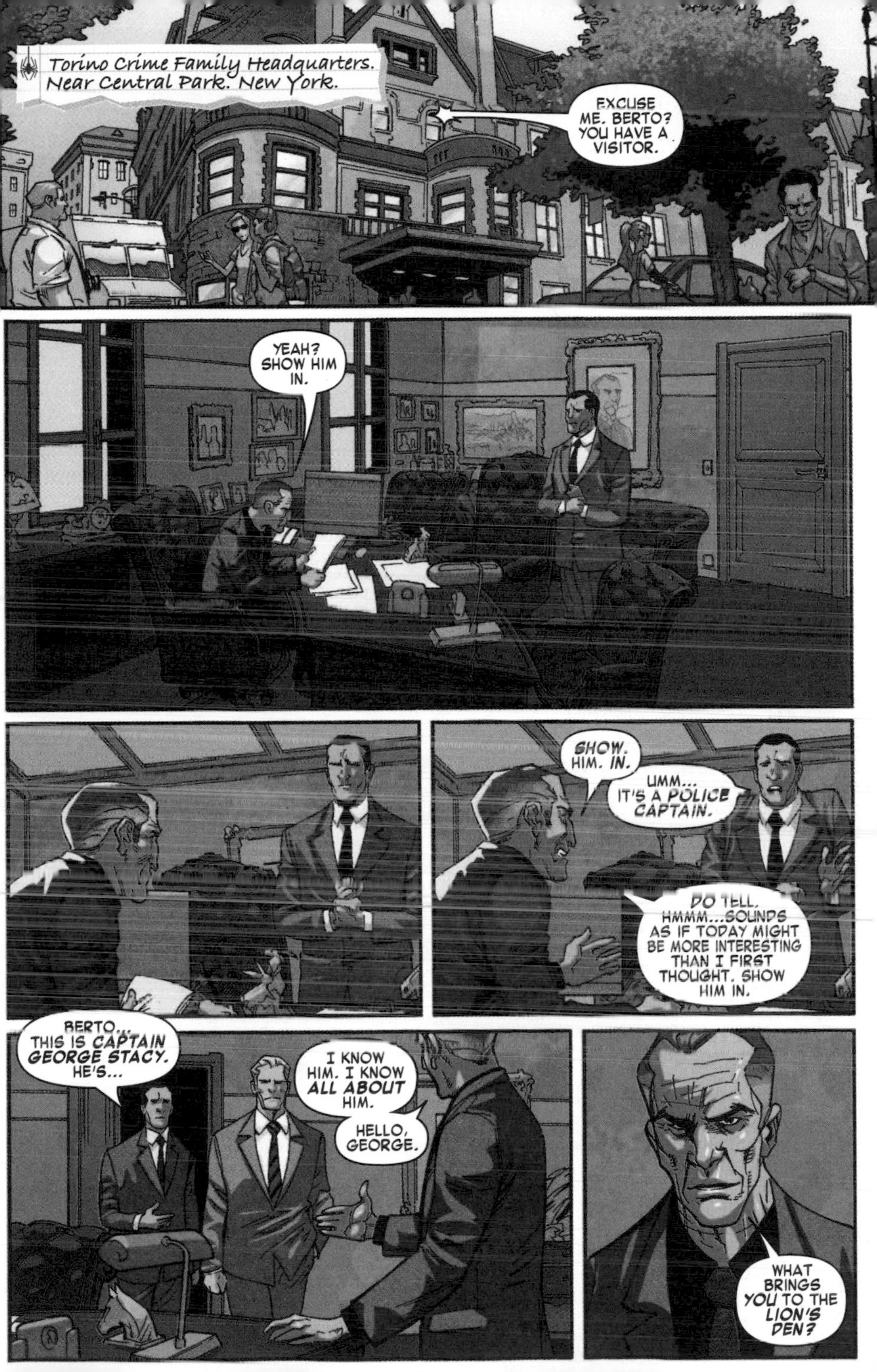
Torino Crime Family Headquarters. Near Central Park. New York.
EXCUSE ME. BERTO? YOU HAVE A VISITOR.
YEAH? SHOW HIM IN.
SHOW. HIM. IN.
UMM... IT'S A POLICE CAPTAIN.
DO TELL. HMMM...SOUNDS AS IF TODAY MIGHT BE MORE INTERESTING THAN I FIRST THOUGHT. SHOW HIM IN.
BERTO... THIS IS CAPTAIN GEORGE STACY. HE'S...
I KNOW HIM. I KNOW ALL ABOUT HIM.
HELLO, GEORGE.
WHAT BRINGS YOU TO THE LION'S DEN?

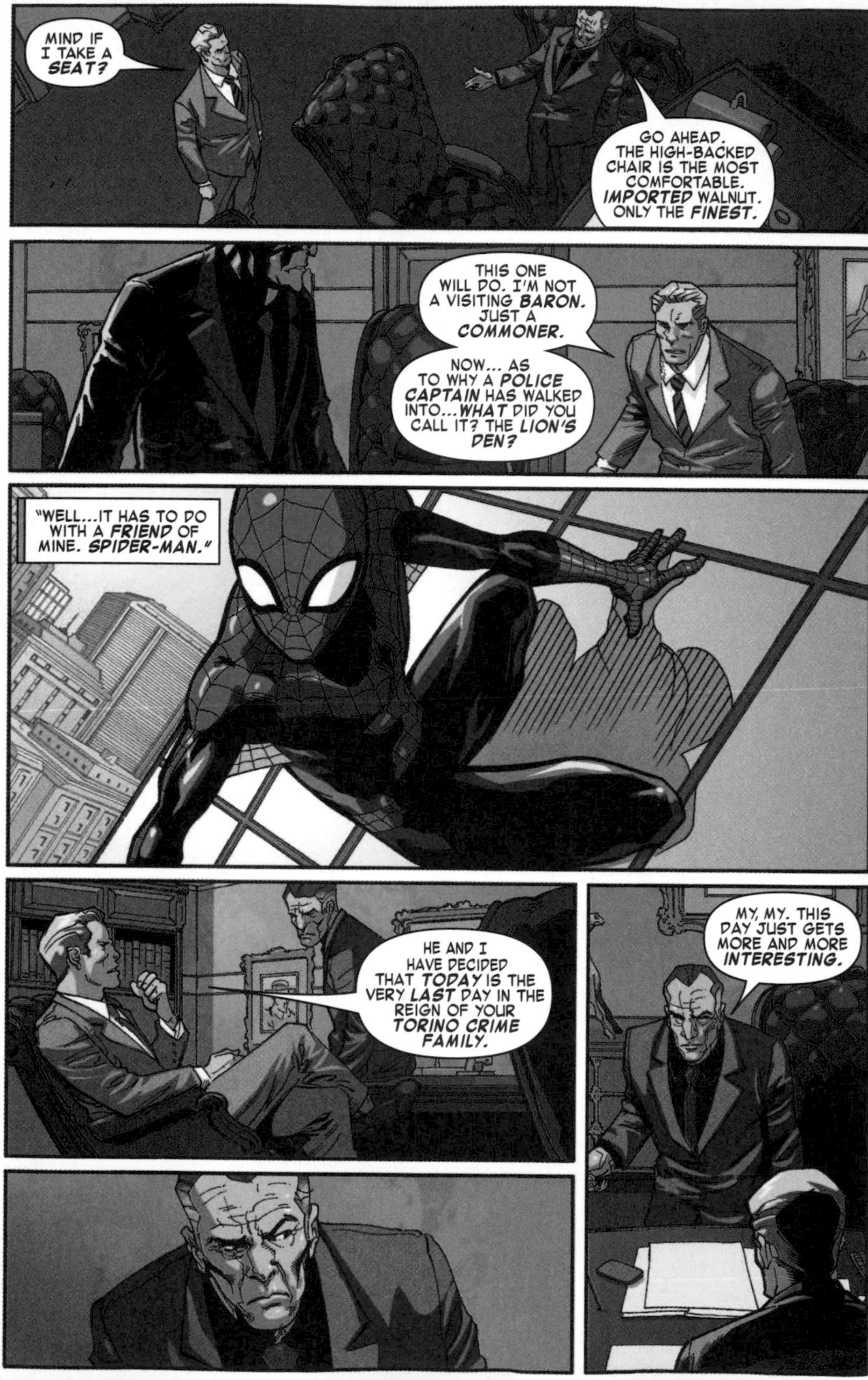
MIND IF I TAKE A SEAT?
GO AHEAD. THE HIGH-BACKED CHAIR IS THE MOST COMFORTABLE. IMPORTED WALNUT. ONLY THE FINEST.
THIS ONE WILL DO. I'M NOT A VISITING BARON. JUST A COMMONER.
NOW... AS TO WHY A POLICE CAPTAIN HAS WALKED INTO...WHAT DID YOU CALL IT? THE LION'S DEN?
"WELL...IT HAS TO DO WITH A FRIEND OF MINE. SPIDER-MAN."
HE AND I HAVE DECIDED THAT TODAY IS THE VERY LAST DAY IN THE REIGN OF YOUR TORINO CRIME FAMILY.
MY, MY. THIS DAY JUST GETS MORE AND MORE INTERESTING.

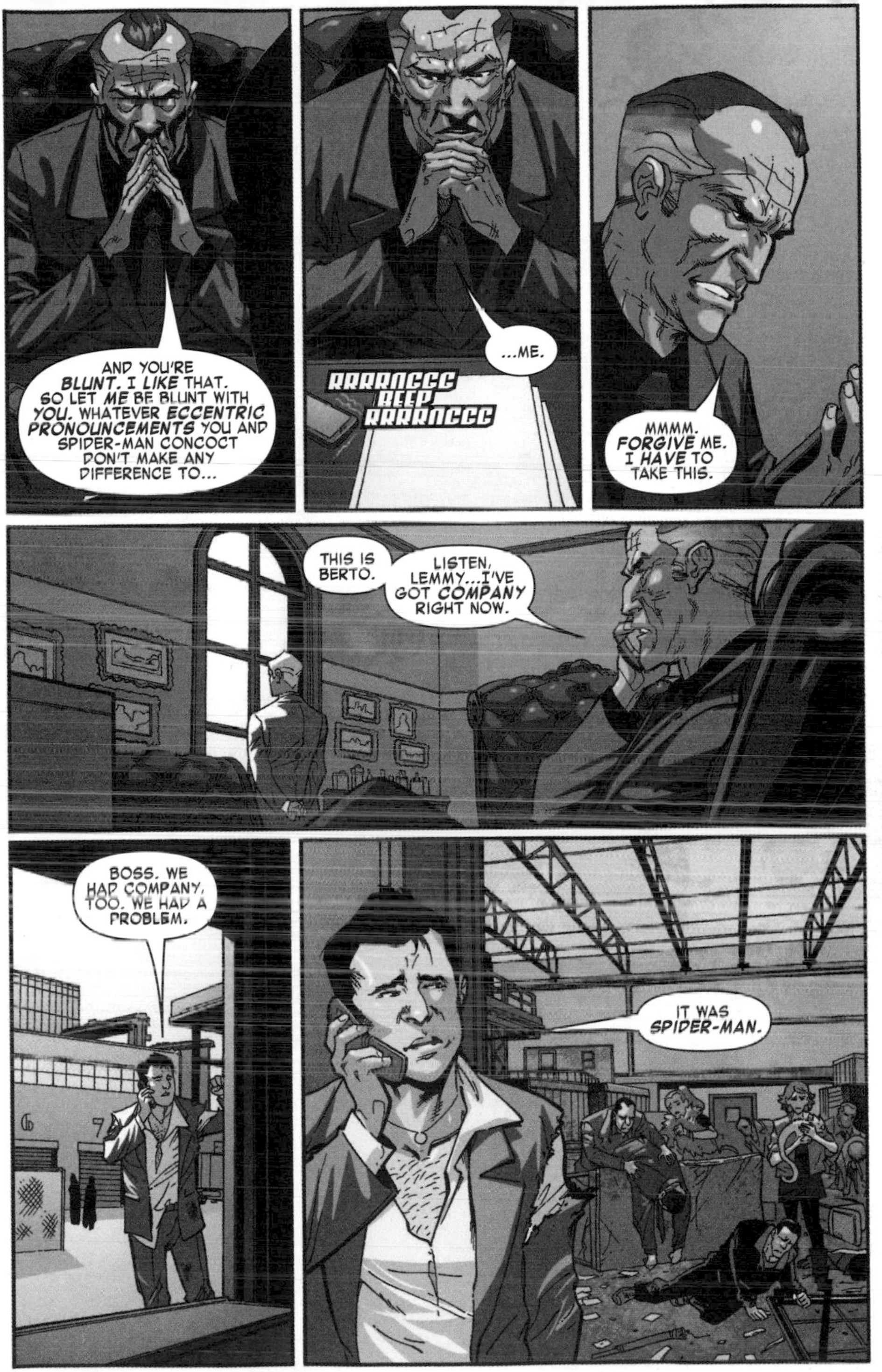
AND YOU'RE BLUNT. I LIKE THAT. SO LET ME BE BLUNT WITH YOU. WHATEVER ECCENTRIC PRONOUNCEMENTS YOU AND SPIDER-MAN CONCOCT DON'T MAKE ANY DIFFERENCE TO...
...ME.
RRRRNGGG BEEP RRRRNGGG
MMMM. FORGIVE ME. I HAVE TO TAKE THIS.
THIS IS BERTO.
LISTEN, LEMMY...I'VE GOT COMPANY RIGHT NOW.
BOSS. WE HAD COMPANY, TOO. WE HAD A PROBLEM.
IT WAS SPIDER-MAN.

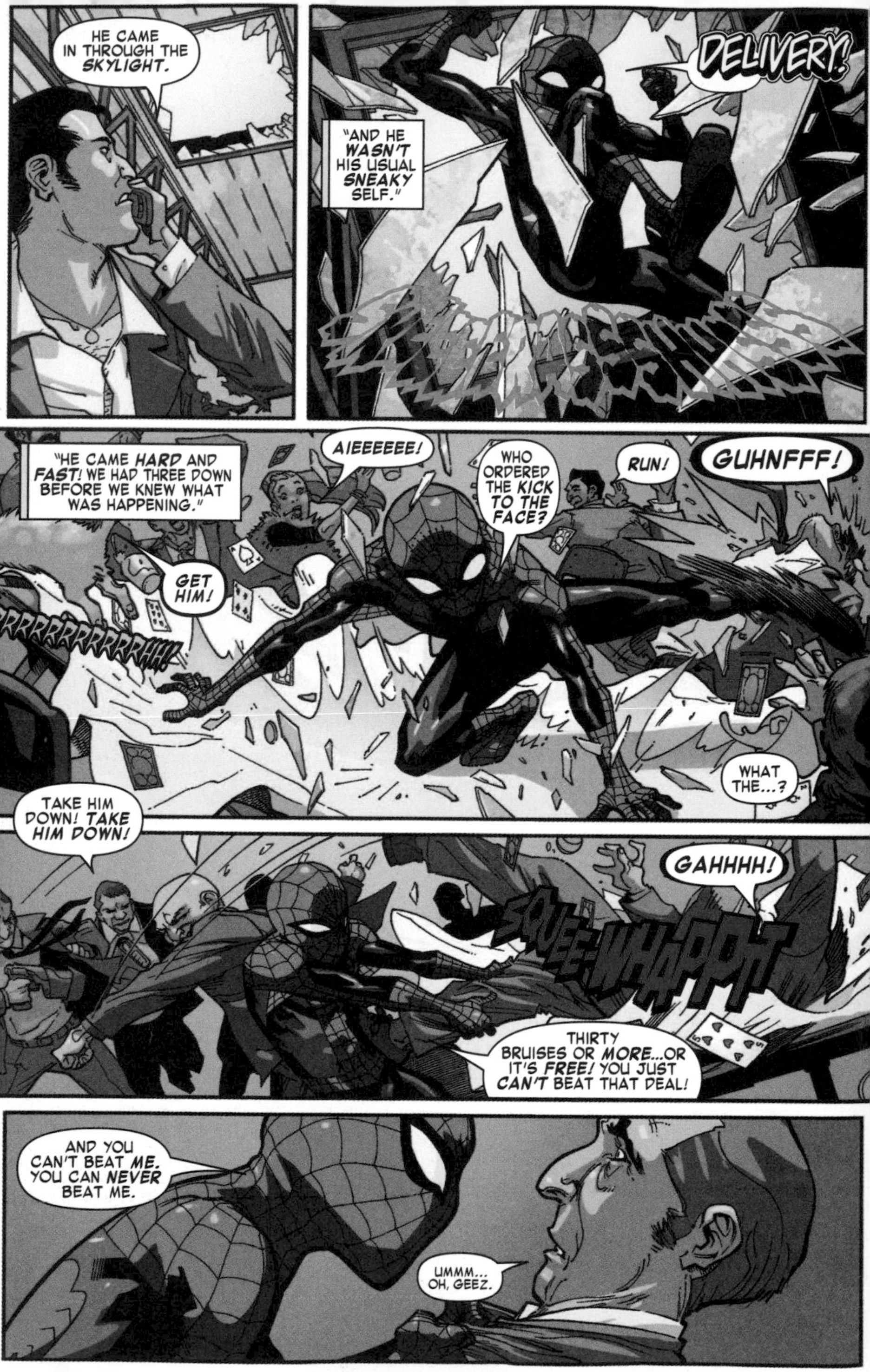
HE CAME IN THROUGH THE SKYLIGHT.
DELIVERY!
"AND HE WASN'T HIS USUAL SNEAKY SELF."
"HE CAME HARD AND FAST! WE HAD THREE DOWN BEFORE WE KNEW WHAT WAS HAPPENING."
AIEEEEEE!
WHO ORDERED THE KICK TO THE FACE?
RUN!
GUHNFFF!
GET HIM!
RRRRRRRRRRRRAH!!
WHAT THE...?
TAKE HIM DOWN! TAKE HIM DOWN!
GAHHHH!
SQUEE-WHAPPPT
THIRTY BRUISES OR MORE...OR IT'S FREE! YOU JUST CAN'T BEAT THAT DEAL!
AND YOU CAN'T BEAT ME. YOU CAN NEVER BEAT ME.
UMMM... OH, GEEZ.

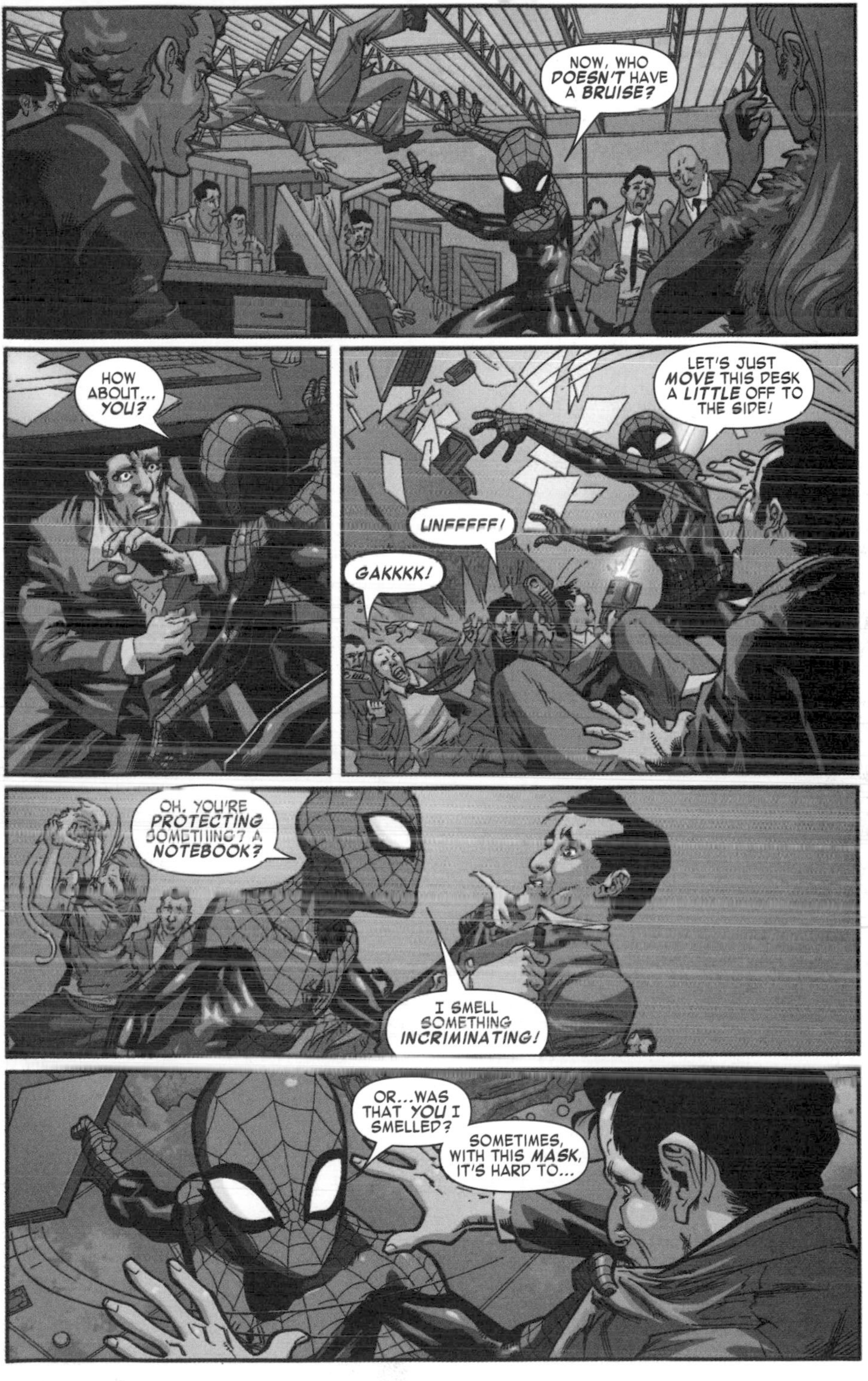
NOW, WHO DOESN'T HAVE A BRUISE?
HOW ABOUT... YOU?
LET'S JUST MOVE THIS DESK A LITTLE OFF TO THE SIDE!
UNFFFFF!
GAKKKK!
OH. YOU'RE PROTECTING SOMETHING? A NOTEBOOK?
I SMELL SOMETHING INCRIMINATING!
OR...WAS THAT YOU I SMELLED?
SOMETIMES, WITH THIS MASK, IT'S HARD TO...

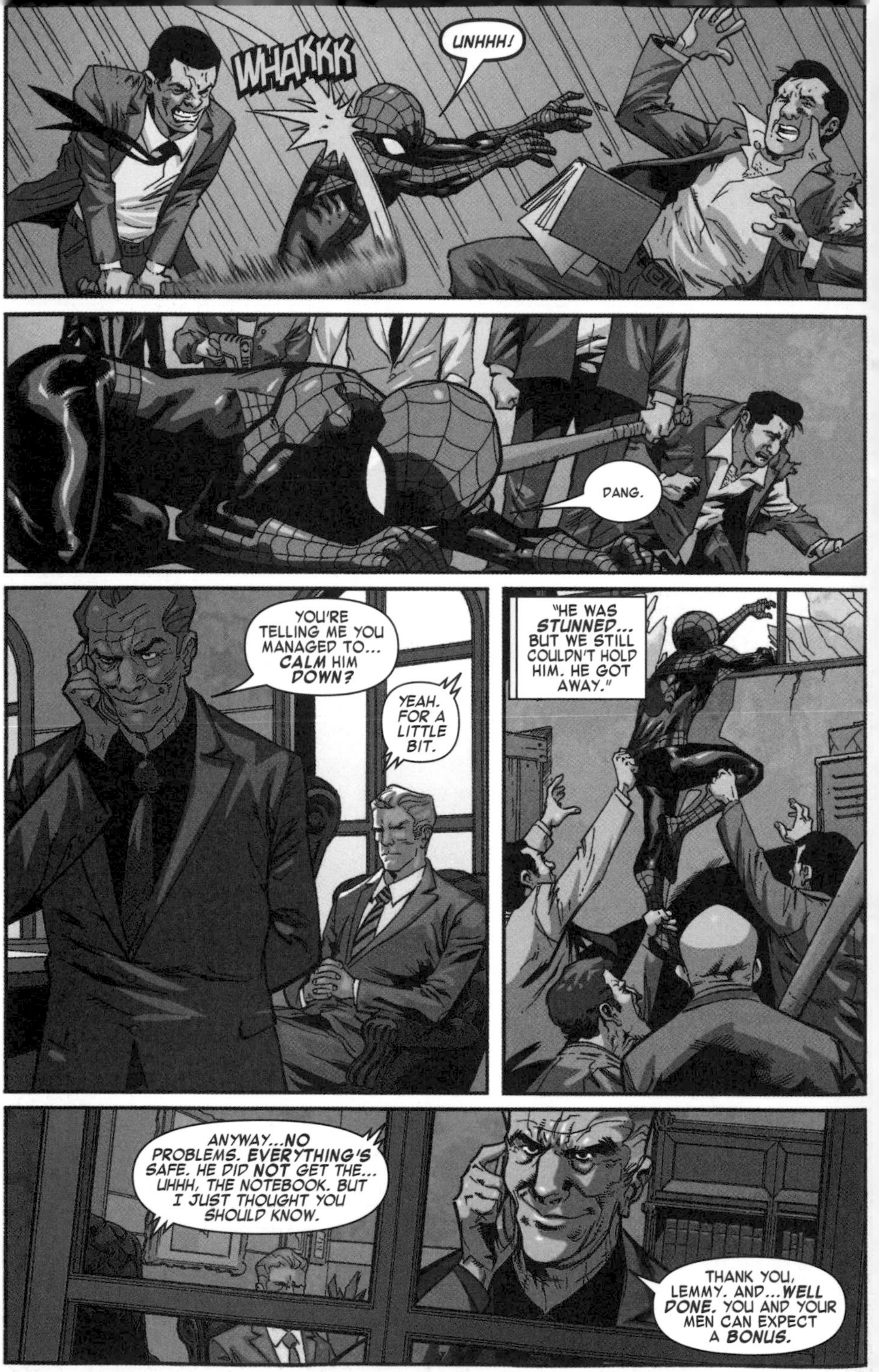
WHAKKK
UNHHH!
DANG.
YOU'RE TELLING ME YOU MANAGED TO... CALM HIM DOWN?
YEAH. FOR A LITTLE BIT.
"HE WAS STUNNED... BUT WE STILL COULDN'T HOLD HIM. HE GOT AWAY."
ANYWAY...NO PROBLEMS. EVERYTHING'S SAFE. HE DID NOT GET THE... UHHH, THE NOTEBOOK. BUT I JUST THOUGHT YOU SHOULD KNOW.
THANK YOU, LEMMY. AND...WELL DONE. YOU AND YOUR MEN CAN EXPECT A BONUS.

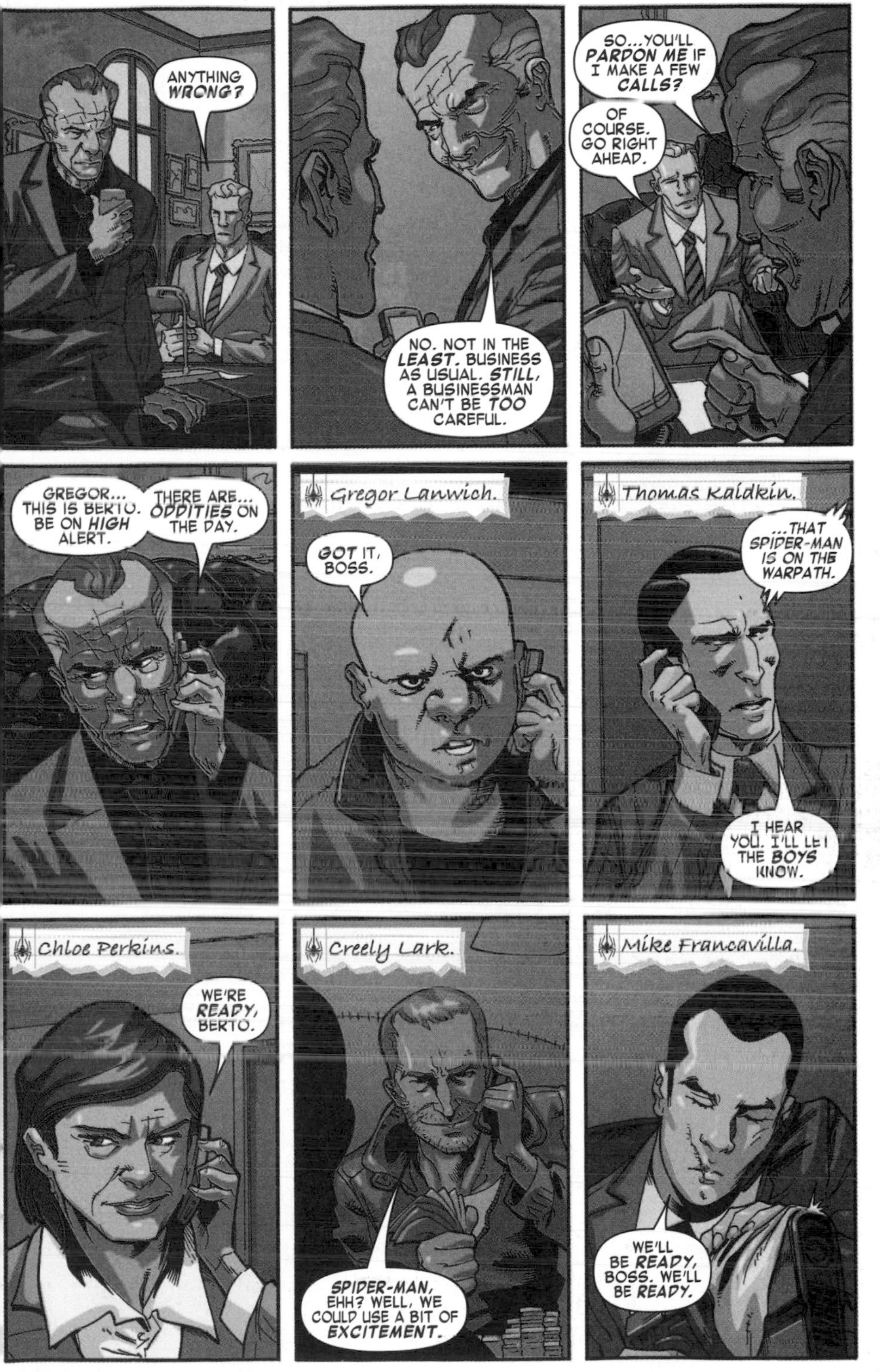
ANYTHING WRONG?
NO. NOT IN THE LEAST. BUSINESS AS USUAL. STILL, A BUSINESSMAN CAN'T BE TOO CAREFUL.
SO...YOU'LL PARDON ME IF I MAKE A FEW CALLS?
OF COURSE. GO RIGHT AHEAD.
GREGOR... THIS IS BERTO. BE ON HIGH ALERT.
THERE ARE... ODDITIES ON THE DAY.
Gregor Lanwich.
GOT IT, BOSS.
Thomas Kaldkin.
...THAT SPIDER-MAN IS ON THE WARPATH.
I HEAR YOU. I'LL LET THE BOYS KNOW.
Chloe Perkins.
WE'RE READY, BERTO.
Creely Lark.
SPIDER-MAN, EHH? WELL, WE COULD USE A BIT OF EXCITEMENT.
Mike Francavilla.
WE'LL BE READY, BOSS. WE'LL BE READY.

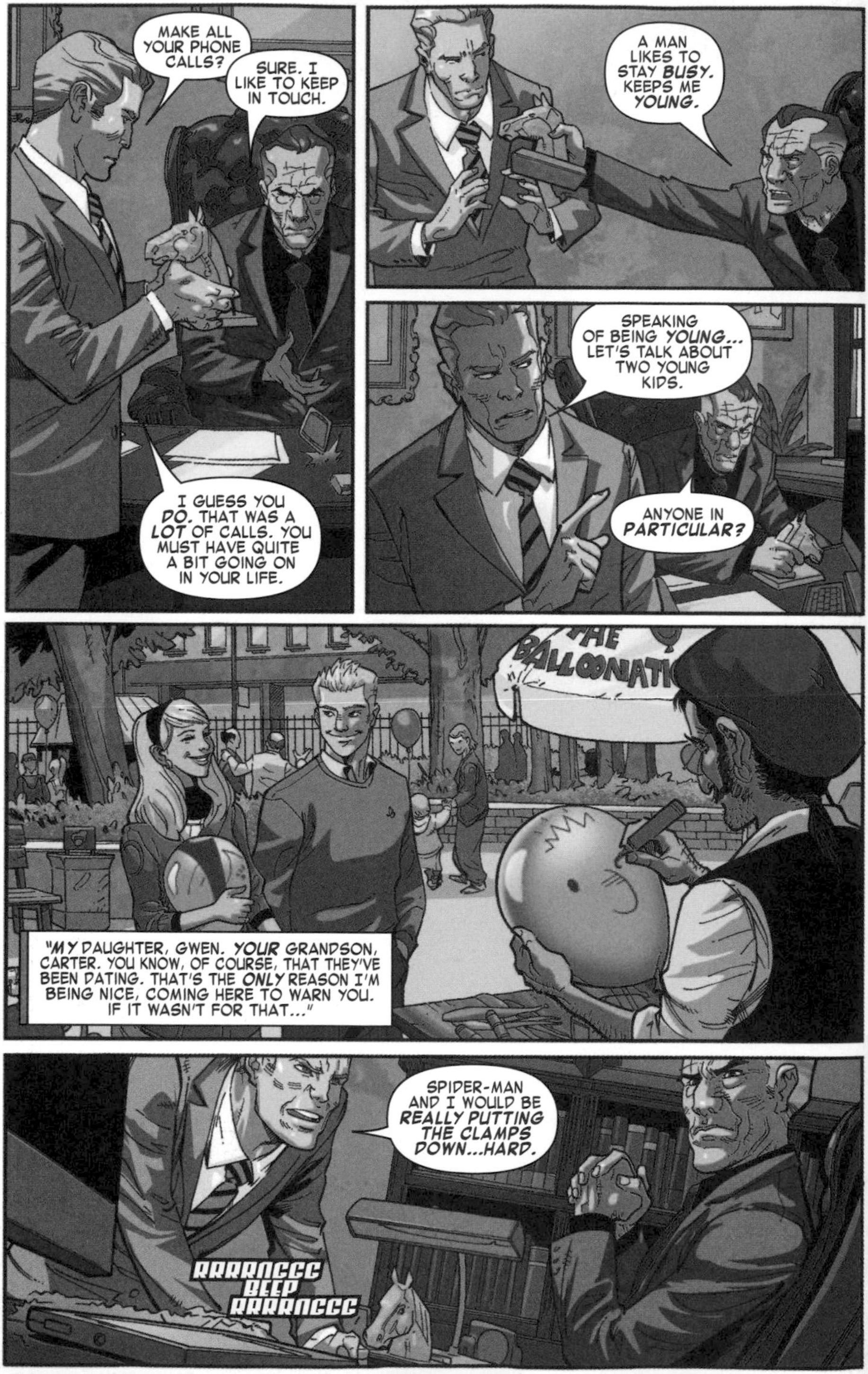
MAKE ALL YOUR PHONE CALLS?
SURE. I LIKE TO KEEP IN TOUCH.
I GUESS YOU *DO.* THAT WAS A *LOT* OF CALLS. YOU MUST HAVE QUITE A BIT GOING ON IN YOUR LIFE.
A MAN LIKES TO STAY *BUSY.* KEEPS ME *YOUNG.*
SPEAKING OF BEING *YOUNG...* LET'S TALK ABOUT TWO YOUNG KIDS.
ANYONE IN *PARTICULAR?*
THE BALLOONATI
"*MY* DAUGHTER, GWEN. *YOUR* GRANDSON, CARTER. YOU KNOW, OF COURSE, THAT THEY'VE BEEN DATING. THAT'S THE *ONLY* REASON I'M BEING NICE, COMING HERE TO WARN YOU. IF IT WASN'T FOR THAT..."
SPIDER-MAN AND I WOULD BE *REALLY PUTTING THE CLAMPS DOWN...HARD.*
RRRRNGGG BEEP RRRRNGGG

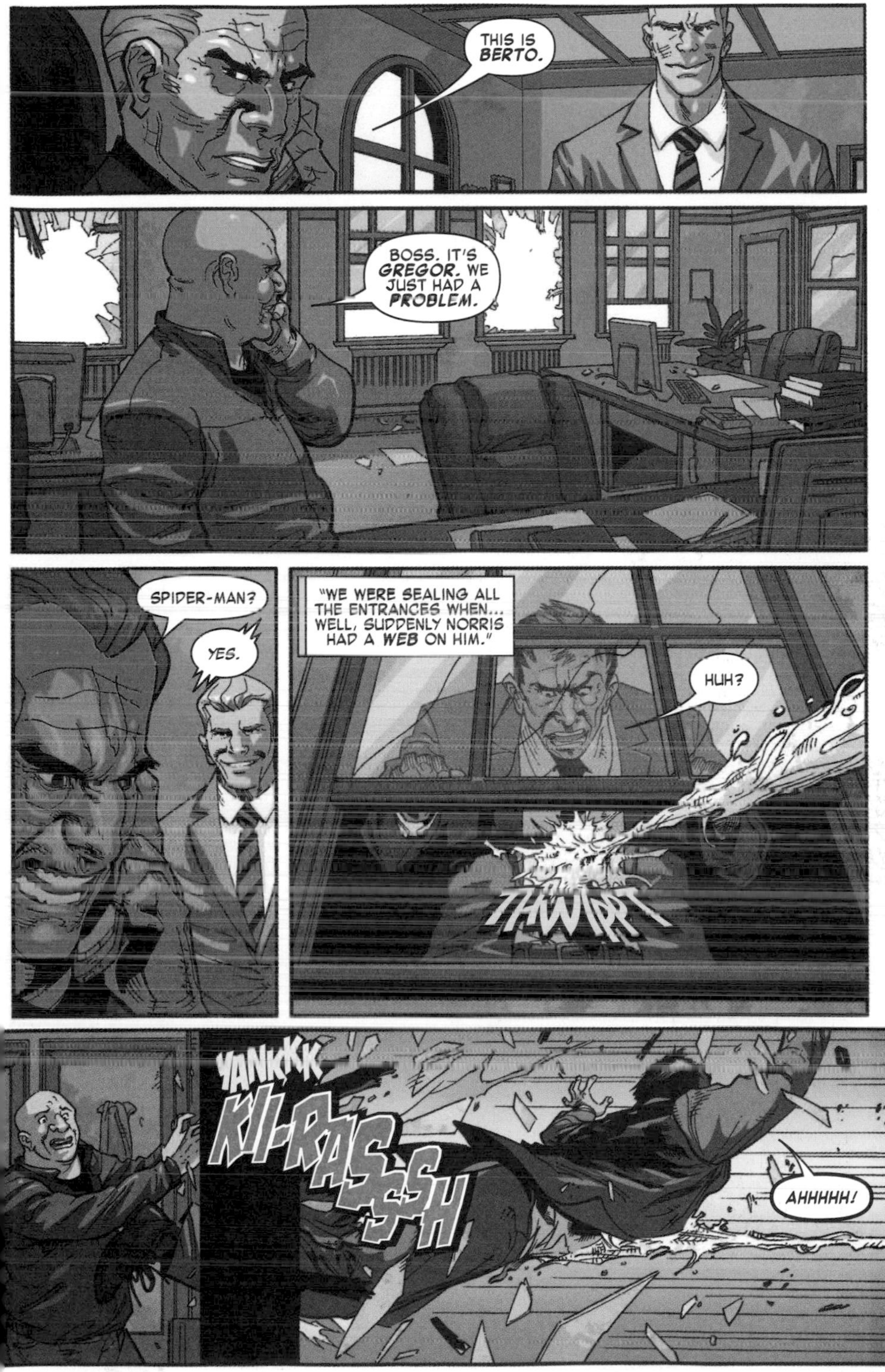
THIS IS BERTO.
BOSS. IT'S GREGOR. WE JUST HAD A PROBLEM.
SPIDER-MAN?
YES.
"WE WERE SEALING ALL THE ENTRANCES WHEN... WELL, SUDDENLY NORRIS HAD A WEB ON HIM."
HUH?
THWIPP!
YANKKK
KII-RASSSH
AHHHHH!

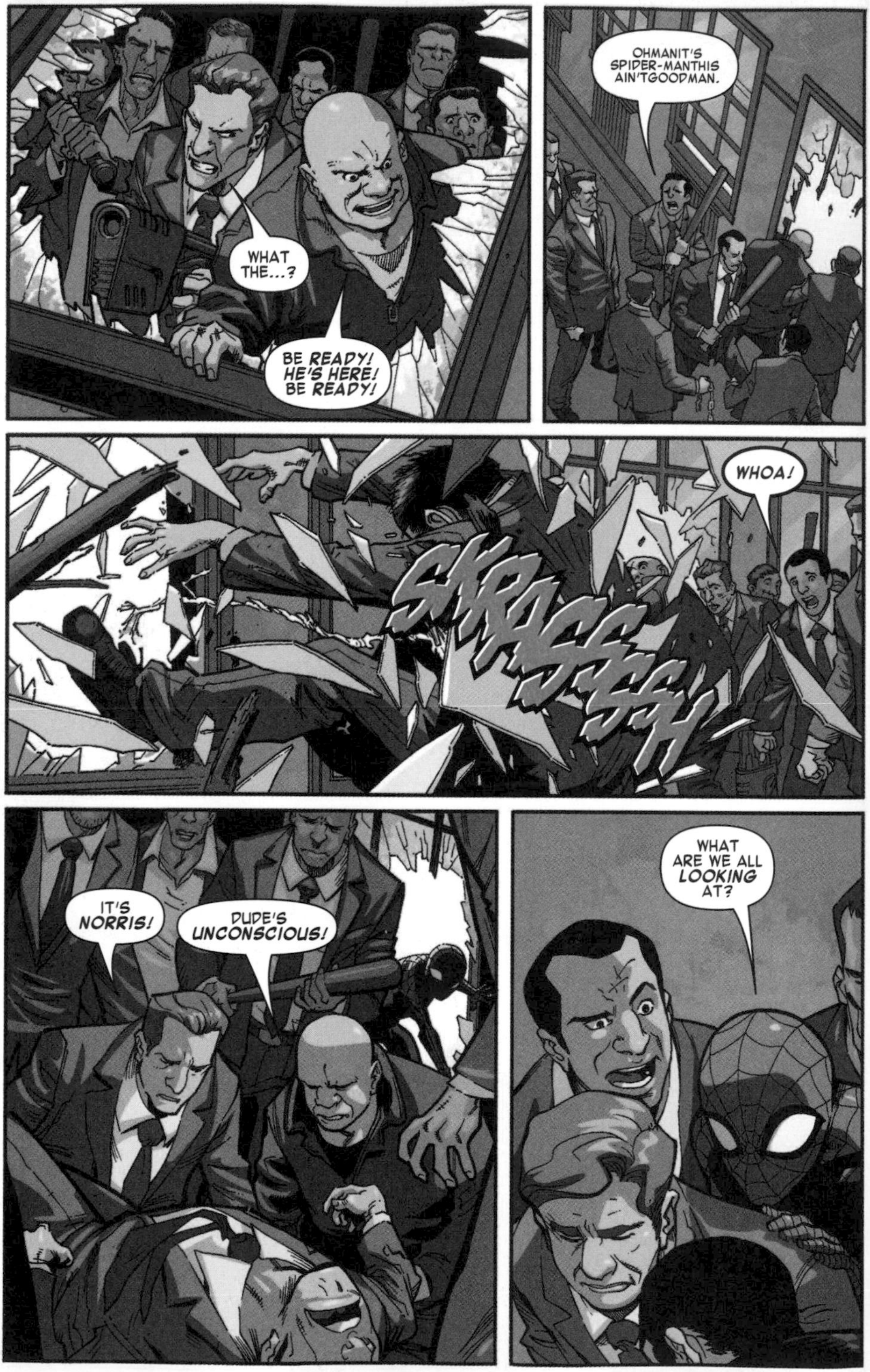
WHAT THE...?
BE READY! HE'S HERE! BE READY!
OHMANIT'S SPIDER-MANTHIS AIN'TGOODMAN.
WHOA!
SKRASSSSH
IT'S NORRIS!
DUDE'S UNCONSCIOUS!
WHAT ARE WE ALL LOOKING AT?

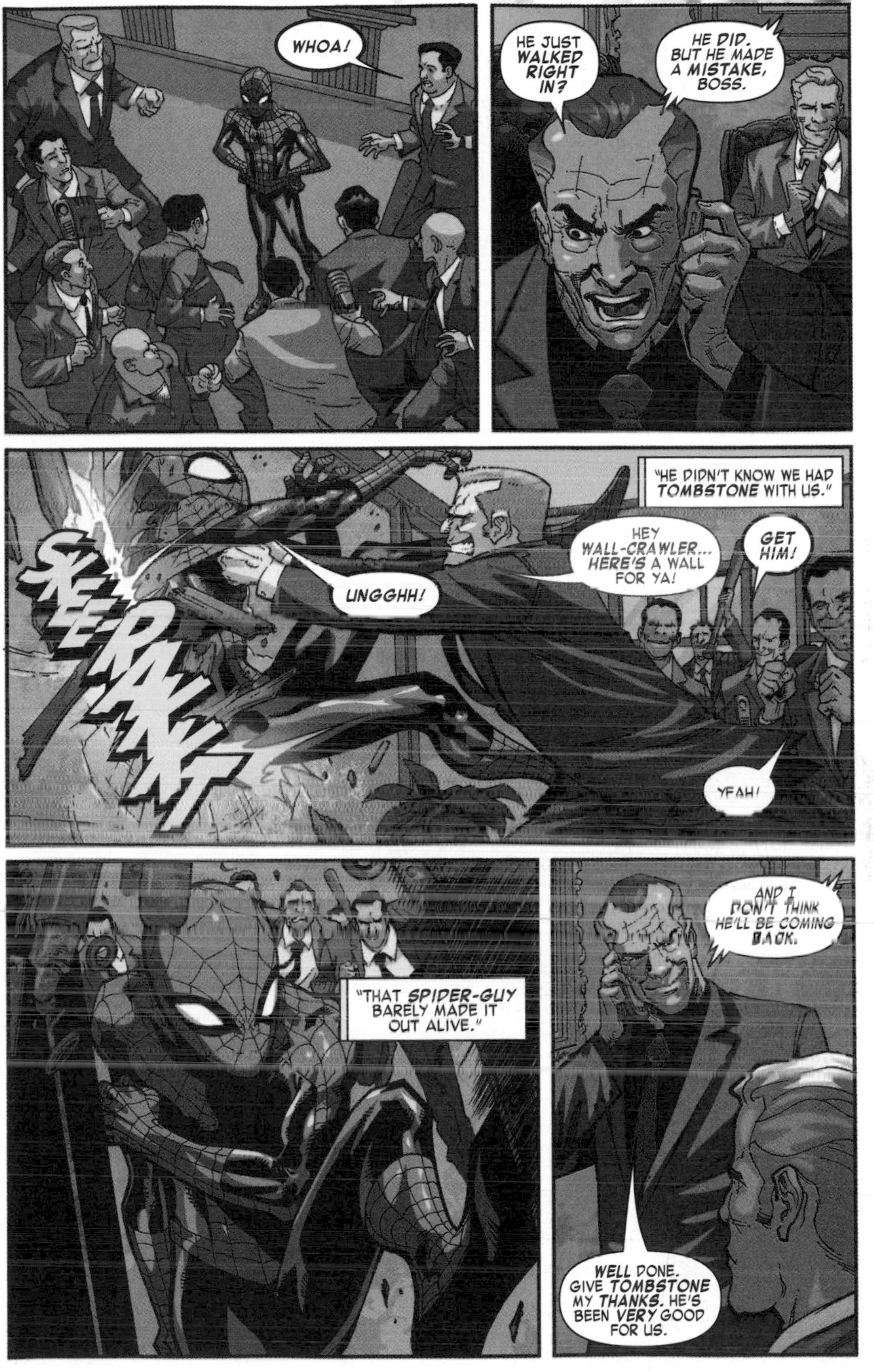
WHOA!
HE JUST WALKED RIGHT IN?
HE DID. BUT HE MADE A MISTAKE, BOSS.
"HE DIDN'T KNOW WE HAD TOMBSTONE WITH US."
SKEE-RAKKT
UNGGHH!
HEY WALL-CRAWLER... HERE'S A WALL FOR YA!
GET HIM!
YEAH!
"THAT SPIDER-GUY BARELY MADE IT OUT ALIVE."
AND I DON'T THINK HE'LL BE COMING BACK.
WELL DONE. GIVE TOMBSTONE MY THANKS. HE'S BEEN VERY GOOD FOR US.

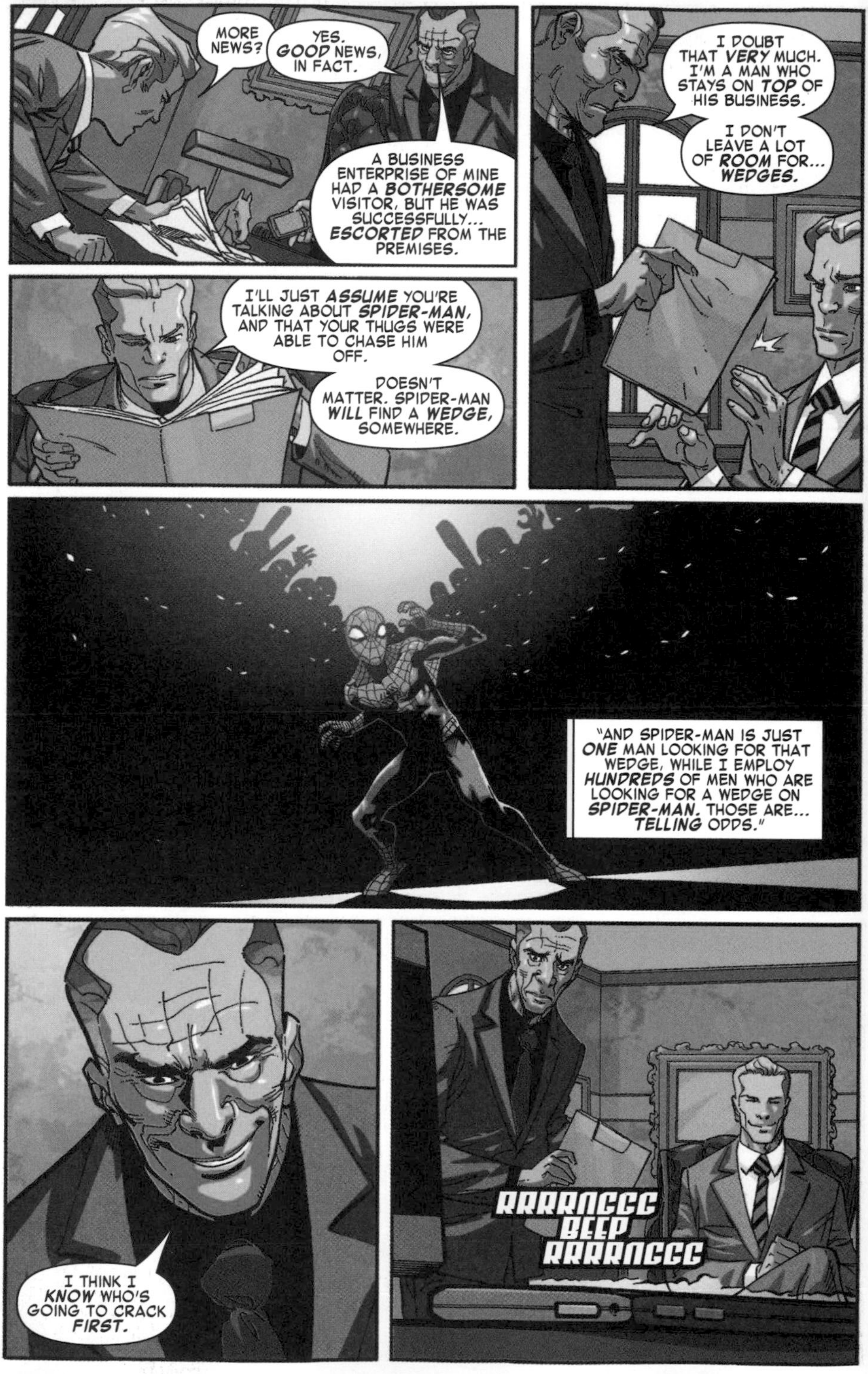
MORE NEWS?
YES. GOOD NEWS, IN FACT.
A BUSINESS ENTERPRISE OF MINE HAD A BOTHERSOME VISITOR, BUT HE WAS SUCCESSFULLY... ESCORTED FROM THE PREMISES.
I'LL JUST ASSUME YOU'RE TALKING ABOUT SPIDER-MAN, AND THAT YOUR THUGS WERE ABLE TO CHASE HIM OFF.
DOESN'T MATTER. SPIDER-MAN WILL FIND A WEDGE, SOMEWHERE.
I DOUBT THAT VERY MUCH. I'M A MAN WHO STAYS ON TOP OF HIS BUSINESS.
I DON'T LEAVE A LOT OF ROOM FOR... WEDGES.
"AND SPIDER-MAN IS JUST ONE MAN LOOKING FOR THAT WEDGE, WHILE I EMPLOY HUNDREDS OF MEN WHO ARE LOOKING FOR A WEDGE ON SPIDER-MAN. THOSE ARE... TELLING ODDS."
I THINK I KNOW WHO'S GOING TO CRACK FIRST.
RRRRNGGG
BEEP
RRRRNGGG

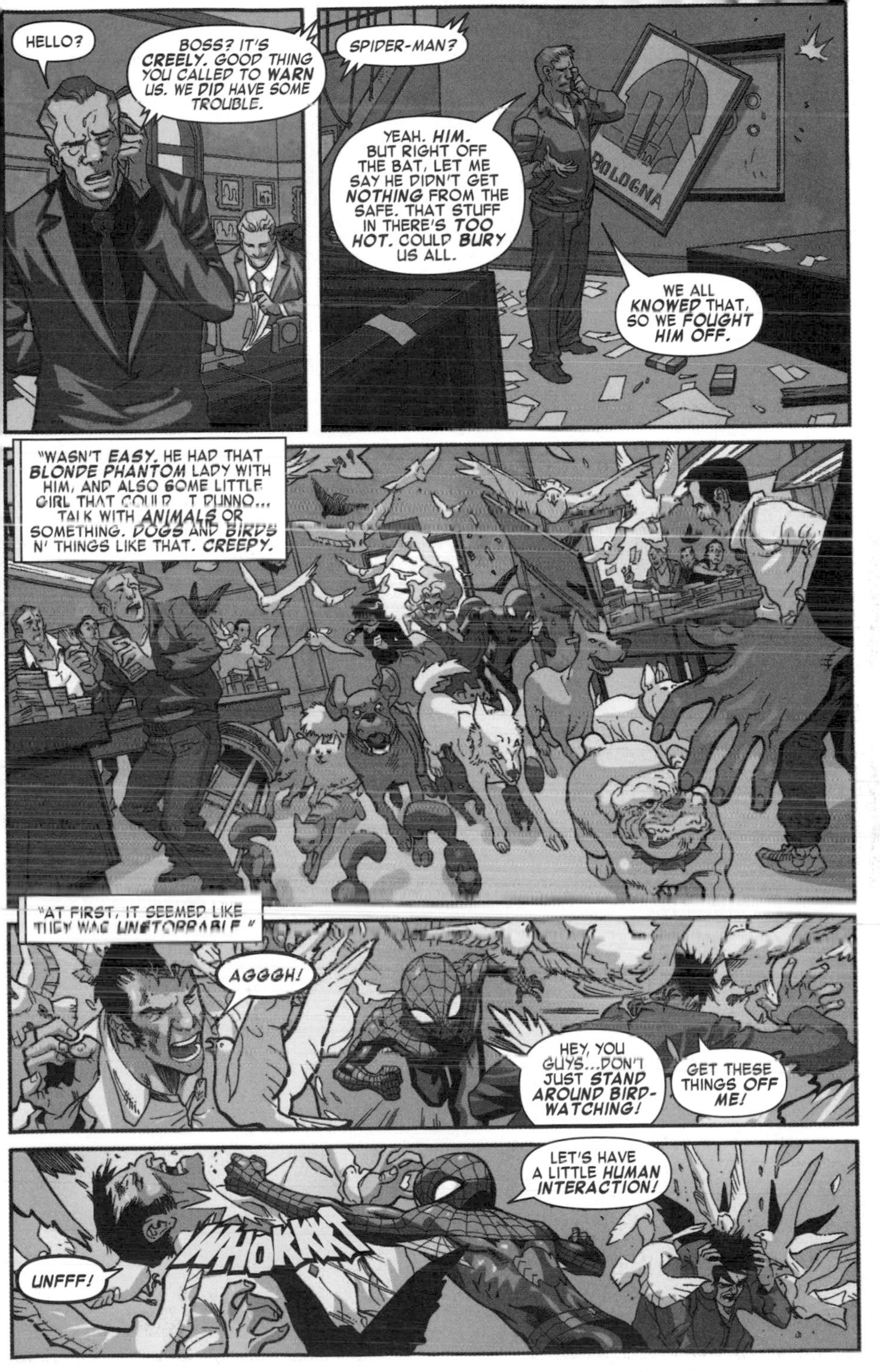
HELLO?
BOSS? IT'S CREELY. GOOD THING YOU CALLED TO WARN US. WE DID HAVE SOME TROUBLE.
SPIDER-MAN?
YEAH. HIM. BUT RIGHT OFF THE BAT, LET ME SAY HE DIDN'T GET NOTHING FROM THE SAFE. THAT STUFF IN THERE'S TOO HOT. COULD BURY US ALL.
BOLOGNA
WE ALL KNOWED THAT, SO WE FOUGHT HIM OFF.
"WASN'T EASY. HE HAD THAT BLONDE PHANTOM LADY WITH HIM, AND ALSO SOME LITTLE GIRL THAT COULD, I DUNNO... TALK WITH ANIMALS OR SOMETHING. DOGS AND BIRDS N' THINGS LIKE THAT. CREEPY.
"AT FIRST, IT SEEMED LIKE THEY WAS UNSTOPPABLE."
AGGGH!
HEY, YOU GUYS...DON'T JUST STAND AROUND BIRD-WATCHING!
GET THESE THINGS OFF ME!
LET'S HAVE A LITTLE HUMAN INTERACTION!
WHOKKK!
UNFFF!

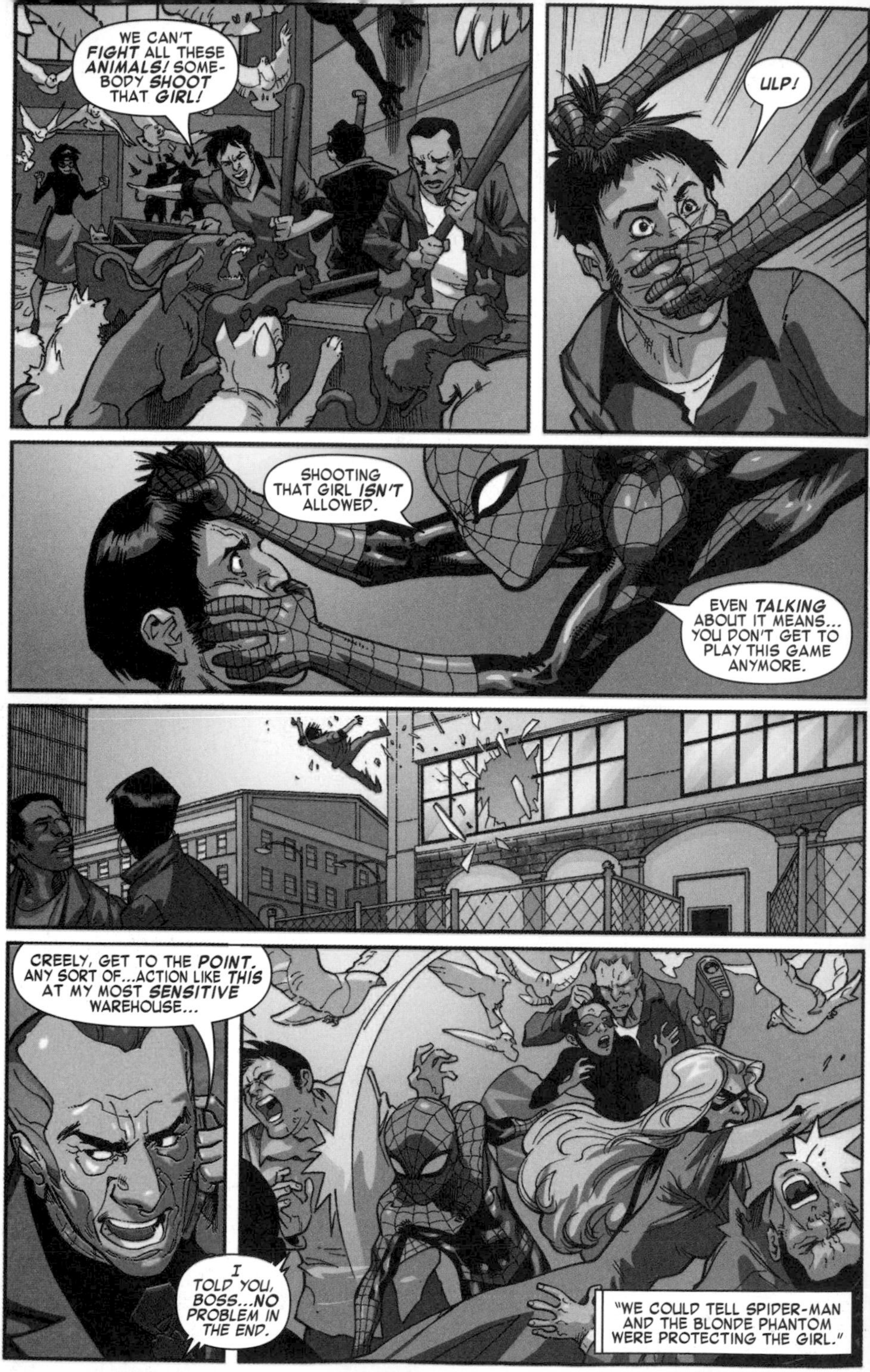
WE CAN'T FIGHT ALL THESE ANIMALS! SOME-BODY SHOOT THAT GIRL!
ULP!
SHOOTING THAT GIRL ISN'T ALLOWED.
EVEN TALKING ABOUT IT MEANS... YOU DON'T GET TO PLAY THIS GAME ANYMORE.
CREELY, GET TO THE POINT. ANY SORT OF...ACTION LIKE THIS AT MY MOST SENSITIVE WAREHOUSE...
I TOLD YOU, BOSS...NO PROBLEM IN THE END.
"WE COULD TELL SPIDER-MAN AND THE BLONDE PHANTOM WERE PROTECTING THE GIRL."

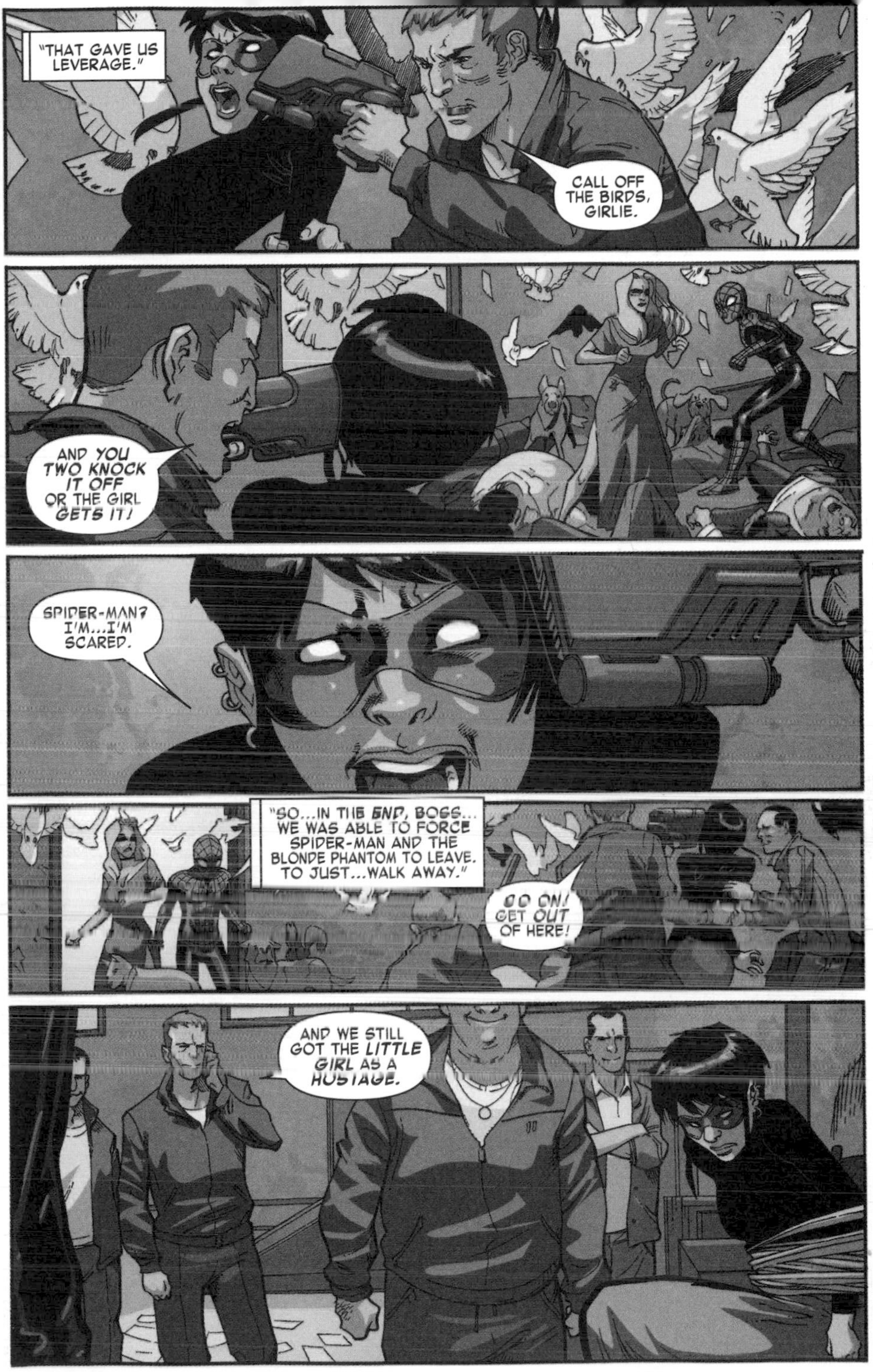
"THAT GAVE US LEVERAGE."
CALL OFF THE BIRDS, GIRLIE.
AND YOU TWO KNOCK IT OFF OR THE GIRL GETS IT!
SPIDER-MAN? I'M...I'M SCARED.
"SO...IN THE END, BOSS... WE WAS ABLE TO FORCE SPIDER-MAN AND THE BLONDE PHANTOM TO LEAVE. TO JUST...WALK AWAY."
GO ON! GET OUT OF HERE!
AND WE STILL GOT THE LITTLE GIRL AS A HOSTAGE.

ANOTHER INCIDENT?

THERE WAS A *DEVELOPMENT*, YES. BUT A RATHER *MARVELOUS* ONE.

YES. PERHAPS. I WONDER, MR. STACY, HOW *MANY* PEOPLE KNOW THAT YOU WERE COMING HERE TODAY?

WELL, THERE'S *SPIDER-MAN*.

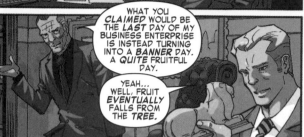

WHAT YOU *CLAIMED* WOULD BE THE *LAST* DAY OF MY BUSINESS ENTERPRISE IS INSTEAD TURNING INTO A *BANNER* DAY. A *QUITE* FRUITFUL DAY.

YEAH... WELL, FRUIT *EVENTUALLY* FALLS FROM THE *TREE*.

BZZZT

NONE OF YOUR FELLOW *POLICE* OFFICERS?

NOT A *CHANCE*. THERE'S NO WAY I COULD HAVE GOTTEN CLEARANCE TO DO ANYTHING LIKE THIS.

THAT'S... UNFORTUNATE FOR YOU.

BECAUSE NOW I CONFESS I'M BEGINNING TO WONDER IF YOU'LL EVER MAKE IT *OUT* OF HERE.

YOU SEE, GEORGE, THE THING IS...WHEN YOU WALK INTO THE *LION'S* DEN...

WELL... THERE'S A *LION* INSIDE.

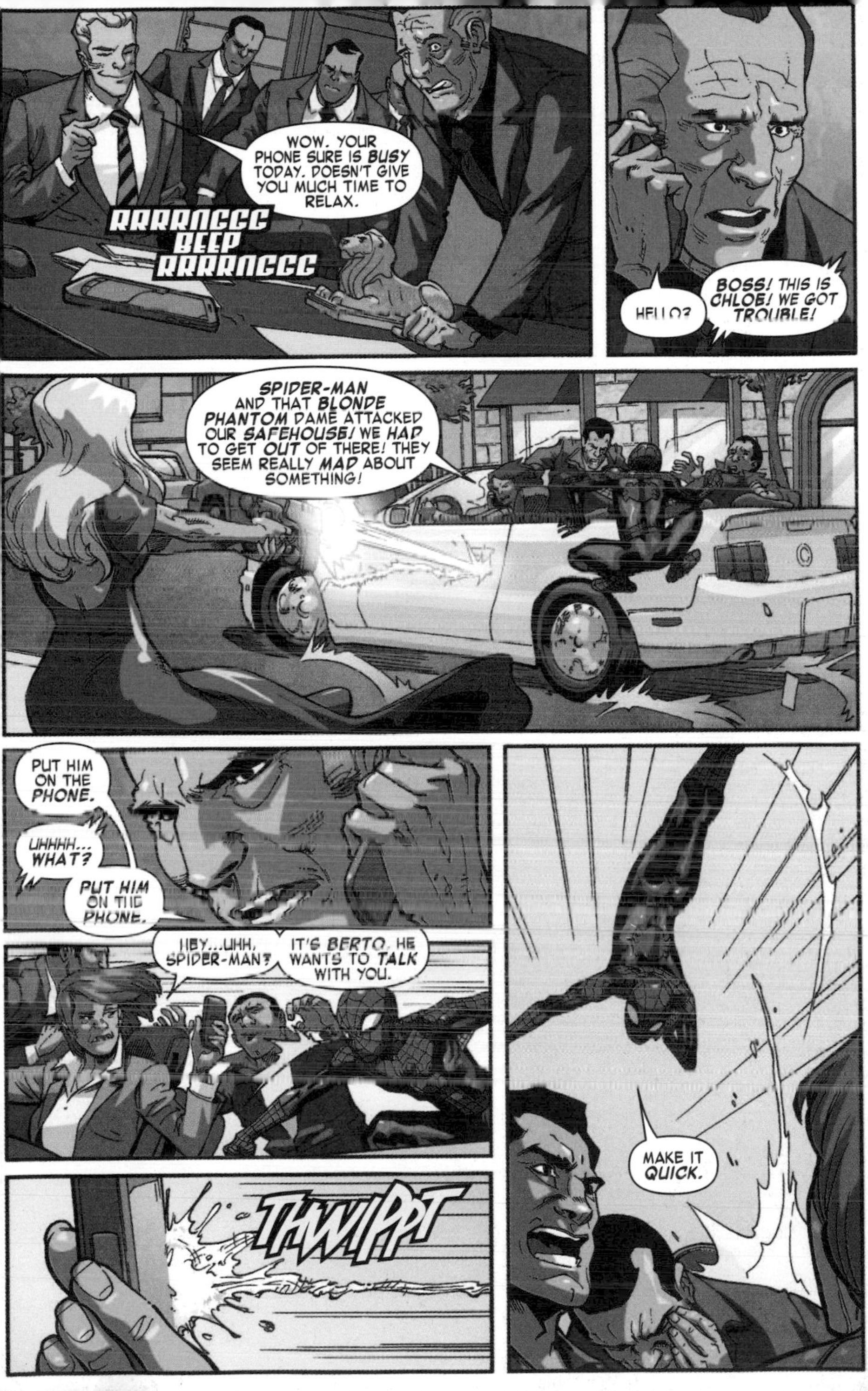
WOW. YOUR PHONE SURE IS BUSY TODAY. DOESN'T GIVE YOU MUCH TIME TO RELAX.
RRRRNGGG BEEP RRRRNGGG
HELLO?
BOSS! THIS IS CHLOE! WE GOT TROUBLE!
SPIDER-MAN AND THAT BLONDE PHANTOM DAME ATTACKED OUR SAFEHOUSE! WE HAD TO GET OUT OF THERE! THEY SEEM REALLY MAD ABOUT SOMETHING!
PUT HIM ON THE PHONE.
UHHHH... WHAT?
PUT HIM ON THE PHONE.
HEY...UHH, SPIDER-MAN?
IT'S BERTO. HE WANTS TO TALK WITH YOU.
THWIPPT
MAKE IT QUICK.

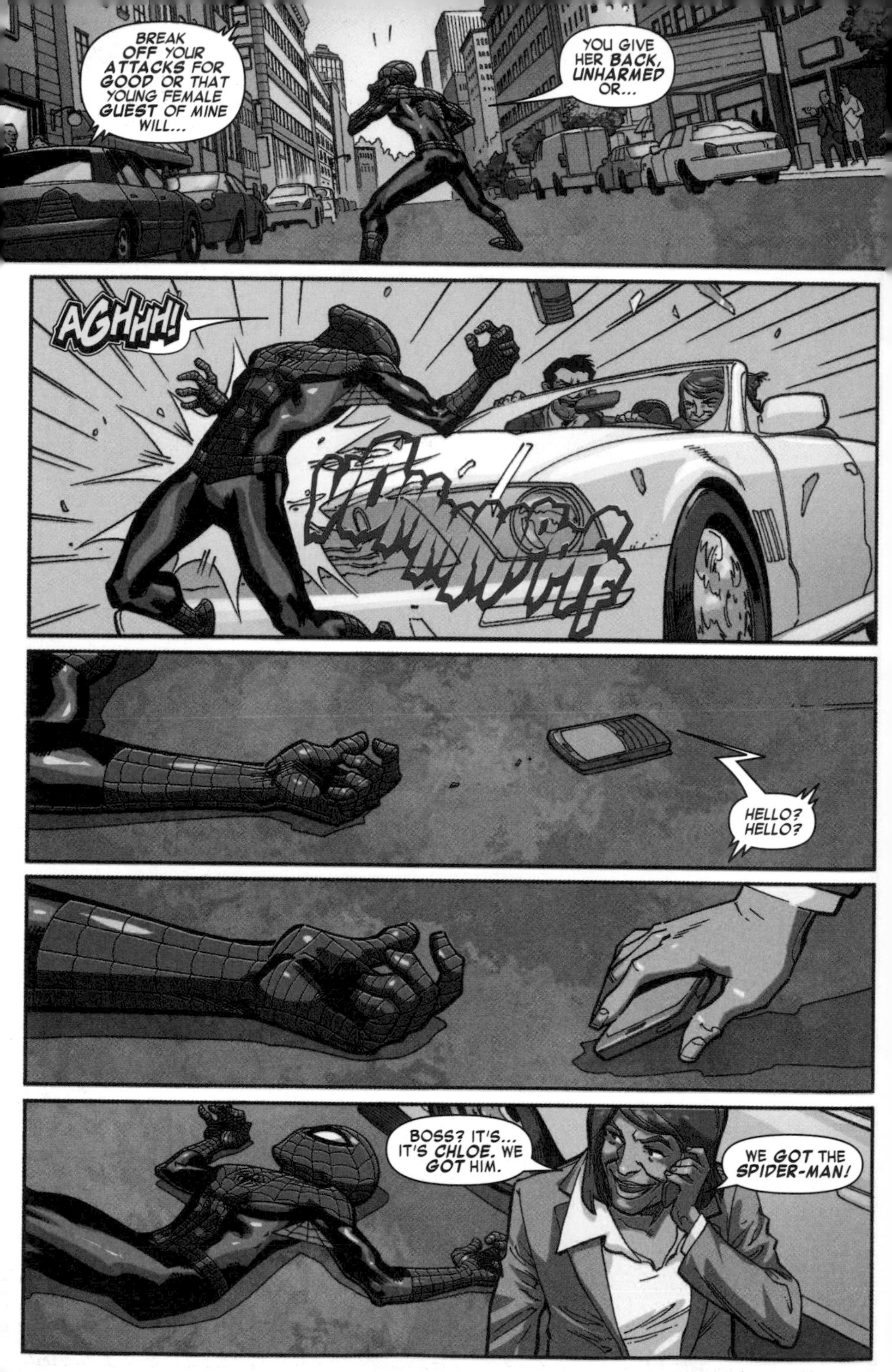
BREAK OFF YOUR ATTACKS FOR GOOD OR THAT YOUNG FEMALE GUEST OF MINE WILL...
YOU GIVE HER BACK, UNHARMED OR...
AGHHH!
HELLO? HELLO?
BOSS? IT'S... IT'S CHLOE. WE GOT HIM.
WE GOT THE SPIDER-MAN!

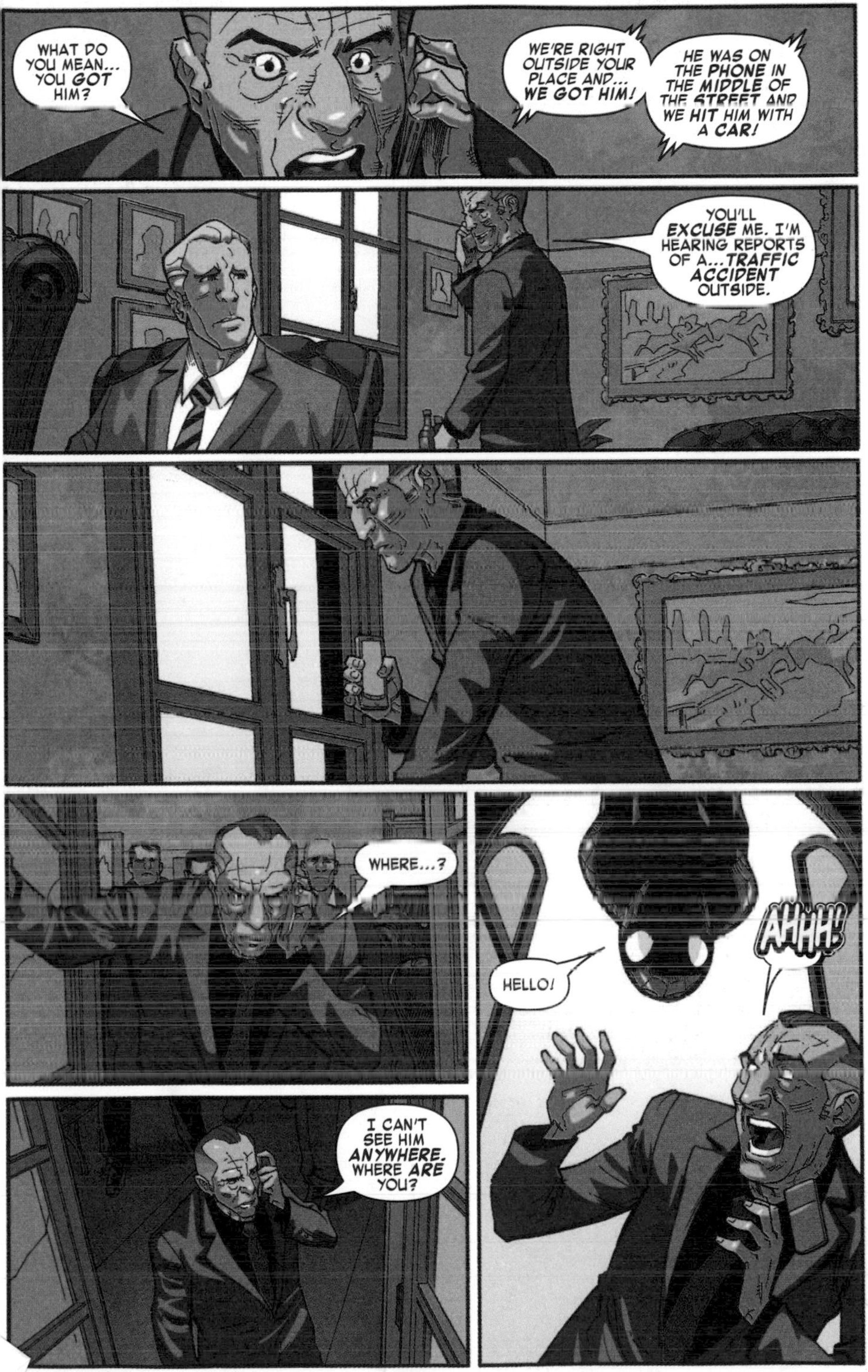
WHAT DO YOU MEAN... YOU GOT HIM?
WE'RE RIGHT OUTSIDE YOUR PLACE AND... WE GOT HIM!
HE WAS ON THE PHONE IN THE MIDDLE OF THE STREET AND WE HIT HIM WITH A CAR!
YOU'LL EXCUSE ME. I'M HEARING REPORTS OF A...TRAFFIC ACCIDENT OUTSIDE.
WHERE...?
I CAN'T SEE HIM ANYWHERE. WHERE ARE YOU?
HELLO!
AHHH!

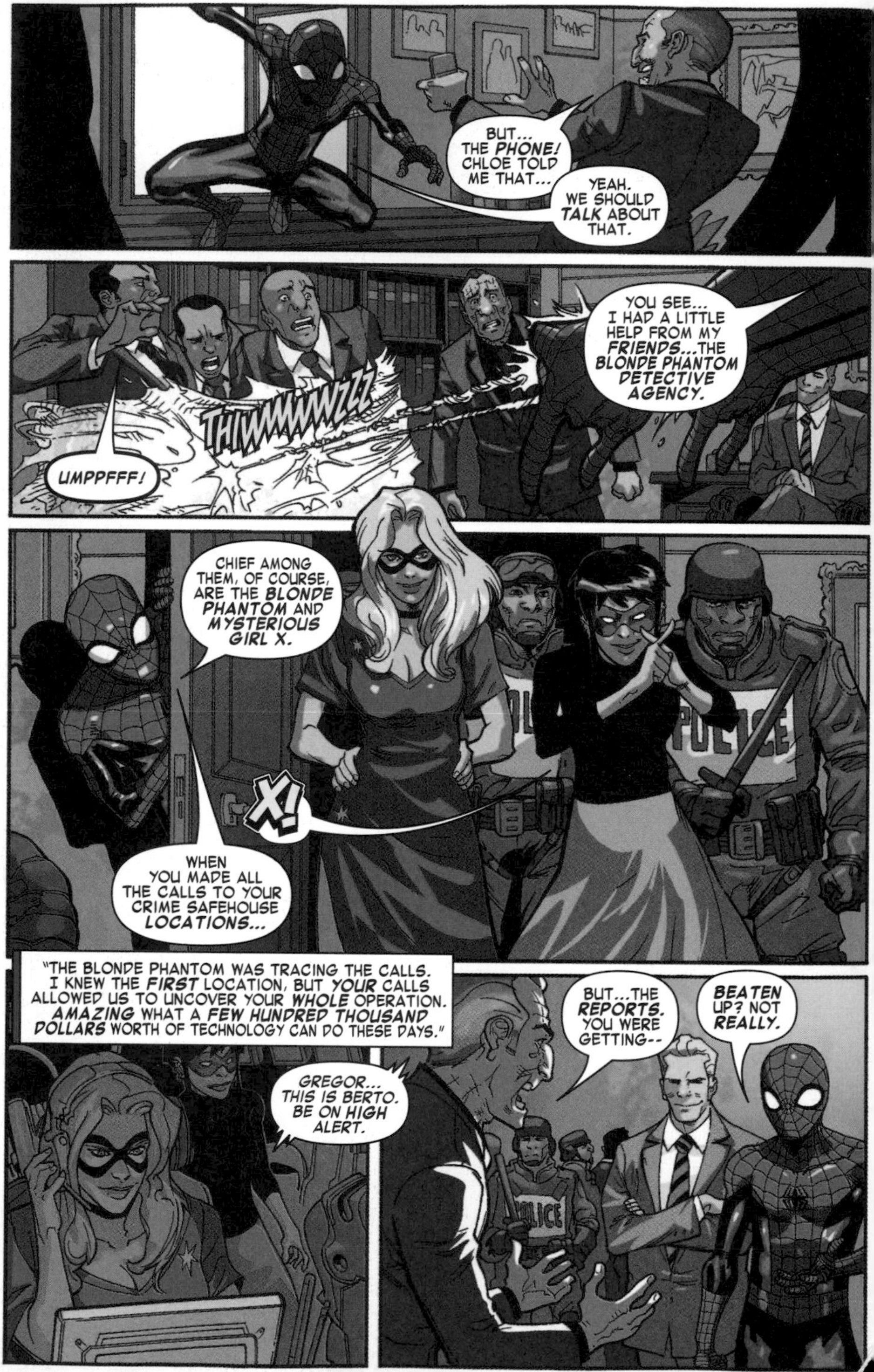
BUT... THE PHONE! CHLOE TOLD ME THAT...
YEAH. WE SHOULD TALK ABOUT THAT.
YOU SEE... I HAD A LITTLE HELP FROM MY FRIENDS...THE BLONDE PHANTOM DETECTIVE AGENCY.
THWWWWWZZZ
UMPPFFF!
CHIEF AMONG THEM, OF COURSE, ARE THE BLONDE PHANTOM AND MYSTERIOUS GIRL X.
X!
WHEN YOU MADE ALL THE CALLS TO YOUR CRIME SAFEHOUSE LOCATIONS...
"THE BLONDE PHANTOM WAS TRACING THE CALLS. I KNEW THE FIRST LOCATION, BUT YOUR CALLS ALLOWED US TO UNCOVER YOUR WHOLE OPERATION. AMAZING WHAT A FEW HUNDRED THOUSAND DOLLARS WORTH OF TECHNOLOGY CAN DO THESE DAYS."
GREGOR... THIS IS BERTO. BE ON HIGH ALERT.
BUT...THE REPORTS. YOU WERE GETTING--
BEATEN UP? NOT REALLY.
POLICE
POLICE
POLICE

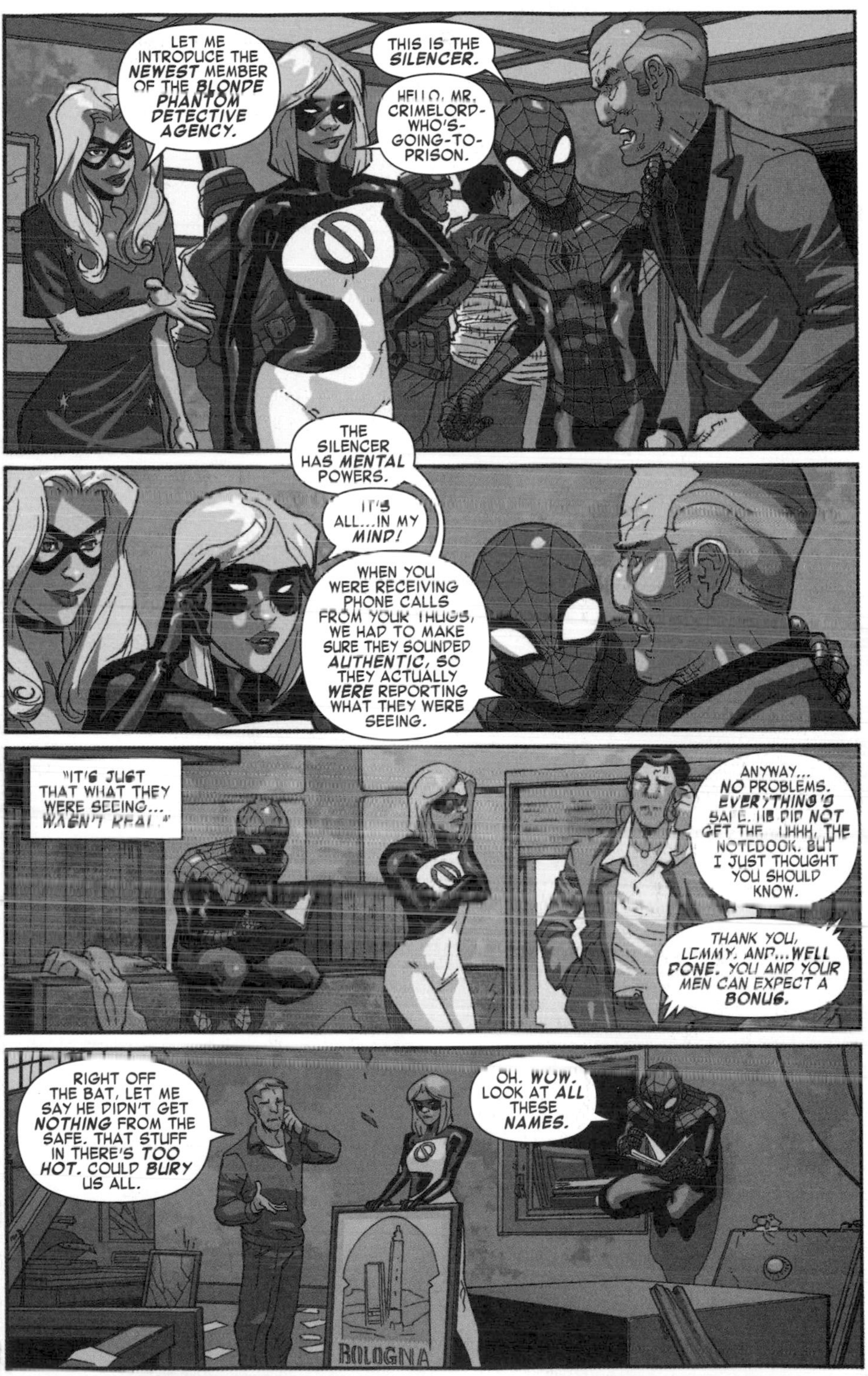

LET ME INTRODUCE THE NEWEST MEMBER OF THE BLONDE PHANTOM DETECTIVE AGENCY.
THIS IS THE SILENCER.
HELLO, MR. CRIMELORD-WHO'S-GOING-TO-PRISON.
THE SILENCER HAS MENTAL POWERS.
IT'S ALL...IN MY MIND!
WHEN YOU WERE RECEIVING PHONE CALLS FROM YOUR THUGS, WE HAD TO MAKE SURE THEY SOUNDED AUTHENTIC, SO THEY ACTUALLY WERE REPORTING WHAT THEY WERE SEEING.
"IT'S JUST THAT WHAT THEY WERE SEEING... WASN'T REAL."
ANYWAY... NO PROBLEMS. EVERYTHING'S SAFE. HE DID NOT GET THE... UHHH, THE NOTEBOOK. BUT I JUST THOUGHT YOU SHOULD KNOW.
THANK YOU, LEMMY. AND...WELL DONE. YOU AND YOUR MEN CAN EXPECT A BONUS.
RIGHT OFF THE BAT, LET ME SAY HE DIDN'T GET NOTHING FROM THE SAFE. THAT STUFF IN THERE'S TOO HOT. COULD BURY US ALL.
OH. WOW. LOOK AT ALL THESE NAMES.
BOLOGNA

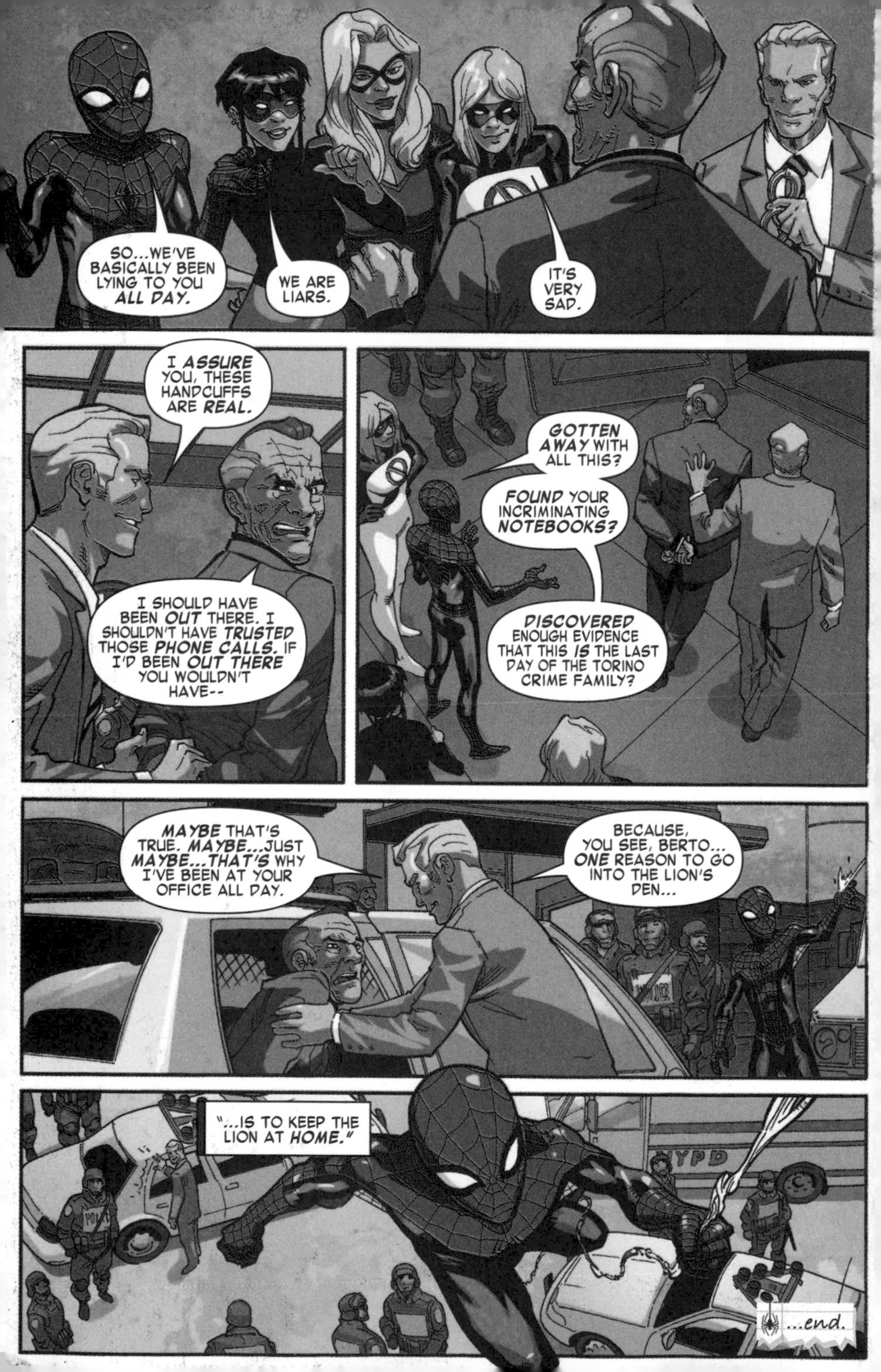
SO...WE'VE BASICALLY BEEN LYING TO YOU ALL DAY.
WE ARE LIARS.
IT'S VERY SAD.
I ASSURE YOU, THESE HANDCUFFS ARE REAL.
I SHOULD HAVE BEEN OUT THERE. I SHOULDN'T HAVE TRUSTED THOSE PHONE CALLS. IF I'D BEEN OUT THERE YOU WOULDN'T HAVE--
GOTTEN AWAY WITH ALL THIS?
FOUND YOUR INCRIMINATING NOTEBOOKS?
DISCOVERED ENOUGH EVIDENCE THAT THIS IS THE LAST DAY OF THE TORINO CRIME FAMILY?
MAYBE THAT'S TRUE. MAYBE...JUST MAYBE...THAT'S WHY I'VE BEEN AT YOUR OFFICE ALL DAY.
BECAUSE, YOU SEE, BERTO... ONE REASON TO GO INTO THE LION'S DEN...
"...IS TO KEEP THE LION AT HOME."
NYPD
...end.